Welcome to the masquerade!

LORD LUCIFER

Lords of the Masquerade
Book One

Jade Lee

Jade Lee

DRAGONBLADE PUBLISHING, INC.

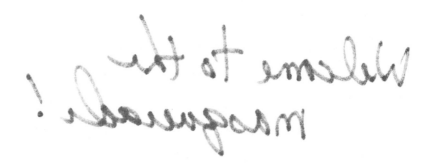

Dragonblade Publishing, Inc. is an imprint of Kathryn Le Veque Novels, Inc.
P.O. Box 7968
La Verne CA 91750
ceo@dragonbladepublishing.com

Produced in the United States of America

First Edition November 2020
Print Edition

ARE YOU SIGNED UP FOR DRAGONBLADE'S BLOG?

You'll get the latest news and information on exclusive giveaways, exclusive excerpts, coming releases, sales, free books, cover reveals and more.

Check out our complete list of authors, too!

No spam, no junk. That's a promise!

Sign Up Here

www.dragonbladepublishing.com

Dearest Reader;

Thank you for your support of a small press. At Dragonblade Publishing, we strive to bring you the highest quality Historical Romance from the some of the best authors in the business. Without your support, there is no 'us', so we sincerely hope you adore these stories and find some new favorite authors along the way.

Happy Reading!

CEO, Dragonblade Publishing

Additional Dragonblade books by Author Jade Lee

Lords of the Masquerade Series
Lord Lucifer (Book 1)

The Lyon's Den Connected World
Into the Lyon's Den

CHAPTER ONE

Seventeen years ago...

THE IVY WAS slick, and it pulled too easily away from the crumbling house, but Lucas Crosse, future earl of Wolvesmead, was determined to scale the wall to reach his damsel in distress. In his mind, he was climbing a tower to rescue his princess. It wasn't far from the truth, and Lucas managed to reach Lady Diana's window without falling to his doom. But once there, he was dismayed to discover that his princess wasn't alone. She was trapped by the evil witch of her mother and her two sisters as they brushed her hair, soothed her nerves, and generally promised her that all would be well.

That was his job, he thought, and he was impatient to get to it. Especially before he lost his grip and fell eighteen feet onto the shrubbery below. He was busy imagining the results of getting impaled by those hard branches when Diana reached her limit. With a harsh voice, she sent everyone away, including her mother. They scurried out like the betraying rats they were, and finally, Diana was alone.

Lucas tapped the window to get Diana's attention, but she had dropped her head into her hands and wouldn't look up.

He tapped again, forcefully enough to make it a knock. That did the trick. His lady love lifted her head to glare out at the drizzly night. Thank God because he was getting chilled. She even stood to approach the window. Excellent! He leaned his face in close so that she would see him. He made sure to smile though it probably looked more like a grimace given the situation. Then she saw him.

She recoiled in horror. Her face went pale, she stumbled backward, and her hands went to her mouth as she squeaked in alarm.

Not the reaction he expected, but what could he do to change it? He tried to slick the wet from his face. "Diana, it's me! Lucas!"

Her brows narrowed, and she peered forward. Then with gratifying speed, she hauled open the window. "What are you doing?" she gasped. "You're wet!"

"I know," he huffed. "Step back so I can climb in."

Stepping back wasn't going to be helpful. The windows throughout London were too small for this type of maneuver. Especially when he was larger than the average burglar. But he managed to wriggle himself inside though he fell on his face in an ungainly heap.

"What are you doing here?" Diana asked as she passed him a towel.

Practical. That was one of the things he loved about her. "Thanks," he said as he wiped off his face.

"Why aren't you in school?"

He straightened up. "Why are you marrying someone three times your age?"

She sighed and slumped over to sit on her bed. "You wouldn't understand."

She was a delicate woman with blonde hair, blue eyes, and a body just starting to ripen. He thought of her as a pixie or a sprite—some tiny, magical creature who had bewitched him while he wasn't watching. He'd only met her a few months past when he'd summered with his friend next to her home. They'd shared tea and gone riding. They'd taken walks by the stream and discussed canals. And he'd left in August expecting to dance with her in the coming season, to flirt with her during musical evenings, and maybe steal a kiss or three.

He'd made plans for just that happenstance and spent many hours daydreaming exactly where and how he would kiss her.

Until her father died six weeks ago and suddenly, in the depths of a cold November, he'd learned she was to be wed on the morrow. It made no sense, and he wanted to tell her that. But looking at her now, he saw that she already knew the illogic of it all. She looked as miserable as he felt, and his soul fired up with the desire to be her knight in shining armor.

He dropped to his knees before her and clasped her hands. "You mustn't do this. How can I help you escape?"

She shook her head. "There is no escape. With Papa gone, Mama needs a man to manage things."

"So, let her marry—"

"He doesn't want her. He wants me."

The level of misery in her voice destroyed him. "Don't do it," he whispered. "They're horrible people. His children are awful. And they're older than you!"

"I know!" she said, her eyes welling up with misery. "They've already said terrible things to me."

He looked into her blue eyes and felt his heart swell. "Marry me. Tonight. We'll run to Scotland together."

He watched her mouth part in surprise and saw hope spark in her eyes. But even as he waited with a held breath, he watched her expression tighten. "How will we get there?"

"What?"

"To Scotland? How will we get there?"

He shrugged. "I have a horse—"

"I don't."

"We'll hire one for you."

"How? It's the middle of the night."

He frowned. "We'll borrow one. I have friends."

"And do you have money for lodging? It's November. We can't

just sleep out in the fields."

He tightened his grip on her hands. She was ruining the moment with her questions. Didn't she see that? It was like being examined by an Oxford don. "We'll figure it out along the way."

"And what about my family? How will they survive if I disappear?"

"Your mother will have to find her own solution. That's what mothers are supposed to do. They shouldn't sacrifice their daughters to—"

"If there isn't an influx of money, then my brother will have to leave school. Elliott is just a boy. And who will take care of my sisters?"

"Your mother—"

"Picked this solution." Diana shook her head. "I can't abandon them."

Loyal. He couldn't fault her for that, and frankly, he was ashamed of himself for not thinking of that sooner. "I have some money," he began.

"Enough to keep Elliott in school?"

He winced. It wasn't enough to keep the two of them in food beyond a month. "My parents will help us."

Diana stared at him, her eyes sheening with tears as she clutched his fingers. "And my family? Will they help them as well?"

Doubtful. His parents hated anything they labeled "untoward." Marrying Diana before he turned twenty would definitely qualify. It would be hard enough to get them to accept the marriage. They certainly wouldn't aid her family, especially since it included her by-blow half-sister. Lilah changed Diana's family from "untoward" to "regrettable," and his mother would never touch anything that was so unseemly.

"How much money?" he asked.

She frowned. "What do you mean?"

"How much money do you think it would take to free you from

this marriage, to support your family, and keep Elliott in school?"

"I don't know. Five thousand pounds per year? Something like that."

He shuddered. Even at half that amount, he couldn't do it. He hadn't inherited yet, and his allowance from his father was barely a thousand per annum. He wanted to promise that he could manage her family's estate, but he knew nothing of farming. In fact, he'd gone out of his way to *not* learn about sheep, crops, and whatnot. It just wasn't in his nature.

"What if I brought you three thousand tomorrow morning? Would you run away with me then? It would be enough, yes? We'd figure out the rest. Would you do it?"

She swallowed, obviously torn.

"It won't be easy," he pressed, "but we could do it together. We're in love, Diana. Anything is possible with love."

He believed that. Indeed, the feeling burned hot inside him, but her eyes widened in shocked surprise. "What?" she whispered. At least that was the word he read off her lips.

"We're in love," he stressed. "Aren't we? Don't you love me?"

"You love me?" she echoed without answering his question. "I…"

She was in doubt, but he knew exactly how to change that. He surged upward and captured her mouth with his. He teased her cold lips and slipped between them with his tongue. And while she gasped in maidenly surprise, he plundered her mouth. He thrust inside and tasted every part of her.

"Diana," he whispered.

She clutched his shoulders in response, then drew him closer.

It was the most natural thing to press her backward, to move over her so that he could lay her down on her bed.

He hadn't meant to be so ardent. He'd merely intended to kiss her doubts away. But lust surged inside him, and love and desire were a potent combination. Especially since she whispered his name with every kiss, and her hands roamed across his shoulders and back.

But while he began to nuzzle down her throat to her breasts, she gripped him hard and held him away.

"Lucas. Lucas!"

"Yes?" He lifted his head, feeling her quick breaths as they merged with his own. He saw the pulse in her throat and meant to nibble it while need throbbed in his loins.

"Yes."

Excellent! He pressed a quick kiss to her throat, and his fingers began to tug at the fabric of her nightrail.

"Lucas, stop!"

He lifted his head. "What?"

"Do you have three thousand pounds? Right now? Do you have it?"

She was talking about money? Right now, when her scent muddied his thoughts, and she was already on fire in her bed?

"Do you?"

"Not just now. I have a little more than a thousand." He'd been saving up to buy a horse. "But I can turn that into three thousand easily. I'm a good gambler, and so many people are bad at it."

She stiffened beneath him. "Gambling? You want me to risk my family on gambling?"

"It's true! How do you think I got a thousand?" He could see that she didn't believe him, and no wonder. What did she know of the kind of money men threw around simply because they could? "I can," he insisted. He straightened up off her, though it physically hurt to do so. "Let me prove it."

"How?"

"I'll come back in the morning with three thousand pounds. I swear it." He could do it. It might be tight, but he knew of a few hells where the play was steep. "Wait for me," he pressed. Then he paused. "And if I show you the money, will you run away with me? Will you refuse to marry him?" He touched her cheek. "Will you be mine?"

"Yes," she said, the word barely audible. Then she straightened up and slammed her mouth to his. It was all he needed.

He plundered her mouth. And when she gripped his shoulders, he tore himself away. There was too much to do. There would be plenty of time for love after the night's gambling was done.

So, he went to the window, frowning as he tried to figure out how to wriggle himself back outside without tumbling to his death.

"Don't be an idiot," she huffed. "I'll take you down the back stairs."

They tiptoed like giggly children down the back stairs. And when they finally reached the doorway, he hauled her close for one last kiss. Her mouth was hot, her body pliant, and he held her so tight, he lifted her off the ground.

"You have bewitched me," he whispered as he let her go.

"Don't fail," she responded. "Please, God, don't fail."

"I won't."

He didn't. He spent the night in four different gaming hells. He played upon his wet-behind-the-ears looks. He pretended to be drunk when he wasn't. And when the players got wise, he slipped out and ran to the next one. And once, he even stole money from a drunkard who had passed out near him.

It was for a good cause, he rationalized, as he became a thief. It was for love and for Diana's family. And when he got the last pound note clutched into his hands, he ran from the hell while his victim screamed, "You better run, boy, but it won't help. I'll find you tomorrow, and then we'll see."

He felt the threat settle low in his spine as his feet pounded away. It held real danger, and he knew he could never return to the hells he'd been in tonight. A man could make a lot of money in one night. He had proven that. But it had required him to be ruthless in a way that he despised. He'd taken money from friends, acquaintances, and idiots.

It left him feeling filthy and ashamed, but he'd gotten what he wanted.

Three thousand pounds.

Wonderful, except he would never be able to do that again. The gamblers were on to him. The monied people and the thieves. He needed to get out of London immediately, which would be fine, except how would he support Diana and her family in the future? How would he cover the other two thousand pounds they needed to survive? This year and then the next and the next?

He didn't know. And he sure as hell couldn't marry her until he had an answer. Cold logic in the morning had replaced last night's romantic passion.

He didn't go to her bedroom that morning. He didn't drop on his knees and shower her with pound notes as he'd envisioned throughout the night. And he certainly didn't stop her from dully speaking her vows to her new husband, though he stood at the back of the church and tried not to weep in despair.

Instead, he used the money to buy a commission and entered the military that very day.

That should have been the end of it. That should have put paid to any relationship between him and Diana. Until the morning, twelve years later, when her brother Elliott walked into his bedroom and said, "I need your help. Diana's in trouble."

CHAPTER TWO

D IANA, LADY DUNNAMORE, smiled as she heard a bird call outside her husband's bedroom window. The sound was piercing enough to make it through the glass and drawn curtains, and she identified the creature as a house sparrow. To her shame, she had not listened to her husband's lectures enough to know whether the bird was male or female, calling for a mate, or just singing about a new nest. But she nevertheless held on to the sound as she held on to the memory of strolling through the gardens with the man who had been at her side for twelve years.

Blessing number seven, Oscar had taught her to appreciate bird calls. It was the one that came right after six—he shaved off his mustache because she did not like kissing it. And before number eight—he did not slurp his soup.

In truth, those should have been numbers one through three of the things she most loved about her husband. But since the priest had asked her to write it, and her mother would undoubtedly ask to see it, Diana had written what was expected of her. Number one was, of course, that he married her to save her family from poverty. It wasn't at all true, and she knew it. But her mother had always needed a man to guide her hand, and so Diana had married Oscar and was expected to be grateful.

Number two detailed her position as a married lady of the peerage. The next items included things that he had bought her, the servants who waited upon her, and the biggest lie of all, the family she was now surrounded by. Not her own, but his viperous children who sneered as they called her stepmama because they were older than she. And who had made her life into hell for the last twelve years such that her only true gratitude came from the knowledge of birdcalls and that her husband had shaved his mustache.

Oscar stirred, and she looked up from where she was pretending to read in the indifferent light. Her husband snorted, grunted, and slowly roused himself. She waited, mentally taking a bet on whether he would settle back into sleep or push himself upright and demand tea.

She bet on tea but hoped for sleep.

She was right, and she counted that a win as he snorted a couple more times and cracked his eyes open.

"Diana."

"Yes, Oscar, I'm here." She stood and tugged on the bellpull. "I've rung for tea."

"Get me tea."

"An excellent idea, Oscar. Would you like me to help you sit up?"

"Don't need your help." He coughed a little, and she handed him a handkerchief. Then she supported his arm as he maneuvered himself upright before she adjusted the pillows to how he liked them.

"Ring for tea," he ordered once he was settled.

"Right away," she responded as she tugged again on the bellpull.

And just like clockwork, there was a scratch at the bedroom door. She opened it quietly, and tea was brought in. Diana sniffed, recognizing her husband's favorite blend, then watched calmly as the tray was set down by the bed. As was their custom, Diana waited until the maid had left the room before sitting down beside her husband's bed.

"Tea, Oscar?"

"Yes, thank you." His voice was stronger this morning, having less wheeze and more breath. That was a good thing, she supposed, but she had been fooled too many times by a strong morning to expect a good afternoon. She simply took it for the gift it was and poured his lordship's tea.

She did not drink. She did not like his blend, and she had broken her fast more than two hours before. But she smiled as he sipped with shaky, arthritic hands and searched for a conversation topic.

"There's a house sparrow outside the window," she said. "Can you hear it? Is it a male or female, do you think?"

"What? No, I can't hear it, but it's female, I should think. They make the most noise in any species, right?" Then he chuckled in his phlegmy way at his joke. He forgot that his first wife had been the chatty one. Diana only spoke when she felt it necessary, which happened less and less these days. At least within this bedroom.

He continued to chuckle while she waited for his valet to appear. She was rewarded after exactly four minutes—she watched the clock specifically—and was surprised because his valet normally appeared after two. What exciting thing had happened to cause the delay?

The man knocked more brusquely than usual. And when her husband bid the man enter, they were both surprised to see not one servant, but two. His lordship's valet Reynolds entered behind a burly footman she did not recognize. The large man kept his head down, but that did not disguise his muscles or the scars along the back of his hands as he carried in the implements used for his lordship's morning toilette. He wore the livery of the house—shabby though it appeared—and he hunched slightly as if he were trying to hide his size.

She arched a brow at Reynolds, but the valet kept his gaze carefully canted away as he smiled too fully at her husband. "Good morning, my lord," he said heartily.

Oscar wasn't fooled. "Who is this?" His eyes cut to Diana. "Are you spending more of my money?"

"Never, my lord," she lied. Since Oscar's illness, she'd had to manage all the bills, including the payments for the staff. She stepped such that she stood directly in front of the new footman. "I'm afraid I've forgotten your name."

"Egeus, my lady," the man said, his voice surprisingly high for such a large man. "But most call me Gus."

"Mr. Egeus, how do you come to help us today?" She guessed that one of their regular footmen had become ill and sent his brother or cousin or something to fill in. That sometimes happened as servants tried to gain employment for their family members. But in this, she was completely wrong as he ticked his head to the hallway.

"Mr. Lucifer hired me on, my lady."

"Lucifer!" she gasped. "What a name!"

"I believe it's meant to frighten those who displease him."

It was ridiculous, and so she meant to tell him. She would not have anyone with such a name in her household. But before she could say such a thing, her husband began to laugh. It was a wheezy sound, but she recognized the fuller notes beneath it. Since being bedridden, Oscar had developed a macabre sense of humor.

"That must be him, then," Oscar said as he waved at the doorway. "Come on in, man. Tell us how you came to be the devil himself."

Diana had been looking at the new footman, so when Oscar gestured behind them, she spun around with a nervous kind of speed. She did not like people sneaking up behind her. And when she saw the man standing in the doorway, she liked it even less. For a brief moment, she considered the truth that it was Lucifer himself come to destroy her life.

The man had dark hair, dark eyes, and dressed to match the sinister name. Though his clothes were worn, they were dark as sin, and he made no attempt to hide the scar that cut through his hair as if a heavenly warrior had cleaved his head a few inches above his right ear. She didn't recognize him, and yet she felt a jolt inside. A shock that cut off her breath and made her heart squeeze tight.

She must have made a sound because his gaze cut to hers. Such weight there in his simple regard. As if living shadows loomed behind his eyes to reach out and grab the unaware. But then she remembered other eyes. A boy tumbling at her feet through her bedroom window and promising to return in the morning with enough money so they could wed.

Lucas.

The memory was so strong that her jaw went slack in shock. But then she blinked and refocused. This man was hard. He stood lightly on his feet, and his eyes caught every movement in the room. And though he bowed to Oscar, she felt as if he tracked her movements as an owl did a mouse. And if she had to imagine him as a boy, he would be nothing like the earnest young Lucas she remembered.

"Do you come to spirit me away to hell?" her husband asked with good cheer.

"Oscar, please!" she gasped. "Don't say such things."

"Oh, come here, my dear." He held out his hand, and she crossed the room to grasp it. His thin skin cool, and the knuckles thick, but it was also familiar, and she found reassurance in his feeble grip. "A man dressed in black cannot scare me," he said. "Tell me your tale."

It sounded as if he were ordering a bard to play for him. And as she expected, Mr. Lucifer did not oblige beyond the most cursory response. "I fought against Napoleon and learned that names had power against the superstitious." He waggled his brows. "And the Frogs were a superstitious lot."

Oscar chortled. "I wager they are. Did they run like babies crying for their mamas?"

"And wet themselves along the way."

Oscar laughed so hard that he began to choke, his breath coming in frightening wheezes. And when he regained some of his strength, he waved Mr. Lucifer closer. "Tell me more," he rasped.

"No, Oscar," Diana interrupted. "You need to finish your tea first. And give Reynolds time to finish your toilette."

Oscar dropped back against his cushions, his breath finally easing.

"She likes me smooth," he said as he scratched at his chin, and Diana felt her cheeks heat. That was not something to discuss with strangers, let alone this dark man.

Mr. Lucifer executed a perfect bow, but when he rose, his gaze was serious. "My lord," he said in a tone that felt like a whisper but was nonetheless heard by all in the room. "I have been sent by the lady's brother to assist for a short time while you are indisposed."

Diana's head snapped up. "Elliot? Why would he send..." Her voice trailed away. She knew damned well why he would send someone to her household. With Oscar in his bed, she had been forced to confront Oscar's greedy heir alone. Geoffrey was a blighter through and through. He gambled, he caroused, and he came often to steal the silver to pay off his debts. And when she confronted him with his crimes, he threatened her.

She shook her head. She was the older sister, Elliot, the younger heir. He might be old enough to manage his own affairs now, but she'd be damned if he insinuated himself into hers. She'd had precious little say in her life. She would not cede control of it to anyone.

Unfortunately, while she was sorting all that out in her mind, Mr. Lucifer took advantage of her silence. "You see," he said as he gestured to her. "She knows, my lord. There are dangers in London, and sometimes they invade a man's home. Especially one who is temporarily weakened by an illness."

"Temporarily, huh?" Oscar scoffed. "Yes, yes," he agreed. "I still have hopes to walk again."

"Of course, you will," Diana soothed, but she was quieted by a wave of Oscar's hand.

"Elliott sent you?" he asked.

"Yes, my lord."

"And does he pay you as well?"

"Yes, my lord."

Oscar's gaze cut to Mr. Egeus. "And him?"

"Yes, my lord."

Then he grunted. "Very well."

"Oscar!" Diana cried out. "We don't need my brother's interference."

Her husband looked at her and shook his head. "He's got a good head, your brother, and a fat purse. If he wants to add to my servants out of brotherly fear, then we shall indulge him." He squeezed her hand. "You need to be protected, my dear. You're too delicate to risk."

She wanted to snatch her hand away at that. She was the farthest thing from delicate, but her petite frame gave everyone the impression that she was a child barely out of leading strings. It was enough to make her want to rip out her blonde ringlets.

She didn't. She'd had long experience managing her husband and her household. So she smiled at Oscar and squeezed back. "But you shall have the ruling over their actions, yes? Elliott may pay for them, but they abide by your rules, do they not?"

Oscar nodded. "Of course. I am the king of my own castle, am I not?"

"Of course, you are." She turned and fixed Mr. Lucifer with a dark stare. "And I am the queen." The smile she gave him was as hard as a diamond. "If you would follow me, Mr. Lucifer, I shall explain your duties while my lord finishes his morning ablutions."

His smile matched hers, though it felt like it glittered with a great deal more relish than hers. "I await your pleasure, my lady." And he made it sound as sinful a statement as if it had been uttered by the devil himself.

Which was ridiculous, and yet the words sent shivers down her spine.

CHAPTER THREE

L UCAS TRAILED THROUGH the house behind Diana. His eyes drank her in as he watched how she moved, how her shoulders were stiff, and her chin held high. And though he walked behind her, he replayed the way she had deferred to her husband and yet still commanded the bedroom. When she said she was the queen, he believed her. The girl in his memory had grown up to be a woman worthy of reverence and protection.

Which was now his job, and he couldn't suppress the lump of joy that he could finally—after twelve years of regrets—be of service to the goddess he had failed so long ago.

He kept pace with her as she descended through the house until he came to the housekeeper's room. As they went, he watched all the servants—even the butler—follow her movements with steady, sympathetic gazes. That told him that she was a fair queen who had made good choices in those who served her. But it wasn't until they stepped into the kitchen that he realized the depth of their devotion to her. Everyone greeted her with a gift. The kitchen-maid held out an apron to her, the cook pressed a scone into her hand, and even the butler set a teapot down just as she entered the housekeeper's room. She smiled graciously at every one of them, thanked them, and then sat down in her chair before pouring herself some tea.

All without saying a word to him. In truth, he felt like he was about to get a dressing down from a superior officer. And so he stood at attention while he waited, his gaze taking in everything about him.

First and foremost, he thought it was odd that she chose to speak with him from the housekeeper's room belowstairs. Wouldn't the female head of the staff be upset by the mistress taking over her place of work? But as he glanced at the papers on the desk, he realized all were written in Diana's neat hand. So, Diana had taken over the housekeeper's duties, probably as a way to economize.

Next, he noticed all the touches of a well-used office. Paper and ink were placed at easy use, and there were the inevitable stains on the dark wood desk. There was a tiny vase for a few spring flowers set on the windowsill. He recalled that she liked wildflowers and—at sixteen—had often woven them into her hair or clothing. But most importantly, he saw that she reclined at ease in this place. A mistress should not be one of the servants, and yet here she was as relaxed as if this were the lady's parlor.

"You should not work as a housekeeper here," he murmured. The words were spoken low such as to not be overheard. "It demeans your station and upsets the servants. They deserve a place to be at ease, and they cannot do it with you here."

Her eyes shot up to his. "You are dismissed, Mr. Lucifer. I shall inform my brother that your services are not needed here."

Dismissed? Good lord, she thought he was here as a true hire and not because she desperately needed some protection. He leaned back and folded his arms across his chest. "So, Elliott was wrong? He didn't witness your stepson assaulting you? And stealing silver from the house?"

Her eyes narrowed. "Just who are you to Elliott?"

He took a moment to absorb her words. Could it be that she didn't recognize him? It wasn't possible! But of course, it was. Just because he'd thought of her every day and night since he'd abandoned her on her wedding day didn't mean that he figured so prominently in her thoughts. It had been twelve years, after all, and yet the blow was so deep as to make his breath catch.

"Answer me, Mr. Lucifer!" she snapped. Then she rolled her eyes. "My God, that is a ridiculous name, and I will not use it."

Her outrage gave him enough time to recover his breath. But when he spoke, it was with an extra measure of coldness. "I will answer when you do, my lady," he said. "Did your stepson steal the silver?"

She blew out a breath. "You know he did." She glanced past his shoulder, through the open door, to where most of the staff loitered within earshot. "I paid off his debts and told him there would be no more quarterly money until after I was repaid. I'm afraid he misunderstood and came looking for his allowance."

He frowned. "You paid off his debts? To whom?"

"His debts," she snapped. "To his landlord, his valet, and even his club. All paid."

"But not his gambling debts."

She shook her head. "Those are his own affair." She snorted. "And he would not suffer the humiliation of having a woman dispense the money."

Of course not. Pride was one of Geoffrey's biggest downfalls. "And so he assaulted you in anger and to make you pay him." The words burned his throat as he said them. The idea of that blighter laying hands on Diana was the only reason he'd come out of hiding.

Diana did not deny it, which made him see red. But he kept it under control even as she tried to turn the tables on him. "I have answered your questions, now answer mine. Who are you to Elliott that he would put you in my household?"

He swallowed, still hurt by her blindness. "Do you not recognize me, Diana? I thought you of all people would remember me."

He watched her eyes widen at his softer tone. Did she recognize his voice? Or perhaps the way he said her name. But just in case, he made it clear.

"I came back," he said. "On the day you married. I came back—"

"Stop!" She turned her head away, but not before he'd seen the glisten of tears on her lashes. "Stop," she repeated again. "That day is long gone. I have ceased thinking of it."

"I haven't," he said. "I joined the army that very day. I couldn't face that I had failed you."

Her hand jerked sideways as if she were shooing away his words. "It was an impossible task. Three thousand pounds in a single night. No one could—"

"I did."

Her head jerked upward at that, but she didn't speak.

"I got all the money, but only by turning everyone I met into an enemy. I played deep and well, but it was not enough. I tricked friends and enemies alike to get the rest. I lost my honor that night, but I counted you worth the cost."

"Lucas," she whispered, his name voiced with anguish, but it still warmed him to hear her say his name aloud.

"So much money, but I could not have done it again. And three thousand was not enough to support you for the rest of our lives. I certainly couldn't have protected you when those who lost everything to me came looking for my hide."

Her breath caught. "You were beaten?"

"I would have been if I'd remained in London."

"So, you joined the army." She sounded as if she couldn't credit the thought.

"I did," he said firmly. "I had to flee. And you..." He swallowed and ducked his head.

"I was married."

He forced himself to meet her gaze and say the one thing he'd been waiting to voice for twelve long years. "I'm sorry, Diana. I failed you."

Her expression softened, and her voice came out with a resigned note. "It is done, Lucas. We were both fools to think it possible."

He couldn't disagree. Indeed, he looked back and wondered at his own idiocy. He'd believed that love would make it possible. Only a fool believed that love was enough. "I regret so much about that night."

She snorted. "Might as well regret the rain. Only children believe that prayers will change the weather." She pushed to her feet. "Nevertheless, I thank you. It is good to see you again, Lucas." She extended her hand for his kiss. "Next time you visit, I shall greet you in the front parlor. A man of your station should not be down here among the servants."

His station? It was below hers. He had yet to inherit his title, and she was already Lady Dunnamore. In fact, at the moment, he was presumed dead, so he had no station at all. He meant to ignore her outstretched hand. Whether she knew it or not, he wasn't going anywhere. But he couldn't resist touching her again, even in so small a way.

He took her hand, but instead of lifting it to his lips, he held her fast in his good hand while his bad one stroked across her skin. He felt her delicate bones and gloried in the warmth of her fingers. He felt her soft skin and wished for the millionth time that things had been different for them both.

And he had the pleasure of seeing her flustered, as if she were a girl of sixteen again, touched so innocently by her beau. Her cheeks heated, and she tried to tug her hand free. He didn't release it, and she wouldn't be so unseemly as to tussle with him.

"Lucas—" she said in a low undertone. "Release me!"

He didn't. "Geoffrey will come back. Surely you see that. He is deep in debt, and his creditors are not kind men."

"How do you know this?"

"I have been working at a place where such things are easily known." He saw her eyes widen again and rushed to reassure her. "It's not a brothel," he said, though, in truth, there were girls, and what they did abovestairs was exactly what one would guess. "I work in a gambling den. That's where Gus is from as well as a few others. They're trustworthy and will protect you well."

She shook her head. "I am in no danger. There is nothing Geoffrey can do to force my hand. Once he realizes that, he will mend his ways. He will have no choice."

She was so innocent and had no understanding of what a man would do when his back was against a wall. And he had no wish to disillusion her. Especially since he had no need to.

"You may be right," he said pleasantly. "But I have promised Elliott to protect you, and so I shall."

"But—"

"I will keep one promise to your family, Diana. Do not think to stop me."

He let her see he would not be moved on this. He held his ground, he looked her in the eyes, and he kept her hand trapped between his larger palms. Once she saw that he would not bend, she would give in gracefully. Such was the natural order of things.

That's what he believed until she abruptly whipped her hand from his, then looked past his shoulder. "Simpson, please see to Mr. Lucifer's departure. Egeus will go as well."

"What! Diana, don't be ridiculous—" he began but stopped at her cold, hard stare.

Meanwhile, the butler stepped into the room, his expression anxious. He was older, thinner, and clearly no match for Lucas, but that wasn't the point. He could no more fight this man than he would his own grandfather.

"This is Simpson," Diana said before Lucas could do more than assess his opponent. "He has a wife, three children, and a grandchild soon to arrive. I depend on him in countless ways, and it would grieve me to no end to lose him even for so much as an hour to an injury.

And that is nothing compared to how his wife and pregnant daughter would fare should he be laid low."

Simpson dipped his chin slightly. "My lady is too kind."

She was being nothing of the sort. She was using Lucas's tender feelings against him. Telling him in clear terms that should he harm Simpson in any way, he would be harming her. And that was something he would not do.

"I would never dream of hurting Mr. Simpson," he said. "I am here to help him coordinate some very large footmen who will see that nothing untoward happens to my lady. And that is something that your brother, your husband, myself, and Mr. Simpson all feel is of value. Is that not true, Simpson?"

The butler blushed a little as he turned rheumy eyes to Diana. "I do find that—at my age—having a few extra strong footmen about makes my tasks easier. And you did just yesterday suggest that I should take a bit more rest when I can."

Excellent. That put the butler firmly in his camp. Now Diana would give in gracefully.

"Mr. Simpson," she snapped. "We can handle things quite well—"

"But as you said," Simpson interrupted, "I should rest more. And I fear your brother would take insult if we refused his generous aid."

Diana stared at her butler for a long moment. When she spoke, it was quietly and with a queen's command. "I am the mistress here, am I not?"

"Indubitably," Simpson answered.

"I control who is allowed in my house and who is not."

It wasn't phrased as a question, but Simpson answered, nonetheless. "Of course, my lady."

"Then I say—"

Lucas spoke up before she could make a declaration she would regret. "How many bruises did Mr. Geoffrey Hough leave on your skin?"

Diana's head snapped up, and she spoke low and angry. "You go too far."

He hadn't gone far enough. "What has he threatened to do to you? Does he stop at a simple beating? Or does he insinuate far worse?"

He saw a flash of fear in her eyes, but she quickly covered it. That told him all he needed to know about the vile things her stepson had said to her. He let the moment hang not so he could draw breath but to control the surge of rage boiling through his body.

"Empty threats," she said. "He would not dare carry them out."

None of that was true. Geoffrey would indeed carry out his threats, and her very pale skin told him she suspected she was being naïve. Which meant he had to force her to admit her vulnerability, not only for her own sake but for everyone else's.

"If something were to happen to you," he asked, "what would become of the servants here? Of your husband? Will your stepson treat them well? Or will he corner the maids in the library? He has certainly done depraved things at the Lyon's Den. How will you keep Simpson safe from an empty bottle thrown at his head? Geoffrey put a three-inch gash in Egeus's forehead seven months ago at the Den. That is why Egeus was the first to volunteer for his duties here." He straightened to his full height. "Refuse my aid if you must, but who will protect your servants? Pride is not reserved just for feckless heirs. I understand that even a mistress of her own home can suffer from the same affliction."

She stiffened at the insult. "It is not pride that makes me want you gone."

He arched his brows in challenge. "No? Then why?"

Her next words cut deeper than anything else she could have said. "Because I do not know you, sir. And I am not accustomed to allowing men I do not know into my home, no matter what promises they or my brother make."

That hurt. Never—not even when they were teenagers—had she

spoken to anyone with that imperious tone. It clogged his throat with surprising pain, but he still got his words out.

"You do know me," he said.

She sucked in a breath. "No—"

"You know that I failed you once, Diana. Which is why I will not fail you again. I swear it."

She shook her head, and her eyes shone brightly. "I put no faith in the promises of men."

Simpson straightened in shock. "My lady!"

"Diana, you are being illogical—"

"Enough!" she snapped as she slashed her hand through the air. He watched her gather her dignity in the way she straightened her spine and lifted her chin. She looked at Simpson first, and his cheeks burned red at her hard regard.

"My lady—" he began, pain in his tone.

"You want him here?" she asked.

He swallowed and nodded. "I think it best."

She did not look at Lucas. "Then you will be sure that I never cross paths with him inside this house. Fill my home to the rafters with his large men, but I will not set eyes on Mr. Lucifer again." She coated his name with disdain. "Do I make myself clear?"

"Yes, my lady."

Then she swept between them, her skirts nearly trapping his ankles as she moved through, only to release him with the force of a whip letting go. She had every right to hate him. Twelve years ago, he had failed her. But in all his daydreams of how they might meet again, never had he expected this. That the very sight of him would fill her with fury.

Except it hadn't at first. Her eyes had softened and... And she had tried to boot him from her home. And while he was thinking about that, Simpson blew out a slow breath.

"It shouldn't be too difficult to keep you two apart. If your men—"

"I'm afraid I'm about to disappoint her ladyship again."

"What?"

"I have no intention of staying apart from her." He hadn't even realized he meant the words until he'd spoken them. So much had changed for them both in twelve years. And yet, the drive to be by her side hadn't lessened one jot. He'd suppressed it for twelve long years, but now, after seeing her again, he could not abandon her again. Not even if she brought in the royal guard to throw him into the street.

"I have promised to protect her, Simpson. That means I will be at her side every minute of every day until that blighter is gone from England."

Simpson was quiet for a long moment, then he pursed his lips. "She won't like that, my lord. And though she might not look like much, she can fight in unexpected ways."

In that respect, they were well and truly matched.

CHAPTER FOUR

*D*AMN, *DAMN, DAMN!* The words sounded in Diana's thoughts with every step she took away from her downstairs desk. Twelve years—*twelve years!*—she had worked night and day to gain respect from the people around her. She'd been a child when she'd taken over the reins of the household, and the staff had run roughshod over her. Her husband had been oblivious to the sleights handed her by everyone from the lowest maid and up through every single one of Oscar's older and crueler children.

She hadn't known how to manage anything, but by God, she'd learned. It had been the mother of her dearest school friend who had taught her that respect came from two things: money and a cool head. She had to gain control of the household finances and wield that money with calm, level-headed authority. No histrionics, no whining. Simple, implacable rules.

It sounded so easy, but learning to do it had been the most exacting lesson of her life. Her mother had taught her to wheedle and simper her way into what she wanted. But that only worked on society men. She'd stood firm against her husband when he complained that she'd upset the house by sacking the insolent housekeeper. She'd used the very same words with him that she had a few moments ago. "I am the mistress, am I not?" and "I control who comes and goes in my own household, do I not?"

Since she had not simpered or been tearful, he had bowed to her logic. He'd had no excuse to send her to her room for being too emotional. And in such a way, she'd gained control of her staff. They were obedient to her wishes, or they were fired, whether they were new hires or lifelong retainers pensioned off without a tear of regret.

That had been the first step, and it had taken two years for her to root out those servants who gave their allegiance to her stepdaughter Penelope, Lady Beddoe. The woman was a vicious shrew with nothing better to do than to make sure Diana felt small as all her plans turned to ash.

It had taken several more years of strict, unemotional management before her husband sought her advice on how to handle his increasingly wild heir, Geoffrey. Even then, he'd asked her advice out of desperation. If he'd listened to her then, she wouldn't be in her current situation, but—ironically—her husband had been too tenderhearted in his dealings with Geoffrey to ever get him under control. Then just last year, her coup de grace.

With Oscar's health failing and Geoffrey's debts becoming an embarrassment, Oscar had allowed her to write his letters for him, most specifically his instructions to his man of affairs. And if either man questioned her directives, she had a well-reasoned answer that forced them to bow to her dictates. The most important one had been that Geoffrey's allowance flowed at her husband's command. And she, of course, managed what he commanded because she was the one who wrote the letters.

After twelve years of thwarting her at every turn, she had indeed become exactly what Oscar's children feared: a managing woman. And she was very good at it.

Until today. Until Lucas Crosse, the future Earl of Wolvesmead, had stepped into her husband's sickroom and brought back feelings long since buried.

Damn him!

He was the one man who had ever tempted her to folly, the one man who had made her good sense scatter. And then he had failed her. Not only failed to marry her but failed to even stand by her side when she was most alone. A young bride of seventeen married to a man three times her age. She needed a friend, and he had been nowhere to be found. She'd shoved him out of her thoughts until today when he'd marched in with a cocky smile and a scar to make him dashing. She wasn't a girl to have her head turned by a handsome man, and she certainly had the experience to know that he could not swoop in and save her from anything.

And yet how her heart had twisted when she realized his identity. How she'd longed to collapse into his arms. *Ridiculous!* She'd spent the last twelve years refusing to collapse for any reason at all.

It infuriated her because he clouded her thinking. All she could think about was to get rid of him, to keep him away from her because he upset everything about her life. He upset her very calm, implacable will, and that was a sin she could not afford.

It was his fault, and she damned him for it even as she reached for the chair of her dressing table with an unsteady hand. She stared at her reflection in the mirror. She had no thoughts except for a silent wrench inside her. It hurt to breathe, so she barely inhaled. And she felt so alone sitting in her bedroom. Through the connecting door, she heard her elderly husband cough. It was a dry sound, ineffective and weak. She would have to kiss him on his mouth soon. She would have to stroke his fine wisps of hair and pretend that she adored him.

Part of her did love him. They had been together twelve years, and he had been kind at times, certainly affectionate, and never brutal. She had found peace in that. In truth, it had been many years since she screamed into a pillow that she hated him, hated his children, and hated everything about her existence.

Was that because she had accepted her fate? Or gotten too tired to scream?

A knock sounded at her bedroom door. She blinked, wondering

how long she had been sitting here.

"Enter," she said, but the word had no sound. She had to clear her throat and then repeat the word. "Enter."

"Simpson said I could come up," her half-sister, Lilah, said. "I hope I'm not intruding."

"Of course not," Diana said, and she meant it.

Her sister was a bastard only by a quirk of fate. In all other respects, she was the best of them. Her mother was irresponsible, her brother was exceptional, but only in the last few years. It helped that he met and married a wonderful woman named Amber. Gwen cared nothing for life except her books, but Lilah was kind and generous. Her smile had a flaw in one tooth that had come in twisted and pushed slightly forward. It gave an uneven look to her mouth that made her all the more endearing. Her hair was a golden blonde with soft curls ruthlessly suppressed. And when she spoke, she used tones so gentle that, at times, Diana had found her annoyingly deferential. Today, she found her sister to be the only person she could tolerate. "I need someone to take me out of my melancholy."

Lilah shut the door behind her. "You don't look melancholy as much as..." Her voice trailed off. It was a trick she often used as she let others fill in the blank, and it worked very well on Diana sometimes.

"It is merely melancholy," she said. Then she glanced at the connecting door. "Oscar is better today, but there is no escaping the inevitable."

Lilah nodded as she sat down on the edge of Diana's bed. "Your feelings are natural. Is there anything I can do to help?"

And there was the question Lilah always asked—if she could help. She twisted in her seat and felt a wave of gratitude for her youngest sister. "There is nothing to do except tell me why you are here."

Her sister shrugged. "Mama wants to know if Amber is pregnant. She thinks you know."

"Me? Why would I know?"

Lilah chuckled. "Because I have no idea and certainly won't ask."

"You can tell Mama that the two are blissfully happy together. And given the way they look at one another, I imagine she will become a grandmother soon enough."

"That's almost exactly what I said, but Mama is—"

"Impatient? Demanding? Tired of meddling in Gwen's life?"

"All of that and more," Lilah responded. "But she also loves us deeply. She doesn't want Amber and Elliott to make babies too soon. She wants them to enjoy their time now before things get more complicated later." She raised her hands in defeat. "She wants to suggest that you speak to Amber. She believes you know about ways of prevention."

Prevention? She did know, but she would never presume to suggest to a married couple what might be good or bad for their marriage. "That is something Elliott and Amber must decide for themselves." She shook her head. "And Mama must accept that her children can decide these things without her interference." Then she paused as she looked at her sister. Lilah would never presume to say something so blunt to Mama. She was the epitome of self-effacing kindness. "I'll speak with her," Diana finally said.

Lilah's expression softened with relief. "Thank you."

Diana smiled. She was happy to help. But as much as she enjoyed seeing her brother ecstatically happy, she couldn't deny a twinge of jealousy. He was a titled man of means. He could afford to find and marry a woman he loved. She, on the other hand, was a woman who had been sacrificed so he could have time to grow up. It wasn't fair, but she'd grown past the resentment. Or she had until Lucas brought everything back.

But rather than return to those thoughts, she focused on her sister. "Tell me something exciting. What have you been doing these days?"

Her sister released a laugh. "There is nothing exciting in my days. Mama wants me to get Gwen outside to someplace other than the lending library."

"You should go to a party. Both of you. Something fun."

Lilah leaned forward. "I will if you will."

Diana shook her head. "My place is here beside my husband."

"Your place was there on the day of your wedding. And now your place is to oversee his household and his care—"

"It is."

"But it is not to hide away." She took a breath and dared touch Diana's hand. It was a bold move for her, but one that was deeply appreciated. "You will need to wrap yourself in crepe soon enough. When he dies, you will be locked away in mourning. Take a moment now to get out of this house just for an evening." Then she shrugged. "And if we can force Gwen to accompany you, so much the better."

It was a tempting idea, to be sure. Gwen was twenty-eight and needed to find a husband immediately. And if she could get Lilah out into society, then the woman might meet a man who was willing to overlook her illegitimate birth. Perhaps there could be happiness for her sisters.

"You said you wanted a way out of your melancholy," Lilah coaxed. "Couldn't this be the way?"

It wasn't her melancholy she needed to escape, but Lucas, who had invaded her home and upset her equilibrium. Then the idea came to her.

She snapped her fingers in triumph. "A masquerade!" she said. That would give time for a gentleman to become intrigued with Lilah before her identity was revealed. Plus, they were known to be more forgiving with the invitations as members of the not-quite-proper *ton* came out to play.

But Lilah shook her head. "Gwen would never go to such a thing. She would find it too frivolous."

"She finds people too frivolous. If we could dress up a book in trousers, then she might be interested." Diana shook her head. "No, I have decided. The very next masquerade shall have all three of us in attendance. Tell Gwen I desperately need the frivolity."

"You do need it."

"And I will not have it unless both my sisters attend."

Lilah frowned. "I might be able to convince her." She sounded doubtful but willing to try.

"The harder part will be to keep Mama away. There can be no fun with her constant interfering." And no chance that Lilah would be able to kick up her heels a bit. Mama was ever vigilant that Lilah did not put herself forward. In truth, Diana thought it cruel to give Lilah all the trappings of gentility but none of the possible futures. Sadly, that was the way with by-blows. If they were lucky, they were given a place in the household as an unpaid servant. It was a difficult life, but at least she was not on the street.

Then Diana had an idea. "I shall ask Mama to reside here for the evening in case Oscar needs something."

Lilah's eyes widened in horror. "Mama abhors a sickbed."

"But I will remind her that it is her motherly duty to help every once in a while." Her tone grew harder in memory. "Just as she told me over and over that it was my daughterly duty to marry Oscar."

Lilah nodded. "Giving you one night away is the least she can do."

"We have a pact then? The very next masquerade—"

"Will see three sisters attend. Yes."

They even shook hands on the bargain.

LUCAS SMILED AS he loitered outside Diana's bedroom door. Now that was a great idea.

CHAPTER FIVE

L UCAS PACED IN the dark, allowing his nerves free rein. He was completely alone here, so he could run a hole in the threadbare carpet if need be. Not twenty minutes ago, he'd sent missives to two of his best friends from school. Aaron and Jackson had been his constant companions until circumstances had thrown them to the four winds. It had been the most natural thing in the world for the three future earls to become steadfast friends, but then he'd gone to war, and he hadn't seen them since.

The missives had requested their appearance in Aaron's own front parlor with no signature provided. That was enough of a mystery that they ought to be here any moment now. And Lucas could only imagine what they would say to finding their supposedly dead friend had unlawfully entered Aaron's home only to wait for their arrival.

He heard them arrive, one through the front, the other through the back. The house was dark because Aaron's lazy servants had long since disappeared to their own entertainments. Lucas forced himself to stand in a relaxed pose next to the cold fireplace, and he waited.

A moment later, Aaron eased into the parlor from the dining room. His dark body was outlined with broad shoulders and a lean waist grown impossibly broader and leaner, respectively, since they last saw one another. Jackson was the overly tall one with the strength of a bull and the stomach of a goat, since he could and had eaten whatever food was put in front of him. At least he had when they were boys. Who knew what either man's habits were now?

When Lucas saw that both men came alone, he squatted down and lit the fire. The coals caught quickly because he had prepared them beforehand, and then he waited as the flames grew and lit his face such that his friends would know him.

Or he hoped they would know him.

Jackson reacted first, his breath expelling on a low growl. "Is that one of your sister's ghosts?"

"Don't think so," Aaron responded. "Unless ghosts smell like the sewer."

Lucas stiffened. "I do not smell like the sewer. I smell like your kitchen waste. Your window stuck as I was trying to gain entry, and I fell. Don't you know that muck will attract rats?"

Aaron lit an oil lamp and brought it forward. His eyes were narrowed, and his brows drew down in confusion, but he was no less intimidating as he loomed close. "By God, Lucas, is that you?"

He raised his hands in a shrug. "Seems so."

"Seems so!" Jackson snapped as he rushed forward to grab Lucas's elbow and spin him until they were face to face. "Seems so? We thought you dead!" He gripped Lucas's shoulders and hauled him into a warm embrace.

Lucas tensed. No one had dared touch him like this in years. And he certainly hadn't been slapped on the back as he if it had been a few months instead of twelve years since they'd last seen each other. But this was Jackson, and he hadn't realized how much he'd missed his friend until he was already in the man's embrace.

"Leave off, Sayres," Aaron said, using Jackson's courtesy title. "Let me see him." He set down the lamp and stood there studying Lucas from head to toe. Lucas had been inspected hundreds of times before. The army was filled with superior officers who had taken his measure with a long heavy stare. He had endured them all, but this was different. This was Aaron, and his insides twitched as he waited to see his friend's reaction.

But as the minutes wore on, Lucas had to say something to break the tension. "Have you gone blind, old man?" Aaron was the oldest of them by seven months.

"Not blind," he said slowly. "Just damned emotional."

The man didn't appear emotional at all. His jaw was set, his gaze was steady, and even his hands were still. But his feet twitched as he shifted slightly forward, then slightly back. Not enough for anyone but his best friend to notice.

"I'm alive," Lucas said gently.

"Thank God," Aaron breathed out. Then the two of them collapsed together, hugging each other as they hadn't for twelve years.

"Call for some brandy, Aaron," Jackson said. "The finest you've got."

Aaron released Lucas and shot the man a dark look. "You're always so free with my brandy."

"Lucas back from the dead deserves—"

"I didn't say you were wrong. Just that you're free with my drink." That was true. Aaron always had the best drink; Jackson had the most charm. And together, they let Lucas devise schemes that entertained them all. And often got them deep in someone's ill graces.

They broke apart, Aaron to tug the bellpull, Jackson to open the sideboard and bring out a half-filled bottle, and Lucas to stand awkwardly by the fire, wondering how to broach the topic of what he wanted. Didn't need to. Aaron knew how things were with him. Always had.

"Here's how it's going to go," he said sternly. "First, you're going to tell us where you've been for the last decade, then you can ask us what you want." He frowned. "Where's Binner?"

"Out to dinner?" Jackson echoed back.

"Binner, your butler?"

"Yes. And come to think of it, where's my sister? She should be home."

"I got her an invite to a séance. It's all very safe, and I knew she'd want to go—"

"What!" Aaron exclaimed. "The devil you say."

"Relax. As I said, it's all very harmless. Should take another couple hours." Aaron's sister, Clara, had a fascination with the occult. And since Lucas had needed her out of the house, this was the safest, easiest way.

"You should not encourage her in that nonsense."

Lucas shook his head. "She's an intelligent woman. Do try to trust in her good sense."

"She believes in ghosts!"

"So did your mother," Jackson said. "The apple hasn't fallen far from the tree."

"That's hardly a recommendation for good sense," Aaron returned as he stepped into the hallway. "Binner! Where are you, man?"

"The house is empty, save us," Lucas said. He'd made sure of it when he got here. "Your butler is at the pub down the way, and the others are gone with him or to their own amusements." He blew out a breath. "You really need to take your staff in hand. How can you run a government if you're not able to keep your own servants in line?"

Aaron was grumbling as he went to the kitchen. He returned a moment later with glasses in one hand and a cleaning towel in the other. He cleaned the glasses one by one before handing them over to Jackson, who poured them all large measures.

"My sister runs the household—" Aaron said.

"Badly," Jackson said.

Aaron shot the man a hard look, but he didn't disagree. "I manage the finances and the..." he waved his hand. "Politics."

Aaron was a member of the House of Commons until such time as his father popped off and he inherited an earldom. Then he'd take his seat in the House of Lords, and some other eager son would find his way into Aaron's vacated seat. The man appeared to love the work—had been an avid student of history since he was in leading strings—and worked tirelessly on the nation's interests. It was a bloody crime that he couldn't have a clean glass in his own household.

Meanwhile, Jackson got tired of tweaking their political friend. "Forget him, where have you been?"

"War, then another war, and now back."

"Yes, but when? Everyone else came back years ago."

"We still have an army," Aaron cut in. "He's probably been serving—"

"No, I haven't," Lucas interrupted. He didn't want to go into details. "I sold out after Waterloo."

"What!"

"But that was two years ago!"

Lucas nodded. He knew. "It took me a while to come back."

"Two years?"

"I…" He shrugged. "I have been waiting until my hand is better before making an appearance." He held up his maimed hand. He normally wore a dark glove over it, but because they were his friends, he pulled it off. The damage wasn't as bad as it could have been. He still had a hand and, for that matter, his life. The thumb and forefinger worked just fine, but the last three fingers were knobby and cramped. His fingers and palm were thick with scars, and the whole thing looked hideous.

Jackson studied the hand with pursed lips. "I've seen worse. Your ugly face, for one, though I'll admit the scar through your hair, is dashing. Aaron, do you think there's cheese and bread in your larder? I've missed supper."

Jackson always missed supper because his ancestral lands were impoverished, and he only ate when attending a ball or because of the generosity of his friends. Normally Lucas would counsel the man to marry an heiress, but Jackson was both canny and unflinching when it came to hard work. He would bet everything that Jackson had a clever plan to restore his ancestral lands. One that did not include charming an heiress.

Meanwhile, Aaron gave a disinterested wave toward the kitchen. "Take whatever you can find."

"Thanks, mate," said Jackson as he disappeared down the hall. Meanwhile, Aaron focused on Lucas.

"Your mother thinks you are dead."

"Yes, I know—"

"Your father and brother as well."

"Yes—"

"And my sister plus—"

"Yes! I know!"

Aaron blew out a breath. "Where have you been hiding?"

Lucas looked down. "I'm known as Titan at the Lyon's Den."

"The gaming hell? The one where—"

"Yes, yes, Mrs. Dove-Lyon's reputation is salacious, but she runs a clean establishment with fair wages. She employs veterans to keep an eye on things, and I supervise them. It's good work with good people, and I have no quarrel with it."

Aaron frowned. "Well, I do. The future Earl of Wolvesmead should not be running tables in a den." He refilled his brandy glass, but his gaze never left Lucas's. "What's really going on?"

How to answer that? Especially since he had no clear understanding of it himself. "You know my family." Most specifically, his mother, who never tolerated anything that was less than perfect. Perfect attire, perfect manners, perfect appearance in every way. She would be horrified by his hand. "I didn't want to see them until after I had found my bearings."

"That answers for a few weeks or even a couple of months. But Lucas—years? Your brother expects to inherit!"

He blew out a breath, then forced himself to speak the truth. "Aaron, I'm an heir who went to war." He looked up. "They wanted me to die." At least his mother had.

Aaron shook his head. "I don't believe it. Your father was ever kind."

If total disinterest could be labeled kindness.

Then Jackson spoke up as he came back to the parlor laden down with cheese, bread, and a few old apples. "It doesn't matter why he's been gone, he's back now, and we should celebrate." He grinned at Lucas. "What did you have in mind?"

Trust Jackson to cut straight to what must happen now. The man always knew how to ignore the past, even when it was all everyone else could think about. "I need you to throw a masquerade."

"Whatever for?" Aaron said, his face twisted into a grimace. "Fancy dress and ridiculous masks. It's just an excuse for the worst sort of behavior."

Jackson grinned. "A capital idea!"

"Nothing too flamboyant. I've rented out all of Vauxhall. That will make it an exclusive sort of thing."

"Nothing at Vauxhall could ever be exclusive."

He nodded. That was true enough, but that was what Diana wanted, and so that was what she would get. And he would make sure that security was tight enough that she was safe. "It's set for Wednesday in three weeks." Thank God the owner of Vauxhall played too deep one night, and Lucas had managed to win his exclusive night. Otherwise, he'd never have been able to manage it.

"That's fast," Jackson said. "You have to give the ladies enough time to get their costumes made."

"It will be a party given by the Lords of the Masquerade." He pointed at Aaron. "You'll be Lord Ares." Aaron had studied every war in detail, and so the name fit. "Lord Satyr for you," he said to Jackson. The man was a dangerous flirt, and so he would embrace the moniker as if born to it.

JADE LEE

"A masquerade just encourages all sorts of knavery," Aaron said.

"I have men to keep the grounds safe."

Aaron arched his brows. "Thieves are not the only danger. It'll be a hunting ground for fortune hunters and reprobates."

"You mean me," Jackson said.

"No, I don't," Aaron snapped. "You have scruples. And some mysterious business plan..." He trailed off to give Jackson a chance to fill in the blank. Instead, the man put on a too-innocent expression.

"I have no idea what you mean."

Aaron snorted. "In any event, you won't hurt a woman. But others will trap young ladies on the dark paths, ravish them quickly, and—"

"I will have security!" Lucas repeated with enough force to show his impatience with the whole discussion. "And once again, you fail to give any respect to the intelligence of the fairer sex. They are too smart to be so easily led astray." At least that had been true of the vipers he saw in the ladies' half of the Lyon's Den. Every one of them was more likely to trap an unwary man than the other way around.

"You're both right," Jackson said in a grumbly voice. "There are plenty of female twits in society. And plenty of women with sense.

"Don't invite the twits," Lucas said. "Would that be acceptable to your high moral standard?"

Aaron gave a short nod, but he didn't speak, as he was more interested in sawing off a piece of bread than objecting to a party.

"Then it's settled?" Lucas asked. "Can you manage the invitations? I am working two jobs right now and haven't managed a full night's sleep in a week. Plus, I don't know the best people to invite, though I do have a few names I'd like to put forward."

"Two jobs?" Aaron said, his voice low.

Lucas blew out a breath. "I'm not ready to come out of hiding yet. I don't want my family to know I'm alive."

"Whyever not?" Jackson said as he drained his brandy glass. "By all accounts, your brother is a genius with the land. Your coffers are overflowing."

He grunted. "They're my father's coffers made full by my brother's sweat. What right do I have to those funds?"

"The right of progenitor," Aaron said. "You're the heir. It's irresponsible of you to hide away like this. And cruel to Nathan."

Lucas thought it might be crueler to come out of hiding. His brother was much better suited to bear the title than he was, and, as far as he could tell, every single one of his family was happier with him dead, himself included.

"You must reveal yourself," Aaron said. "At least to your family."

"No."

"Lucas—"

"I'll pay for everything," Lucas interrupted. He had enough money saved up. "But I can't host it. There would be too much attention on me. And I can't put together the right guest list the way you can, Aaron. And I can't make it popular among the right people the way Jackson can. And I certainly can't get invitations written and sent while working night and day." He blew out a breath. "I've taken a big risk coming to see you tonight. Please, for our old friendship, can you not find a way to help me?"

"Of course, we'll help," Jackson said.

"And I'll pay my fair share," Aaron snapped. "But that's not the point."

Lucas grabbed a hunk of cheese. "What is the point?" he asked before biting hard into the cheese.

"The point is I won't help you hide from your family."

Jackson snorted loudly. "He doesn't need your help to hide. He needs it to get a lady." Then he waggled his eyebrows at Lucas. "I'm right, aren't I? Who's the woman at the center of this?"

Lucas tore off some bread and matched the last of his cheese with it. After he'd eaten and swallowed, he spoke in a casual tone, though he doubted either man was fooled. "I should like you to invite Lady

Dunnamore and her two sisters."

Aaron refilled his brandy glass. "Lord Byrn's sisters?"

"Yes."

Jackson chuckled. "Does Elliott know you're planning to seduce his married sister at a masquerade?"

Trust Jackson to sort out the truth. "I'm not going to seduce her!" he snapped. "I'm just going to give her a spot of fun."

"Exactly what I said—"

"I need her to think kindly toward me. She's in trouble, and I can't protect her unless she ceases to fight me at every turn." He lifted his head and pinned his friends with his heavy stare. "Will you help me?"

Jackson laughed. "Will I host a scandalous party that you pay for? I believe I can bestir myself to make such an effort."

That, he already knew. But the party wouldn't work unless it had the stamp of someone completely respectable, like Aaron.

The man took his time, but in the end, he nodded. "I will do it—"

"Excellent—"

"On the condition that you host as well."

Lucas's head jerked up. "What? I can't host it."

"Pick a name. Something sinister."

Lucas groaned. "I'm called Lucifer at Diana's house."

"The devil you say," joked Jackson. He'd always been good at puns.

"But hosting a party defeats the whole purpose. I will not reveal myself."

Aaron leaned back in his seat. "You shall be the mystery that gets everyone to attend. They'll figure out quick enough that Sayres is Satyr, and I am Ares. If we're to get the right people to come, I'll have to tell them who we are."

Jackson nodded. "The smart ones will figure it out."

"And we'll invite your family—"

"You will not!"

"Your brother then. Nathan always loved you."

It was true. His younger brother had adored him almost as much as Lucas had cherished his tag-a-long sibling. Nathan was the one family member he missed.

"You must tell him you're alive," Aaron pressed.

"I will," he said. "In my own way, and on my own time."

"On the night of the masquerade."

Lucas shook his head. "If I'm the big mystery, then everyone will try to expose me. I won't be able to talk with Diana at all."

Jackson shook his head. "You'll have a better chance speaking with her as the host of the party than as some random bloke wearing black. We'll each pick a lady for the opening dance. You can select her."

"It's the only way I'll agree," Aaron said.

Lucas blew out a breath. "You're just trying to expose me to the *ton*. You think that someone, somehow, will figure out who I am."

Aaron grinned. "You always enjoyed a challenge. Surely this will make for exciting sport."

"I didn't intend it to be sport for me. Just for Diana."

Jackson clapped his hands. "Now, it'll be sport for you both!"

CHAPTER SIX

D IANA SETTLED INTO the boat that would take them to Vauxhall.
She kept her expression serene, but inside, her heart was
pounding with excitement. It was ridiculous, really. It was just a
masquerade party, but she was here with her siblings, and it felt like a
treat that had been so long denied. Even Gwen's grumbling as she
maneuvered to her seat gave Diana a happy glow.

"I don't see why you need me here tonight," Gwen said as she
adjusted the dark brown of her dress. "I have a new botany book that
is waiting for me at the house. If I took a hackney now, I could be
happily reading within a half-hour." Gwen was dressed as a dog
tonight, complete with a canine mask. Diana was sure that her sister
had a very specific breed in mind for the animal—with some heavy
symbolism attached—but she didn't dare ask about it. The answer
would devolve into a lecture on the poor lot of women in this world.
Since Diana already agreed with the statement, she had no wish to
revisit the litany of abuses set upon the fairer sex.

"Because no outing would be complete without you," Diana answered, carefully avoiding the topic of her sister's choice in costume.

"Yes," agreed Lilah as she settled down beside Gwen. "So stop
talking about leaving. If you go, then as your companion, I shall have
to leave as well. And I have been so looking forward to this treat."

Lilah was dressed simply but to great effect as a lilac fairy. Her
dress was green, she was just now tying on her lavender mask, and

sprigs of lilac adorned her hair and bodice. On anyone else, it would have looked silly, but Lilah carried herself with such quiet elegance that she never looked ridiculous, ever. It was a quality Diana envied.

Last into the boat came her brother, Elliott, and his new wife, Amber. She wore a simple domino and mask of bright red, but the feathers in her hair suggested she was some sort of bird. And Elliott, Diana was happy to see, was not in all black as was his usual custom. His mask sported red feathers, and he pulled at them irritably.

"Stop fussing with them," Amber instructed her husband. "They look quite fetching."

"I do not wear feathers," he groused, but the smile he bestowed on his wife was tender and indulgent.

"I am, as always, grateful for your attempts to expand your attire." The words could have been cutting, but they were said with such love and humor that Diana felt a twinge of envy. Especially as Elliott caressed his bride's face.

"Will you reward me for suffering these damnable feathers?"

Amber's expression grew mischievous. "I shall indeed."

"Then, I am content."

He was besotted, and Diana was so pleased that her brother had found happiness. She looked away to give them some privacy only to see both her sisters watching the pair as well. Gwen frowned as she studied them as she might a strange plant, for botany was her passion. Lilah, on the other hand, seemed to lean forward with such unguarded yearning that Diana was surprised. How sad that the sister most unlikely to find a husband was the one who so obviously wanted it.

On impulse, Diana leaned forward and clasped her hand. "It is possible for you, too," she whispered.

Lilah started and immediately ducked her head to cover her embarrassment.

"All creatures yearn for love," Diana continued. "I do not believe God would give us such desires if it were not possible to find it. We only need the courage to reach for it and accept no substitute."

Her attention had been on Lilah, but she saw Gwen's frown at her words. The woman was about to chastise her for her romantic notions, and she tensed to defend her thoughts. Instead, Gwen added her hand on top of Diana's. "It should have been me," Gwen said to Diana. "I haven't a romantic bone in my body. I would have been content in a loveless marriage."

"You marry Oscar instead of me?" Diana said. "You were fifteen."

"I wouldn't have cared. Give me my books, and I would have been exceedingly content."

"As am I," Diana said. It wasn't a full lie. She had found her own kind of equilibrium inside her marriage. "Come now, we are here for a party, one that I have been looking forward to for three long weeks."

Everyone seemed to agree, even Gwen, and soon Diana was settling into the joy of a night out. She hadn't realized how much she had missed until they were stepping into the pleasure gardens. Elliott found them seats in a box near the orchestra, and the five of them settled in with minimal fuss.

"Look! There's Lord Ares!" Lilah said, pointing to the box opposite them where a large man in a Roman outfit sat on a throne befitting a warrior god.

"Lord Satyr's over there," Gwen said as she pointed to a man wearing trousers meant to resemble a goat's legs, and instead of a mask, he wore a headpiece with goat horns. He was right now dancing with a jolly flair that made everyone clap, Diana included.

"But where is Lord Lucifer?" Amber asked as she scanned the crowd.

Diana didn't want to look. She already had one Lucifer in her life; she had little interest in adding another. But the fun was infectious, and she couldn't help herself. Eventually, Elliott spotted the man and pointed him out to everyone else. Lord Lucifer stood near the orchestra with his arms crossed and his face covered entirely by a black mask. His clothing was equally black, as were the bat-like wings that extended behind him. As Diana studied him, she saw a pair of ladies approach him and try to engage him in conversation. He must have said something rude as they gasped, then backed away with scandalized giggles.

"No one knows who he is," Diana said.

Even she had heard the gossip regarding the three hosts of the party. The other two were generally understood to be Lord Kittrell and Lord Sayres, but Lucifer was the mystery that had spawned enough gossip to intrigue even Gwen, who stared hard at the man. But it was Diana who abruptly gasped as Lucifer flicked his wrist at someone in a gesture she recognized well. It was a tiny movement, as crisp as it was restrained, and yet it carried such a note of command that it could not be anyone but the very same Lucifer who plagued her household.

Good God, what was he doing here? Could she not escape her home for one night without its unnerving aspects following her here as if to stalk her. Because at that very moment, Lucifer looked across the grass to stare long and hard at her.

She drew back. She was in the company of her family. Surely he wouldn't...

"He's coming over," Amber whispered. "Do you think he means to talk with us?"

Of course, he did. After all, Diana had taken extra pains to see that she never crossed paths with him in her own home. Naturally, he would plague her on the one night she truly escaped. So Diana took pains to look elsewhere, most specifically at the dance floor. If someone asked her to partner with him, she would immediately agree. But no one presented themselves, and so she stood stiffly by as Lord Lucifer approached the box.

"Good evening, beauties and sir," he intoned.

That was definitely Lucas. She would recognize his voice anywhere.

"Good evening, Lord Lucifer," Amber responded. "Do you come to tempt us to sin?"

"Most definitely." He turned and looked straight at Diana. "What of you, my lady? Would you indulge the devil with a dance? I would allow you to flit about me to your heart's content."

Diana's gown was themed as a butterfly, the dress expertly dyed, and the mask fitted with wings of blue and black. "I am afraid I am not a lady to be tempted by sin, my lord," she said darkly.

"Oh, go on," Gwen said as she dug her thumb into Diana's thigh. "You love dancing. And as we are here specifically for fun, then you cannot decline."

Beside her, Lilah agreed with a daring smile. "If you will dance, then I shall dare to find a partner myself."

"Perhaps you and Lord Lucifer—" Diana began, but Lilah cut her off.

"No! I shall find my own gentleman. Come along, Gwen, let us go hunting for dance partners."

Odd to see Lilah so forceful, but it was a welcome change. And as the two ladies departed, Elliott asked his wife for her hand, and that left nothing for Diana to do but accept the inevitable.

"Very well, Mr. Lucifer," she said. "I see, I have no excuse."

If he noticed she had called him by his name in her household, then he did not react. Instead, he gestured to their now empty box. "If you prefer to sit here, we could talk—"

"Definitely not." In truth, the music was calling to her. She wanted to be on her feet. It would help her work off the disquiet she felt whenever he was near. She stood as calmly as possible and even took his hand to allow his escort.

"I mean no insult, Diana," Lucas said. "I merely wanted you to have an evening's fun."

She turned to look at him, her heart lurching. "Surely, you did not arrange for this whole evening merely for me."

"I did."

She stared at him a moment. Her gaze swept across the park as she calculated the cost of a party like this, even if it were split with the other two lords. The amount was staggering. Unless…

She blew out a breath. "You have made up with your family then." Accessing his estate funds was the only way he could have had the money for this. "I am so pleased. They should know that you live."

"They do not." Three words, spoken with implacable coldness, as he pulled her into the opening stance.

She faced him, her mind scrambling. "But Lucas, your family deserves—"

"I am Lord Lucifer, madam," he said sternly. "The great deceiver. Do not think you know the purpose of my actions."

That was rubbish, every bit of it. "You are merely being dramatic, as you are wont to do," she said. But even as she frowned sternly at him, her insides were twisting with a warmth she couldn't deny. "Did you really arrange all this—"

"For you. Yes."

"But how did you manage it?" she asked. "It must have cost the Earth."

"And the sun and the moon," he said. "All for you."

With a gesture at the orchestra, there was a loud clang as if to announce the opening of the masquerade. In truth, they'd been playing for a bit, but suddenly, everyone separated as Lucifer led her onto the dance floor. And—to her shock—Gwen and Lilah came as well, partnered with Lord Satyr and Lord Ares, respectively. It was a stirring moment as Lord Satyr made some opening remarks—a plea for everyone to enjoy themselves to the fullest—and then the three couples began their dance. Other couples quickly followed, but Diana had never opened a ball before, and this was a marvelous experience.

There was no more talking, per se, but certainly touching of hands, moving of feet, and shoulders. Their eyes met and held when it was appropriate, and even when it was not. Diana couldn't believe such extravagance, and yet wasn't he the one who had climbed her wall in a rainstorm, then tumbled at her feet just to beg for her hand in marriage? Lucas was a man of extreme passions. Or rather, he had been twelve years ago. It was certainly in character for him to arrange an entire masquerade party for her.

But really...just for her?

The idea kept tickling her insides and made her smile in the most embarrassing way. Her cheeks flushed, and not from the exertion of the dance. And when they came together as the steps proscribed, she allowed him to pull her a little too close and touch her a little too long. This was a masquerade, after all, and she could be forgiven for a bit of fun. There were no society matrons here to judge the distance between couples, and several pairs were already far closer than propriety allowed.

Lucas did not speak to her, nor she to him. Everything was done by way of their bodies. When he held her hand, his smallest finger slipped beneath to caress her palm. When he was meant to swing her around, he squeezed her tightly and put more effort into pulling her close than in drawing her around. But all of that paled in comparison to his gaze. Hot, dark, and so appropriate to his Lucifer moniker. His eyes smoldered when she met his gaze. Unwavering, unnerving, and so delicious to have his attention riveted upon her.

By the end of the dance, her heart beat much too fast, and her lips felt parched as she wet them with her tongue.

His gaze fell to her mouth, and she remembered the way he had kissed her that night before her wedding. The way his tongue had invaded her mouth and their bodies had pressed together with a desperation that nearly swept them both away.

Sometimes—like now—she wished she hadn't stopped him. At least she would have known one night of true passion. One night unchained from responsibility. One night with a man she desired and who made her think of nothing but their two bodies becoming one.

"Diana," he rasped. "The way you look at me. It's like—"

"Hush!" she whispered, the word aimed more at herself than him. Such thoughts were inappropriate to a married woman. But more importantly, they only brought pain in their wake. She had not indulged that night, and she could not do so now. Her marriage to Oscar wasn't perfect, but they had grown to respect each other. She would not cuckold him. She had too much honor for that.

She pulled away, or she tried. Lucas would not release her, but he allowed her to rest her fingers lightly on his arm as he escorted her back to the box. They maintained a polite distance, which he did not fight. And for that, she was grateful.

Until the moment she saw who else had come to join their party. Geoffrey, her horrible stepson, lounged at the entrance of their box as he sipped on a glass of wine. He wore no costume, but his evening attire was new and of the finest cut. And he grinned as he watched her approach, the expression making her feel like she'd been touched by a vile brush.

"Dearest, Mama," he drawled.

She sighed. She had wanted one night of fun, one night's escape from Oscar's sickroom, and the ugly battle with Geoffrey. Clearly, that was not in the cards.

CHAPTER SEVEN

Diana felt a change in Lucas. He said nothing, but suddenly he seemed sharper and a great deal more menacing. Yet all he did was stand beside her as she confronted her stepson.

"Good evening, Geoffrey. I hope you are enjoying the party." Then she turned as if to move past him, but the man straightened up, effectively blocking their entrance into the box.

"I would like a word, Mama." As usual, he sneered the word Mama. Years ago, that had hurt. She'd had no choice in becoming his stepmother and saw no reason he should hold it against her. Now it merely bored her.

She sighed. "Very well, what is it?"

"A family matter," he said as he glared at Lucas. "Call off your dog."

Strangely enough, Lucas didn't stiffen at the insult. In fact, it made him smile, and for a moment, Diana was struck by the differences between the two men. Geoffrey was all too aware of his dignity, spending and gambling exorbitant amounts of money just to maintain an image. Lucas, however, did not dress to his station and certainly didn't rise to any taunt. Except to poke back in the mildest of ways.

"Shall I growl at him?" Lucas asked her. "Would that amuse you?"

"A little," she had to admit, but then she shook her head. "Perhaps another time."

"Do not toy with me," Geoffrey snapped. And there was his prickly ego lashing out. "Family matters should be discussed in private."

"Then you should not bring them up at a party," she said. But sometimes, expedience was the better choice. And she definitely wanted to be done with this unpleasantness *expediently*. So, she turned to Lucas and gave him a curtsey. "I thank you, Lord Lucifer, for a delightful dance and your wonderful fare, which my stepson definitely seems to enjoy." She gestured to Geoffrey's now empty wine glass. "I will not detain you when so many other guests beg for your attention."

"I'm not leaving you alone with him," Lucas said, and now his voice was a low growl.

"But I am not alone. There are guests everywhere. And we shall sit here and converse like civilized people." And with that, she did brush past Geoffrey, though he made sure one of his hands clutched her thigh as she went past. It was too low for Lucas to see and hidden by her skirts, but the skin-crawling violation was clear.

She ignored it, though it made her stomach clench in fear. The man had no shame. And she quickly sat down at the front edge of the box before her knees gave way to their trembling.

Meanwhile, Lucas studied her and then Geoffrey. Then he said, "I think I shall watch the dancing." Then he moved a few feet away—far enough to give her the illusion of privacy—without leaving her alone. And then, contrary to his words, he stood with his back to the dancers as he stared hard at Geoffrey.

"*Salope*," Geoffrey said under his breath. As if calling someone a bitch in French made it any more appropriate. Especially if he was referring to her and not Lucas. Either way, it made her angry.

"Is this who you wanted to be, Geoffrey? When you were a boy and thinking of your future. Did you want to be someone who terrifies women and wastes his life in meaningless games?"

The words had come out spontaneously. They were borne of frustration from looking at a man with all the advantages who still decided to waste his life. Her words must have hit him hard because his face purpled in rage.

"How dare you—"

"How dare I?" she scoffed. She was never this bold with him. It was too dangerous, and yet knowing Lucas watched from a few feet away made her reckless. "Forget your father and me," she said with a slash of her hand. "You are destroying yourself. He would be very generous with you if only you would show him something. The tenants need a landlord who will help them."

"You want me to go slop pigs alongside the unwashed, un—"

"So farming is not for you," she interrupted. That was no surprise. "Surely there is something you care about. Something worthwhile that is not endless gambling to no point. Show your father anything, and he—"

"He is the one who made me who I am," Geoffrey rasped. "Constant criticism. A blind eye to my pleas for help. He is to blame."

She threw up her hands. "Blame anyone you like, Geoffrey. Only find some way to make a future for yourself. After all, you are the one who has to live it."

It was a reasonable argument and the most generous offer she had given him so far. Before she had told him to make good on his commitments to the estate. Now she would happily pay him to pursue any kind of worthwhile endeavor.

But again, his pride prevented anything she said from getting through. His eyes narrowed, and he threw his wineglass such that it shattered against the table. "Last chance," he growled. "Release my funds now or suffer the consequences."

How many times had she heard that threat from him? And she answered as she always did. "What consequences, Geoffrey? You have already hurt your father as much as any son could. You have threatened me inside my own home such that I have had to surround myself with guards. What can you do to me that is worse than you have already done? This is not the way to change your circumstances."

He leaned close enough that his breath was foul in her face. "I can tell one and all what a whore you are, and I can slip into your bedroom and be upon you before you scream. I can puncture my father's lung with a knife between his ribs and blame the crime on you. I can poison your drink, turn your servants against you, and set the Watch to demand your arrest." He lowered his voice. "I can send footpads to kill you tonight, and no one would be the wiser."

His words were so clear that she could tell he meant everyone. He'd obviously spent a great deal of time thinking of how he could hurt her, but she had been dealing with him too long to crack under threats no matter how menacingly he spoke.

She might have said something back to him. She wanted to but feared her voice would crack. She couldn't show any weakness. He was a bully who would pounce on any weakness. So, she held his gaze and said nothing more. She would give him nothing.

It was the hardest thing she'd ever done. She held firm until he realized his threats would not sway her.

"So be it," he said.

Then he spit on the ground by her feet before quitting the box. He even whistled as he strode away, the insolent sound scraping against her raw nerves. The man was a spoiled child. Thank God she was numb to his threats. *Numb*, she repeated to herself. She was not afraid. Except her hands were shaking, and she couldn't seem to catch her breath.

She'd barely gasped twice before her brother appeared at her side, gripping her shoulder as she steadied her breath. Amber joined her a moment later with a glass of sherry in her hand.

"Drink. It will help," the woman said as she pressed the glass into Diana's hand. "Lilah and Gwen have gone to find you something to eat. Lilah thought it would settle your stomach."

It probably would, as did the sherry. But even as she sipped, her gaze went to the place where Lucas had last stood. His dark silhouette was gone. Had he abandoned her?

"He's following Geoffrey," her brother said. "Wants to be sure the man leaves."

She looked at Elliott. "He's what? But Geoffrey's furious. He'll strike out at the nearest target—"

"Lucas can handle him," he said quietly. "He also prevented me from joining you earlier. Afraid I would punch the blighter right here."

"And get locked up for it," Amber said. "Lucas was right. Geoffrey was hoping one of you would punch him because any fight would increase the pressure on her." Amber gently urged Diana to drink more sherry. "Did you promise him his funds?"

Diana shook her head. "If I crumble to his tactics now, he will never learn that he has to behave better if he wants any kind of money from his father."

Elliott snorted. "There comes a time when a man is too old to learn."

Diana shot her brother a sad look. "Surely you don't believe that." She swallowed the last of her drink. "He has to learn. He *has* to." She could not stand much more of this.

Her brother merely looked grim. It was left to his wife to voice the words everyone was thinking. "You can take a horse to water, but you cannot make him drink."

"He will learn or go to debtor's prison." She blew out a breath. "Why will he not simply apply himself to something? Anything! I would release his money if he showed the smallest signs of control."

At that moment, she saw Lucas return to the main path. His dark figure appeared like an avenging angel as he strode up the way. A few tried to catch his attention, but he moved with too much purpose to stop them. And he headed straight for her.

Damn her traitorous heart. Her spirits rallied with every step that brought him closer to her. But her sister-in-law sat where he might, and her brother hovered over her as if she were a lost child. Neither of them moved as Lucas came near, and she saw a quick flash of frustration tighten his jaw, but it was covered quickly. Instead, he crouched down across from her such that he could speak to her eye to eye. Or rather eye to masked eye. He still wore his costume as Lord Lucifer.

"The blighter has left," he said softly. "And I have instructed my men to watch for him, but I doubt he'll come back."

She shook her head. "No, he'll go home to threaten Oscar." Geoffrey had made a habit of catching her husband alone and saying all manner of horrible things until he got the money he wanted. Oscar had always been lost when it came to his son, and it wasn't until he'd given Diana control of the money that any type of discipline had arrived. But it was a hard thing to put restraints on a dissolute man in his thirties.

"I have men there at the house as well. He will not be allowed in." His gaze was somber as he looked at her. "I heard what you said to him, Diana. It was the bravest thing I have ever seen."

She jolted. "You heard? But..." She looked to where he'd been standing. She'd thought he'd been too far away.

"I have very sharp ears, and neither of you took pains to be quiet." He blew out a breath. "It was very brave—"

"It was foolish," her brother snapped. "You are under siege, Diana, and it is impossible to stay safe all the time. What does it matter to you if he gets his money now? Come live with Amber and me. We will keep you protected and—"

"And Oscar will be completely vulnerable. Geoffrey will burn through the money, and his tenants will have nothing, and our servants will be terrorized. Oscar will live his last days in misery. Is that what you would have me do?"

"Yes!" her brother huffed. "I would have you safe. The matters between Geoffrey and his father are not of your making."

Diana closed her eyes, feeling the weight of her responsibilities as never before. She daily fought for her husband and the people he cared for—servants, tenants, and even his grandchildren, who might one day inherit the estate. The last thing she wanted was to fight her brother as well. But before she could voice any of that, Lucas rose up in her defense.

"Don't you think she already knows that?" he said. "That she hasn't considered minute to minute that she could ditch everything and run to your home? The fact that she stays and fights is a credit to her strength. That she is a woman and has little responsibility beyond vows forced upon her make her the bravest, truest person I have ever known. You belittle her by suggesting otherwise."

Her breath caught at his words. How was it that Lucas saw what even her own brother did not? It melted her. From inside to out, her rigid muscles gave way until she heaved a breath as if for the first time in ages. It was embarrassing, the sounds she made as her body shuddered in reaction.

Lucas dropped down before her. His hands grabbed hers, and he merely waited while she found some control. And since he did not demand anything from her—no words, no answers, just his solid presence—she found the strength to weather the storm. In time, her shoulders relaxed, and a shudder rolled through her entire body. She disentangled one of her hands and swiped at the tears that were drying on cheeks. And where she wiped one side, she felt his thumb caress the other. Then she took a deep breath that brought her heartbeat back to its usual steady rhythm.

"Diana," he said softly, "tell me what you would like. Do you want to go home? Do you want food, drink? Name it, and it shall be yours."

She wanted things that could never be. She wanted to step back in time, never marry Oscar, and have the Season that she had been denied. She wanted her father to have lived so she and Lucas could have courted in the normal way of things. She wanted children with a father who would care for them and not allow them to become spoiled, angry boys that grew into men who threatened those around him. But most of all, she wanted someone to walk with her and perhaps ease her burden for a time.

She lifted her chin and looked Lucas in the eyes. "I should like you to take off that ridiculous mask and perhaps take a turn with me through the pathways here."

Amber shifted uncomfortably. "Are you sure you want to stay? There's Gwen and Lilah with plates for everyone. They'll be here in a moment. Or we can all go home—"

"Pray do not shorten their fun on my account," Diana said. "Or my fun." She smiled at her sister-in-law as she tried to explain. "This is the first night I have gotten away in..." She couldn't remember how long it had been. "Don't force me back into the sickroom just yet."

Lucas straightened up to his full height and held out his hand. "If you should like a stroll, then I would be honored to accompany you."

Elliott shifted uncomfortably. "Of course, we will all take a stroll."

Thankfully, his wife tapped him on the arm. "She is perfectly safe with Lord Lucifer. If we walk, my husband, let us walk to the refreshment table to help your other sisters. They cannot carry all that themselves. Leave Diana and Lord Lucifer to their own amusements."

Diana could feel Elliott stiffen. He did not like abandoning her even in so little a thing as a stroll about Vauxhall. Ever since Elliott had grown to manhood, he lived with the guilt that her marriage had allowed for his freedom. And that guilt—well-intentioned though it might be—tended to stifle her at the worst possible moments.

"You hired Mr. Lucifer to protect me," Diana said. "Do you say now that I am not safe in his care?"

Elliott blew out a breath. "No, of course not."

"Then it's settled," Amber cut in. "We shall help Gwen and Lilah, and you shall go where you wish. Though—Lord Lucifer—it would ease my husband's mind if you would remain on the more popular paths? One where—"

"He can keep an eye on me," Diana interrupted as she pushed to her feet. It galled her that she was the shortest one here and had to look up at the men, and perhaps that gave extra stridency to her tone. "I am a grown woman, Elliott. And Lucas will see that I am safe."

She was so focused on facing down her brother's overprotection that it took her a moment to realize what she'd just said. Lucas would keep her safe? She had only once put her faith in Lucas, and he had failed her. In her mind, she knew that she'd set him an impossible task. She was always going to marry Oscar, and two naïve teenagers could not have stopped it.

And yet, until this moment, she hadn't acknowledged the anger she still harbored against him for failing her. It was irrational, but it was there. And yet, she felt safe with him. The warmth of that thought burrowed into her bones. He would do everything in his power to keep her safe.

She looked up at Lucas. "Geoffrey is gone," she said firmly, "and I would like to take a stroll with you." What she really wanted was to take this time to acquaint herself with the man Lucas had become, not the teenager who had failed to save her years before. And she counted an evening stroll in Vauxhall an excellent way to begin.

"As you wish," Lucas said with a bow. Then he extended his arm to her, and she took it. What would come now was up to the two of them, and only them.

CHAPTER EIGHT

"**W**OULD YOU PLEASE take off that silly mask?"

Lucas sighed as he escorted Diana down the main Vauxhall walk. The musicians were behind them, the lanterns illuminated them, and everywhere people speculated on his identity. "I cannot let people know who I am."

"Why not? Lucas, you cannot wish to be hidden from your family. They think you're dead."

"I absolutely can," he said softly. "You know my mother. How can you think—"

"No," she interrupted him. "Your mother is a lovely woman. A bit high in the instep, I suppose. I hear that if you cross her, she does not forgive. But you are her son—"

"She once directed the gardener to drop me in a well and not retrieve me until morning. All because I had appeared before her in dirty clothes. I was seven and had escaped my nanny."

Diana blew out a breath. "Parents often get exasperated with their children. I cannot think she was serious."

Lucas didn't answer. That was always the explanation that people gave, especially his nanny. But to him, his mother's pronouncements had always held a degree of truth. She would probably never truly drop him in a well, but part of her wanted to. She would never do any of the thousands of threats she used, but on some unspoken level, his mother hated him. He felt it, he knew it, and perhaps right now, he didn't want to see the disappointment on her face when she realized he was alive.

"Oh dear," Diana said as she squeezed his arm where her fingers rested. "She did mean it, didn't she?"

Lucas jolted. How quickly she guessed the truth when no one else had wanted to even acknowledge the possibility. And then she guessed even more.

"Was it just you or your brother as well?"

He looked away, feeling too raw to see the pity in her expression. "Just me. I don't know why."

Diana released a mew of sympathy. "I don't suppose it matters. Such a thing from one's mother..." She shook her head. "That's the very definition of irrational. To try and look for a reason is just a waste of time. What you felt was real. *It is real*, and I'm sorry if I ever suggested otherwise."

He stared at her a moment, shock riveting his feet to the ground, and his breath held tight in his chest. She hadn't said anything beyond what he'd said a million times to himself. He wasn't crazy. His mother *did* hate him, and the reasons why didn't matter. The truth was that it *hurt*, and no amount of denial changed that. He knew because he'd tried.

But no one else had ever said such a thing. Never. And her words spoken so simply unraveled his control. His defenses crumbled, and pain spilled out. Not in sound or action, but it poured out of him, nonetheless. He felt crippled by it, and yet he couldn't let it show. He was supposed to be protecting her.

"Diana," he rasped.

She turned to him and stifled a curse. Without warning, she pulled off his mask. He flinched and tried to stop her, but she insisted, and he would not tussle with her now.

"We are in shadow. No one will see," she said. "No one but me, and I already know who you are."

She did. And to a depth he thought no one could possibly reach.

"I want to see your face," she said softly.

"And now that you do," he said, the words forced out through a throat tight with emotion. "What do you gain?"

She smiled, though the expression was wistful. "What I've always seen." She touched his cheek. "Such passion. Such a pure force of feeling."

The heat of her palm seared him. The sight of her gaze on his face cut him to the quick. She knew him too well, and he felt too vulnerable this way. And yet, he couldn't force himself to move away. The feel of her hand was like a brand, and he leaned into it rather than away. He wanted her carved into his very bones, and yet the pain of it weakened him. He had no idea how he managed to stand strong against her caress when every part of him crumbled.

"There it is," she murmured. "That burn in your eyes. When everyone else seems to be looking for themselves even as they glance at me, you always saw me."

"You speak in poetry," he said. "I am a simple soldier now, and a damaged one at that." He held up his crippled hand, less deformed in appearance now because he wore stiff leather gloves.

She grabbed his hand, enfolding it with both of hers. That meant her touch left his face, and he was bereft by the loss. Then she turned, still holding his hand, as they resumed their stroll.

"Your hand does not seem to limit you. Have you found it a problem?"

How to answer that? It certainly hindered his use of a pistol and a sword, but his other hand compensated well enough. Even deformed by the scar tissue, he could make a fist, and though he could not open his hand completely, he could grasp things and pluck at his guitar, which is what he did to improve his dexterity.

"It is getting better with time," he finally said. "I exercise it regularly, and it has become more limber."

"How did it happen?"

He shrugged. Everyone asked him that. "The honest truth is that I don't know. It was Waterloo. Everyone believes that there is an order to a battle, and there is. But not always, and not for everyone. We were in chaos, and I was grabbing men, trying to get them to hold, to fight, to work with one another. Two men fight better together than apart. Five men can block a horse and its rider with ease. If a company can hold their position, then the battle can be won. But it takes many men working together."

"And a leader who can make it happen when bullets are flying everywhere." She turned to him. "You impress me."

So many emotions continued to tumble around inside him. He did not like thinking about that day, much less being praised for it. In the end, he said what he always did. "I survived. So many did not."

"And I am grateful that you did."

He let those words sink in. After her earlier animosity, he had not thought she would say such a thing. After all, he'd been expressly forbidden to cross paths with her at home, for all that he managed the footmen who protected her.

"Why did you block me from coming abovestairs? Surely you understand that I can protect you better with full access to the entire home."

She slanted him a wry look. "Do not pretend that you have been limited in any way. I know you come upstairs to check the windows and even the roof."

He had, but he'd had to be scrupulously careful that they not cross paths. "I would never harm you."

She was silent for a long time, then she sighed. "It took me a long time to accept my marriage. Longer still to find my way. I had to fight with the housekeeper about the smallest things." She shook her head. "I didn't know it at the time, but Oscar had dallied with her, and she imagined that she would become his wife."

"The devil you say!"

"I don't blame her for thinking it. Oscar often says what is convenient for him. Her fault was in not seeing him clearly enough to know the lie."

His estimation of her husband was dropping by the second. Up until now, the staff had been universally supportive of the master, for all that he was bedridden. "Now you impress me," he said. "You married into a disaster."

Diana nodded. "It took me a year to realize that I would rather be respected than loved. From there, it became easy."

"Nothing about that sounds easy," he said. He knew. He'd had to earn the respect of his men, and that had been the hardest battle of all. "Now, you have both—respect and love."

She snorted. "You have been listening to the flattery."

"I don't think so. Especially since they believe you despise me."

She blew out a breath. "I don't despise you," she said tartly. "I don't know you. This is the first we have talked in years."

He acknowledged the point. "Will you allow me abovestairs now? May I check the windows and the roof without sneaking around behind you?"

"You may. Provided there is no familiarity in your attitude toward me."

"Familiarity?" he teased. "You are the one who pulled off my mask."

"Here at Vauxhall, you are Lord Lucifer. There, you are simply Mr. Lucifer, my servant. I would not link arms with him nor stroll anywhere at his direction. No more than I would with the bootblack." She glanced at him. "Surely you understand that."

"I understand that a bodyguard is not a bootblack. If I direct you to stroll to Haymarket, you will do it immediately and not question it."

She stiffened at that, and he could tell she wanted to argue. She'd fought hard for the right to direct her own life—in a small way—and she was loath to give that up. "Lucas—" she began, but he cut her off.

"I am there to protect you, and you will listen if I have to carry you out over my shoulder."

"You exaggerate the danger," she huffed.

"You are naïve." He didn't say that to hurt her. His statement was pure fact, but she was too innocent to realize that.

"You overstep," she snapped. "As did my brother to hire you in the first place."

He snorted. "Your brother did not hire me. I came of my own free will, and I will see the job done no matter if I offend your sensibilities or not."

Her body stiffened against him. "For how long, Lucas? How long will you hide beneath your mask and your silly moniker? How long do you intend to play dead and skirt the responsibilities of your title?" She narrowed her eyes. "How long shall I have you underfoot when you should be standing in the House of Lords?"

"Until such time as I deem it safe," he said flatly.

"And when will that be? A month? A year?"

"I will not leave you until it is safe," he said firmly.

She shook her head. "You are using me to avoid your own family."

He laughed at that. The sound burst from him in a harsh bark of levity. "I assure you," he said, "I do not need any excuse to avoid my family. I have been doing it quite well long before I was needed in your household."

"I can attest to that," said a voice to the side.

Lucas jerked around at the words, damning himself for being so distracted by her that he paid too little attention to his environment. With his damaged hand, he pressed Diana behind him while his good hand tightened into a fist. His heart beat hard as he searched the shadows for an enemy. There was but one person, and he did not appear threatening at all. At least not to Diana.

"Nathan," Lucas said.

His brother.

CHAPTER NINE

L UCAS'S ONLY BROTHER, Nathan, stepped out of the shelter of a large tree. He was dressed roughly in worn boots and muddy clothes. If it weren't for his dark green cloak, Lucas might have mistaken him for one of his tenants.

"What are you dressed as?" That wasn't even remotely important, but somehow the words blathered out anyway.

Nathan spread his hands. "A farmer. What else?"

"That's not a costume. You are a farmer."

"Not in London, I'm not." His expression tightened. "Apparently, in London, I've been playing at being a titled lord."

Lucas swallowed. There was only one courtesy title for his family, and it went to the eldest son. Lucas knew that Nathan had waited a year after Waterloo to take the title. On the anniversary of that battle, crepe was wrapped around their door knocker, his mother showed herself in public dressed in black, and his brother took the courtesy title of Lord Chellem. In such a way, his family declared him dead before society, if not in the courts just yet, and the *ton* accepted it as fact. In truth, he'd just returned to England after months of a devastating fever, not to mention a broken leg and mangled hand. The news that his family had declared him dead had crippled him more than his mangled hand.

But none of those thoughts came out. Instead, he studied his brother and saw that the lanky youth he remembered had filled out into a man. His shoulders were broad and thick with muscle. His hands were far from the dainty kind fops prized. His brother was large and strong in all the best possible ways.

"You look good," Lucas said. And he meant it.

"So do you. Especially since I thought you were dead." And when Lucas had no response to that, Nathan spoke with his usual blunt honesty. "I couldn't understand it when Aaron insisted I come to this masquerade. And then Jackson challenged me to find Lord Lucifer. He bet me money that I would account it well worth my while." His jaw clenched as he shoved his hands into his pocket. "Damn it all. Now I owe him a monkey."

Five hundred pounds? "What made you do that? You were never a betting man."

Nathan glowered at him. "I thought it an easy win. There's nothing here that could possibly be worth my time."

The words sat heavy in the air. "There still isn't, Nathan. Go home. Pretend—"

"What? That my only brother is dead? Is that what you were going to suggest?" Fury burned under his words, and Lucas held up his hands as much to defend himself from the lash of it as to quiet his brother.

"Hush! Don't draw attention."

"Don't draw attention?" his brother sputtered. "You're alive!"

Thankfully, Diana interrupted, hooking both brothers by the elbow as she drew them down the dark path. "Let us have this discussion more privately, shall we?"

Fortunately, a glance around told Lucas that they were somewhat alone. He had walked Diana to the very end of the main pathway. It was a few steps more to the path where lanterns were spaced infrequently, and there were dozens of tiny breaks in the shrubbery for all kinds of illicit behavior.

He doubted though that the greenery had ever been host to a discussion such as he was about to have with his only brother. A man who even now refused to lower his voice. "How long have you been back?"

"I arrived in London a year after Waterloo." He blew out a breath, struggling to express why he'd made the choices he had. "I did come to the house. I saw the crepe on the door and..." He shrugged, ashamed to admit his actions. "I followed you on a walk about Hyde Park."

"What?" The word was barked out.

"I heard Mama tell everyone to call you Lord Chellem. She was so proud of you."

"Proud that my brother was dead? Are you daft?"

He had been, perhaps. Feverish from the crossing and ashamed of his hand and his limp. He hadn't worked that out yet, and he'd kept looking at his brother. "You looked splendid, you know. Every inch the future earl."

His brother turned around to face him. "That's it then. You think I wanted the title, and you thought you'd let me—what? Play at it for a time?"

"No!" He blew out a breath. How did he explain? "At first, I was so sick from the crossing that I ended up at a..." He didn't want to confess that he'd gone inside a gambling den simply to escape the rain. And when he'd collapsed with fever, Mrs. Dove-Lyon had given him a room and cared for him. And when he'd recovered, she'd offered him a job as her door guard.

Being no fool, Diana already knew what he did. "He works at the Lyon's Den managing the men who watch the tables and hold the doors."

His brother recoiled. "You work at a gambling den?"

"And as my bodyguard," she huffed. "Even though I don't need it."

His brother frowned at her. "You need protection? From whom?"

Lucas waved that all aside. None of that was important right now. Looking at his brother, he realized the magnitude of what he had lost when he'd refused to reconnect with Nathan. He'd hurt the man, and he could see the burn of that pain in his brother's eyes. "Nathan, I'm sorry," he blurted. "I never meant to hurt you."

It was a poor response, but an honest one. Unfortunately, the damage remained. Nathan looked at him with heavy regard. His hands were shoved into his pockets, and his gaze darted around in confusion. "Why would you hide from us?"

"Not you," he said. "Never you. I just..." He raised his damaged hand and pulled off his glove. Even in the shadows, his brother would see the thick scars on his palm, the mangled way his fingers twisted. "I had a limp, too, but I've worked that out," he said. "It's better, but I'll never win a footrace."

"Does it hurt?" Nathan asked. He gestured to the hand and also to Lucas's face, where a scar cut down by his ear. "Are you in pain?"

"Not often. And I forget about the face scar except when I shave."

Nathan nodded. Once. Twice. Then he blew out a breath and stared hard at his brother. "And what does that have to do with anything?" He asked it with confusion, not anger. And if that didn't show Lucas how wrong he was, nothing else would. His brother honestly didn't understand how his parents would view his disabilities.

"Nathan," he murmured, using that same tone of exasperation he'd used when they were children.

"Lucas," his brother echoed, in exactly the same way.

And then it was done. They were kids again, facing off after one of them had made a mistake. "I'm so sorry," Lucas said.

Nathan took the step forward and embraced him. His arms were thicker than when they were children, his grip a thousand times more welcome. And after the emotional moment he'd had with Diana, this felt like another tidal wave of feeling. He hugged his brother, using the time to let the tears slip free because he could hide them in his brother's rough cloak. And when Nathan shuddered in his arms, Lucas felt his own breath release.

He was welcome. His brother didn't wish him dead.

"Damn you," Nathan said against his ear. "Father's going to—"

"No!" He jerked back, out of his brother's arms, feeling his chest tighten. "No," he said more calmly.

"But they deserve—"

"Let me tell them in my own way. Give me that, at least."

Nathan didn't look like he would agree, so Lucas took a stab at explaining.

"Imagine it, Nathan. The moment Mama sees me alive and comprehends the truth."

"She'd be so—"

"Happy? Truly? Certainly, she'll make a show of it, but remember how happy she was when you took my title. Can you remember one time when she ever looked on me with such joy?"

He waited, his breath held as Nathan finally let his head drop. "Very well," he said, "but Papa—"

"He's not a man for change—for good or ill. You know that. He won't like it simply because—"

"It's not what he is accustomed to." Nathan nodded. "But you must tell them. You must take your place."

Lucas let the thought hang. Did he really need to take his title? Truly? He had some money and work that he was good at. It wasn't the life of leisure most titled peers enjoyed, but he'd never lived that. Not even when he was in school and his friends were future aristocrats. In many ways, the life of a soldier had suited him better, as did the management of men who watched over a gaming hell and the workers within. He had grown so used to not having any of the responsibilities of his title that he wondered if it was something he truly needed.

"You wear it much better."

"The hell I do," his brother spat.

What happened next came by luck, not because he'd been paying enough attention. He heard a rustle in the shrubbery and a muffled grunt. If he hadn't been arguing with his brother, he would never have allowed Diana to stand so far apart from him or so near the shadows. The noise was all that alerted him, and even so, he was too slow.

A hand came out of the shrubbery and grabbed Diana. She gasped in surprise as she was jerked back, but another hand covered her mouth, and any noise she made was muffled. Didn't matter. Lucas was already leaping forward, knocking the bastard back—*two* bastards. No, *three*, all stepping out of the shadows. He tried to pull Diana sideways toward his brother. It didn't work. She was held too fast. Worse, he saw the glint of a blade in the lamplight. He was about to stab Diana!

He tried to knock the blade aside, but he already knew he was too late. Almost at the same instant, he saw a coin flash almost as bright as the blade. Nathan had thrown it, his accuracy uncanny ever since he'd learned the trick as a boy. It zipped past Lucas's vision to land square in the attacker's eye. The blackguard cried out and recoiled, which gave Lucas the time he needed.

He knocked the blade aside, then grabbed the man's wrist and twisted hard. It was enough to free Diana, especially as she slammed her elbow into the bastard's chest before dropping down below the grip of his arms.

She was on the ground, rolling to safety. That gave room for Lucas to release his full fury. Even with a damaged hand, he was a fast fighter. Whatever power was lost because of his mangled hand was made up for in speed. He moved quickly as he steadily pummeled the man. And as Nathan took on one of the blighters, Lucas managed to handle the other two. He fought as he had been taught—with hands, feet, and any other weapon that could be brought to bear. In this case, he made sure one tripped over a tree root, and the other got tangled in the shrubbery. Not to mention the steady pelting of sticks and pebbles that Diana threw at their faces.

It was over quickly. The moment the brutes realized they faced true opponents and not a frightened woman, they scrambled back into the bushes and away. Lucas meant to go after them, but he checked the impulse. His first priority was Diana. He spun around to see her launching two clods of dirt with impressive speed. He even heard the grunt of one of the attackers as her missile landed. But then she stopped, her breath coming in quick gasps as she looked around.

"Is that all? Are there more?" she asked.

Nathan hadn't stopped when Lucas turned back for Diana. They could hear him now crashing through the underbrush. But a moment later, he returned with a grim expression.

"They're gone," he said. "There's a path that leads back to the river."

Lucas had already guessed as much. Meanwhile, he scanned Diana from head to toe. "Are you all right? Did he hurt you?"

She slapped her hands together to brush off the dirt. "Only my pride. I had heard that Vauxhall could be dangerous, but I never thought—"

"That was no common footpad, Diana," he said as the reality of what had nearly happened sank like ice into his bones. "That was someone hired to murder you."

Her head jerked up in shock. "Don't be ridiculous. A common thief—"

"Would have cut your purse," Nathan said, his voice grave. "But that knife..." He stopped speaking as his gaze cut to his brother's. "I thought you were exaggerating. I thought..." His gaze hopped to Diana and back with a guilty shrug. "I am sorry I doubted your motives."

His brother thought he'd created a danger so that he could seduce a beautiful woman. Well, obviously, his brother thought him a cad. "The danger is real," he said grimly. And he damned himself for thinking her safe once Geoffrey had left the gardens. The man had obviously hired common thugs to kill her just as he'd threatened before he'd left. "Come quickly, Diana. We need to get you to someplace safe."

Nathan's eyes narrowed as he scanned the shadows. "You think they will return?"

"Of course not," Diana said, though her voice trembled.

"I don't know," Lucas said as he began walking Diana quickly back to the main path. His brother went to her other side, a large bulwark of defense.

"Lucas..." she began, but her voice trailed away as he pushed their speed. Then she caught her breath. "You don't really think that, do you? That..." Apparently, she couldn't even voice the possibility.

Lucas shot her a grim look. "Yes," he said. "Yes, I do." Whatever she was thinking, whatever she meant, he considered it possible. And a real threat.

At that moment, he redoubled his focus, he tripled his determination, and he swore to all that he held holy that he would not fail to protect her. Even if it meant locking her away until he saw Geoffrey dead.

CHAPTER TEN

DIANA WASN'T A fool. She'd felt the man's rough hands on her, smelled his rank sweat, and—worst of all—seen the blade as it skittered away thanks to Lucas's fast fist. But, at the moment, she'd focused exclusively on getting away and then clobbering her attackers from a distance. She was a good throw, and those stones had distracted them a little, she thought. However, she knew that Lucas and his brother were the real heroes. She'd merely survived.

But as the immediacy of the fight wore off, as the two men braced her from either side and walked her quickly back to the well-lit center of Vauxhall, panic began to claw its way into her thoughts. Had she truly been attacked? Had she nearly died but for Lucas's lightning-fast reflexes?

She brushed at her arm, where it throbbed. She could still feel the hard grip of the man as he'd jerked her toward him.

It wasn't possible, and yet, it had happened. That was terrifying enough, but the idea that someone she knew wanted her murdered— even someone as difficult as Geoffrey—was too far for her to go. Geoffrey might threaten, but he'd never actually do it...right? The attackers had been simple footpads. Dangerous, naturally, but the danger was over. They'd been frightened away, and Diana was safe again.

Anything else was simply too terrifying to contemplate.

Then memory burst into her thoughts despite how desperately she tried to bury it. She saw the flash of the knife above her. It burst into her thoughts no matter how many times she repeated to herself that Geoffrey was a petulant child, not a murderer.

Meanwhile, Lucas whisked her through Vauxhall. She saw people point at him and belatedly realized he had not put his mask back on. More than one tried to stop them, but Lucas would have none of it, except when he stopped long enough to leave a message for her brother, Elliott.

While they paused, she failed to suppress a cough. It was a silly thing. Just a need to release the feeling of a hand over her mouth, but it was hard to catch her breath. She forced herself to slow down, to inhale with dignity, and exhale with poise. By the time Lucas was done with the servant, Diana had regained her breath.

"We can use my carriage," Nathan said. "I told my man to wait close because I wouldn't be long."

Lucas responded with a clipped nod.

"Don't be silly," Diana said. Or at least she tried to. Her words came out as an unintelligible squeak. She had to clear her throat while Lucas's gaze riveted on her. She smiled reassuringly at him, but she didn't think it worked. His expression grew even grimmer as he shook his head.

"Don't try to speak," he told her. "Wait until we are in the carriage."

That defeated the purpose, she thought, since she'd meant to tell him that there was no need to upset his brother's plans. And then she felt an irrational giggle bubble up. She strangled it with an awkward kind of choke, and all she could think was that this was certainly humiliating. Having two men muscle her through a party and out the Vauxhall gates, as if she were threatened royalty. Her mother would say she was making too much of herself for all that she tried to slow them down.

She knew—in a distant kind of way—that her thoughts were circling. Every time she felt pressure on her mouth or saw a flash of light such as what had been reflected on the blade, her mind spun out in bizarre directions focusing on something—anything—that wasn't attempted murder. Someone's costume had gone awry. Someone had failed to drink their lemonade. Someone laughed, and another soul gasped. These things filtered through her splintered consciousness until the moment Lucas handed her into Nathan's dark carriage.

She sat down quickly, Lucas at her side. Nathan had barely stepped into the interior before Lucas was pounding on the roof for them to leave. Nathan shut the door and dropped inelegantly in the seat across from them. Both men exhaled in relief as the steady clop of the horses' hooves began. And though Diana desperately wanted to say something, all she seemed able to do was grab Lucas's hand in a tight grip. He covered her hand with his other, but his gaze was on the window as he watched for she-didn't-know-what out there.

"This is ridiculous," she finally said. "Completely ridiculous." She wasn't exactly sure what she meant. The dramatic carriage ride through London? The way her mind kept spinning forward and back? She kept feeling that man's hand on her mouth as she tried to scream. And she kept focusing on Lucas by her side, his brother across from her, as both men stared out the windows with deep frowns.

"Your safety is not ridiculous," Lucas said.

"I'm in no danger," she retorted, and she so desperately wanted to believe it.

He turned and looked at her, his expression grave. She wanted to flinch away. She didn't want his steady regard forcing her to face something she didn't want to believe. Not yet. Not until she could breathe without feeling that man's hand on her face.

"My lady," Nathan said, his voice calm, "perhaps there is somewhere you could stay for a bit. Somewhere to rest and settle your nerves."

Diana's temper ignited. "Do you know how many times men have said that to me? To sit down, be quiet, and steady my delicate nerves. You think because I am female, I have no logic? My husband hasn't been well for months. I have had the running of the estate, and that task is considerable."

Nathan blinked, his expression contrite. "I meant no offense—"

"Men never do," she groused. "And yet, I am offended."

"No, you're not," Lucas cut in. "You're just looking for a target because you are frightened. Aim your darts at me. My brother doesn't deserve it."

Lucas didn't deserve it either. She swallowed, and damn if she didn't feel that grip on her face again. Hard, punishing, and smelling so foul that she felt her stomach revolt. *No, no, no!* She could not cast up her accounts here. That would be awful for everyone! She felt hot and sick and—

Lucas abruptly shoved her head down between her knees. Her skirt muffled her breath, but he was quick to pull it up and out of the way. Her legs were exposed in the most undignified way, but no one seemed to care, especially not her as her breath came in stuttered gasps.

"Just breathe, Diana. Breathe until it passes."

"I am. No weakling." Her words came in gasping pants.

"Never said you were," Lucas answered.

Then Nathan spoke. "Did you see the rocks she threw? Damned fine arm you have, my lady. Bloodied one of their noses."

"Truly?" Lucas asked. "I didn't see."

"That's what made him run. It was her shot that made him turn tail."

Nathan's fists had certainly been a factor. Still, it made her feel better to hear his praise.

"Did you see her last throw? Right at the back of the bastard's head. Rang his bell quite properly. I'm sure he would have gone down if there hadn't been a tree there propping him up."

"Impressive," Lucas said, admiration in his tone. "I'd turned away."

To look to her safety. She remembered seeing him come for her just as she released her missile. He'd been at her side to protect her the moment his attacker ran off. And though Nathan had dashed after them, Lucas had stayed by her side. At the time, she'd merely been grateful he hadn't been hurt. But now she realized how alone she would have felt if they'd both run off.

It was enough to make her shudder.

"Diana?"

"I'm better now," she said. "Please help me up."

After that first push to shove her down, he'd gentled his hold, supporting her as her stomach settled. Now he eased her upright, and she was grateful to realize that she did indeed feel better. Her temperature had come down, her heart rate, too. And most especially her temper.

"Thank you," she said. Then she looked at Nathan. "And my apologies. Your brother was right. I was lashing out to no purpose."

"Perfectly understandable," Nathan said. "Think no more of it."

But she couldn't stop thinking of it. The attack, the blade, the hand on her arm and face. She'd felt Geoffrey's menace before, but she hadn't actually believed herself in danger. Not until someone grabbed her arm. The memory made her lightheaded.

Lucas's grip tightened. "Do you feel sick again?"

"No, I'm fine," she lied as she adjusted her skirt down.

"Your family will be with you soon. I left word for Elliott. I'm sure they will follow as soon as—"

Diana held up her hand, and Lucas immediately quieted. "I don't need my family." She'd been going her own way for so long, the idea that they would suddenly descend now made her shrink into herself.

"They will want to see you safe."

"I'll send a message as soon as I am home." And she would, but rather than focus on that, her mind skittered back to exactly where she didn't want it to go. "I just cannot think that anyone would…" She couldn't form the rest of the words. It was inconceivable that anyone would wish her dead. She wasn't royalty or political or even deeply religious. Those were the people who were targeted for murder. "I'm just not that important!"

"But you are," Lucas countered. "To Geoffrey, you are the only thing standing between him and his inheritance."

"Really?" Nathan asked. "I would think that was Lord Dunnamore." Then he answered his own question. "But if she is handling the purse, then that would stand to reason."

There was a moment's silence when the two brothers exchanged a significant look. Diana didn't understand it at first. She was still grappling with the shock of it all. But she was steadier now, and it only took a few more breaths before she realized what they were thinking.

"So you think Geoffrey…" She still couldn't say it.

"I believe he hired those men, yes," Lucas said.

Not a surprise. He'd said as much. But the next step, the very horrid next thought, was that if Geoffrey had turned evil enough to attack her, then what would he do to Oscar? After all, she merely held up his quarterly income. As long as Oscar lived, Geoffrey could not inherit.

She straightened with dawning horror. "We must get home immediately."

"We're nearly there," Lucas soothed.

"I must see to my husband. He is bedridden. If someone were to—" Her words choked off, the memory of that hand over her mouth suffocating her. If someone were to do that to Oscar, he would have no strength to defend himself.

"We're nearly there," Lucas repeated.

She looked out the window and saw the truth. A few more streets and they should arrive. "It cannot be possible," she said. "Geoffrey is spoiled. He's not murderous."

Neither men responded, and she knew with a sick kind of dread that it was possible. In the past two years, she'd dealt with a tenant who was violent toward his family when drunk. Another who had gone into a jealous rage at his wife and her lover. But both of those men were violent when their passions overcame them. What Lucas suggested spoke to cold-blooded premeditation. That was a thing for lurid gothic novels, not real life.

And yet, she couldn't stop the cold dread in the pit of her stomach. Why couldn't the horses go faster?

She sat in tense silence while staring out the window. She noted every passing house, every inch that brought her closer to home. And when the carriage stopped, she threw open the door. She would have run up the steps if Lucas hadn't prevented her.

"Steady, Diana. Let me be sure that no one waits in the dark here."

"What? Here?" She had put the danger in Vauxhall, not her front steps. Or upstairs with Oscar, not out here where everyone could see.

"With me," he said sternly, and his gaze brooked no argument.

"I'll lead," Nathan said. Then he hopped out and scanned the shadows as he moved. Lucas went next, his gaze about him as he drew her tight to his side. Then all three of them rushed forward to the steps.

Fortunately, her butler Simpson was just then throwing open the door. Safety beckoned from the bright lights within. But one look at the man's face told her that something horrible had already happened inside.

CHAPTER ELEVEN

"**W**HAT HAS HAPPENED?" Diana demanded as she crossed the threshold. Simpson barely had time to grab her cloak before she was heading toward the stairs. "Is it his breathing?" Oscar had been coughing lately. Weak rasps in his dry throat that made her wince every time it happened.

"No, my lady," Simpson answered. "His lordship is resting peacefully."

She exhaled in relief, stopping her forward movement with one foot on the stair. "Then what has happened?" she asked.

Simpson didn't answer beyond a gesture to the front parlor. Diana looked there, only now seeing that a burly footman stood at the door to the parlor, and both Lucas and Nathan were turning with grim expressions to what or who was inside.

Diana took a step closer and grimaced.

Geoffrey lounged against the fireplace with an arrogant smirk. "Home at last?"

The bastard! Three words, but his attitude implied that she spent all her time at parties and masquerades while her husband lay dying. It wasn't true, and he knew it. But she'd long since learned not to rise to taunts of any kind.

"It's late, Geoffrey. What are you doing here?"

"I came to visit my father at a time when I knew you wouldn't be here."

"Because she'd be lying dead in a ditch?" Lucas asked, his voice low with threat. "Sorry to disappoint."

"Lying in a ditch? Whyever would you say that?" Then the man smiled. "I assumed her dishabille was because she'd been cavorting in a ditch with you."

She heard Simpson gasp in shock behind her. Nathan, too, no doubt appalled by the despicable insinuation. Diana didn't even roll her eyes as she stripped off her muddy gloves. She'd heard worse things from Geoffrey, and by comparison, this was mild. Except for this time, she heard something underneath his tone. Disappointment, perhaps?

"Did you do it?" she asked, gratified to hear that her voice didn't shake. "Did you hire people to kill me?" Good God, the words surprised her even as she said them.

Again, her butler gasped, but her gaze was trained on Geoffrey. She needed to see his reaction for herself. He didn't disappoint her.

His lips curved into an echo of a smile as he looked at her. "Would that I had. Indeed, I'd likely give the thieves a guinea for doing me such a favor. But alas, no, I did not. I came here directly from Vauxhall to speak with my father." His eyes narrowed murderously on Simpson. "But it seems I am not even allowed that in this household. You truly have everyone wrapped around your despicable finger."

"What is all this unseemly commotion?" a voice interrupted. Diana sighed. It was her mother. She'd asked the woman to sit with Oscar this evening so she could have an evening free, and now that indulgence was coming home to roost as her mother gave her a disappointed frown. "Diana, what have you been doing? You look as if you've been in a barn."

Fortunately, she'd learned to outwardly ignore her mother's jabs. They still stung, but she didn't allow that to show. "Hello, Mama. Is Oscar all right?"

"The noise woke him. I ordered some of that tea he likes and came down to see what all the fuss is about."

"It's about me," Geoffrey said. "I am my father's heir, and yet I have been refused into his presence."

"Well, of course, you were. He was sleeping." Diana's mother lifted her chin for her most disapproving look. "Come back at a decent hour, and I am sure you will be admitted."

Diana wasn't so sure. Geoffrey always managed to upset his father. "So, he's alone?" she asked as she turned to go upstairs. She tried to keep someone with him at all times, just in case.

"There's a footman with him. The one who brought the tea," her mother said with a dismissive wave. "And you shouldn't see anyone in that state. There's mud all over your skirt." She shook her head. "I've told you that Vauxhall is no place for any decent woman."

"Then it is perfect for her," Geoffrey sneered.

Diana's mother curled her lip. "You are being repulsive. I insist you leave immediately."

As if that had ever made a difference to Geoffrey. And yet, he bent in a deep and mocking bow. "As you wish, my lady." Then he turned to Diana with a clear smirk of triumph. "I will see you in the morning, stepmama." He sneered the last word, infusing all the insult he could into every syllable. He wormed his way through the room, past Lucas and Nathan, who bristled with every breath. Simpson had his hat ready, and Geoffrey grabbed it with a grin. And then he plopped it on his head and left, whistling a merry tune.

"He's planning something," Nathan said the moment the front door shut behind him.

"No," Lucas said. "He's already done something." His gaze cut to the waiting footman. "I want every room, every window checked for something out of place. And Diana—"

She was already on the way upstairs to check on Oscar. She found him sitting up in his bed and drinking his favorite tea. She had it made special for him from a tin kept solely for his use in the kitchen. Her breath eased out the moment she saw him smile at her, and she barely noticed when the footman bowed and bid a hasty retreat. Few people liked being in a sickroom, and so she tried to keep the staff in here to a minimum.

"Oscar," she said as she came close. "How are you feeling?"

"Very well, very well indeed," her husband said. "Well enough to take you dancing very soon, I should expect."

"I shall look forward to it," she said. He always promised that, as he was always hopeful of a recovery. Meanwhile, she settled onto the chair by the bed and carefully arranged her skirts so the worst of the mud wouldn't show. Oscar wouldn't likely notice, but she did try to appear neat before him. "Did you have a nice time with my mother?"

"She's a chatty thing, isn't she?"

"Always."

"All sorts of advice on how to get the better of this damned illness."

"I can imagine." Her mother did love to give advice.

"I think she mucked about with my tea," he said as he set his empty cup aside. "It tastes sweet."

Diana frowned. "She shouldn't be allowed to do that."

"Never mind. It's not so bad. You can tell her I drank it all," he said as he showed her his empty cup. "But throw it out, will you? And get me my usual mix."

"Of course."

He settled back against the pillows. "Actually, we talked about your father. Reminisced, as it were." He paused as he coughed but soon regained his breath. "I miss him, you know. We were boys together at school, and he had the kind of charm that got him the best treats from the cook."

Diana nodded as she eased into her seat. Oscar often talked about her father. She had heard his stories about their schoolroom antics a thousand times. It seemed to calm him, and she could let her mind wander as he spoke. Usually, that was a happy time for her, but tonight she flashed back to the attack. She heard in her head the smack of Lucas's fist as he slapped the knife away and his grunt as he was punched in return.

Those memories returned with every breath, and the more she tried to focus on something else, the more insistent the details became. She couldn't inhale without smelling her attacker again, and she scratched at where the man's hand had gripped her arm.

"Are you listening, Diana?"

"What?" She jerked her attention back to her husband. "I am so sorry. I'm afraid it's been a long day for me."

"A happy one, I should think. You've been looking forward to that masquerade for weeks now."

"Um, yes." No point in telling him the truth. It would only upset them both. "Are you feeling all right, Oscar? You seem a little pale."

"My stomach seems a bit tetchy. Whatever your mother put in my tea, no doubt. I think I'll have some laudanum tonight. Enough to get me back to sleep." His eyes already appeared somewhat unfocused, but that could be her own exhaustion.

"If you'd like," she said as she poured him a full measure. If nothing else, she needed a night's rest. She needed to make a decision about Geoffrey, especially if he intended to visit in the morning. Did she bar the door to him? Did she tell her husband about her suspicions? He wouldn't believe that his own son would try to murder her, but didn't he deserve to know the truth? Not tonight, obviously. She was too unsettled to speak rationally, and he needed his rest. But she had to tell him in the morning. He had to know that he could be in danger from his own son.

"There," he said as he swallowed down the laudanum. "Now go get cleaned up. There's dirt on your chin that makes you look like a naughty child."

Her hand went to her face, and he chuckled as he pulled his covers up. She waited a moment until his eyes had closed, then she slipped out of his bedroom to head for her own toilet. Both her mother and husband delighted in treating her as if she were still in leading-strings when that was so far from the truth as to be laughable. But every time she tried to assert her independence, they chuckled and referred to any of a dozen tiny infractions.

She could hear their conversation now. "Remember when you appeared before company with mud on your skirts and face? Why that was just yesterday!" It was irritating, and she was furious that she had appeared so before them. Never mind that no one had asked why she looked as such. Likely they'd not believe there had been a knife at her throat, a ruffian choking off her breath, and Lucas the one who kept her alive through it all.

She stepped into the hallway only to be met by her entire family, hovering outside Oscar's room. It was mortifying to see them all there, each looking awkward or anxious or furious, depending on their wont. Fortunately, Lilah came forward first.

"We came as soon as we could. What do you need from us?"

"Nothing," she said. She wanted silence, not hovering.

"You cannot want us to leave at a time like this," her mother huffed. "I am your mother—"

"Stop, Mama. Please go home." Her words came out as an agonized whisper. Thankfully, Lilah understood exactly what she wanted.

"We'll take Mama home," Lilah said. "Try to get some rest, if you can, and send a messenger if you need anything."

"Thank you," Diana answered, truly grateful. The only person she wanted to see was Lucas, and he wasn't currently in the hallway staring anxiously at her.

Lilah began chiding her family back down the hall. Her brother hung back, though, his expression dark. "I'll speak with Lucas before I go."

Diana wanted to speak with Lucas, not have her brother acting on

her behalf. But she had no wish to have that argument now, so she
held her tongue.

"I need to get Amber home, but then I'll—"

"You'll stay with her, Elliott. Keep her safe."

His eyes shot wide. "You don't think there's any danger to—"

"No, no!" she rushed to say. "I just..." She wanted someone big
and strong to rush to her side tonight, to hold her steady when she
thought she might shatter. "Be with your wife. I'll be with...Oscar."
Her husband's name felt heavy in her mouth. He had never been a
comfort to her.

"Very well," Elliott said, his voice crisp. "If you need anything—"

"I'll send a messenger," she agreed. Then she watched as he reluctantly left her side.

Finally, she slipped into her bedroom, where her maid waited. She
was quick to clean her face, then strip out of her gown. "Give it away,"
she said when the woman tsked over the state of her skirt. "Burn it if
no one wants it."

She knew that someone would take it. The fabric was still good. It
only wanted a thorough cleaning, but she could not see it without
remembering. She would have it gone from her sight. She had just
changed into her dressing gown when the knock came. She already
knew it was Lucas. No one else would come to her now. Fortunately,
her attire was respectable enough, serviceable for sleep but also
enough coverage in case she spent the night in the chair by her
husband's side.

"Enter," she said.

He opened the door but did not come in beyond a single step. It
was because her maid was still in the room as she brushed out Diana's
hair. Lucas was no doubt maintaining his respectful distance as her
servant. It was logical, but that did not stop the wave of yearning that
buried her the moment she set eyes on him. He'd discarded his Lucifer
costume in favor of simple black pants and shirt, and somehow that

made him look even more dashing. There was a shadow on his face, whether from a bruise or the beginnings of his beard, she couldn't tell. But she saw the hard cut of his jaw, the barely leashed fury in his expression, and—most seductive of all—the way his gaze took in every aspect of her appearance as if reassuring himself that she was whole.

"Mr. Lucifer," she said. Then she grimaced. "You really must choose another name."

"I have checked the house and can find nothing amiss."

She could tell by his narrowed brow that he didn't like that. They both knew Geoffrey was up to something, but neither could guess what. "I'm sure we will find out by morning," she said, her voice weary. "I should check downstairs. You might not know if something was amiss."

"The cook would. She has seen nothing. And Simpson made the rounds with me. He saw nothing."

"Perhaps it was only Geoffrey making his usual threats. He delights in making me question everything. He would no doubt laugh that we have searched the house from top to bottom when he did no more than cool his heels in the parlor."

"He had you attacked." Fury burned through his words, and she could see his need to fight for her. It tightened his hands into fists, stiffened the muscles in his entire body, and made him look all the more like the devil with every breath. And yet, as she looked at him, she never felt safer.

It was enough to make her eyes water with gratitude. No one but Lucas had ever leaped to her defense. It didn't matter that twelve years ago his attempt had been fruitless. He had tried. And tonight, he had saved her. That made her breath stutter inside her as she ached to be in his arms. She needed the comfort of his touch and the safety it brought as well.

"Thank you, Tina," she said as she pulled the brush from her maid's hand. "Go rest now. It will be a long day tomorrow." It was always a long day in this household as they cared for Oscar.

"Yes, m'lady," Tina said as she curtseyed.

"Oh, and please tell Mrs. Hopkins to throw out his lordship's tea. It's gone off somehow. I will order more in the morning."

Her maid nodded and departed, leaving her alone with Lucas. Finally.

He stood awkwardly just in front of the door, his expression tight, and his gaze unsettled. When he spoke, he kept his words low, but they seemed to fill the room, nonetheless.

"I'll be sleeping just outside your door tonight. I'll know if anything happens."

"What? In the hall?"

"Yes." And from his tone, there would be no arguing with him.

"You really think—"

"Yes, Diana. I really do."

She bit her lip and gripped her hands together to keep them from trembling. "I suppose we should call the constable then. Tell him about... About..." She didn't want to think about the attack, much less speak of it.

"Yes. I sent Nathan to make the initial report. I expect the constable will be here first thing in the morning."

Of course, he had. While she'd been listening to Oscar's rambles, he'd been protecting the house, searching for answers, and proceeding with the next steps even without her thinking of them. How wonderful to have someone who thought ahead, who acted intelligently on her behalf, and who now remained nearby just in case.

Normally, she'd bristle at such impertinence. She was the mistress of the house. She should have ordered these things. She should have *thought* of them. But right then, she could feel nothing but gratitude. He was here. He was helping her. And finally, she had someone who could shoulder some of the burdens for her.

It was a miracle, and if she hadn't been sitting down, her knees would likely have given out from her own silly weakness.

"Diana!"

He was across the room in a second, squatting down before her, even as he put one hand on her neck.

"Do you feel faint?" he asked. "Are you hurt?"

She knew he meant to shove her head between her knees again, but she shook her head. "No," she said quickly. "No, that's not it."

"Then what?" His hand relaxed on her neck to slide down her arm. In a moment, he was gripping her hand. "Tell me." It was as much an order and a plea, but how could she put it into words? How could she express any of the feelings inside her? Fear, gratitude, relief, and need—all that and more churned inside her with no true outlet. Except for one.

"Hold me," she whispered. "Please." She put everything she felt into that last word. Then she waited to see if he would fail her or be exactly what she needed.

CHAPTER TWELVE

LUCAS WAS IN a dark place. It was a military state of mind where he assumed every shadow held an enemy, and every sound was a predator. His mind was quick, and his muscles were ready to erupt into violence at a moment's notice. This was how he'd stayed alive during the war.

Civilians did not understand this place where he was as sharp as the knife he wielded. And they certainly couldn't comprehend the danger they were in from the simplest human interaction. A hand extended in friendship would be seen as an attack. A smile was a lie to cover betrayal. And even the scent of a woman was a misty fog that concealed danger.

And an embrace—well, that wasn't simple under normal circumstances.

He hadn't come to Diana's bedroom to report. It was a ruse. He didn't see her as a commanding officer, but he knew the value of doing something innocuous in order to protect what was most valuable. But never during his entire military career had anyone asked for an embrace. Never had he been in this place in his mind and yet assaulted by the softness of a woman's plea or the scent of her body.

She looked up at him. "Please," she said. And he knew what that request cost her. She'd fought so long to be a woman in control. To ask for his embrace now meant she was in desperate need.

He touched her arm, wrapping his larger hand around her slender forearm. He knelt before her, so close their bodies could be entwined. But all he could do was hold her arm because she was not part of his dark place. He could not touch her softness when he was this sharp. He could not have a woman so perfect when he was so ugly.

And yet here she was, bowed before him in her pain. When she gripped his shoulders to pull herself up, he supported her without thinking. He could not let her fall, so he wrapped an arm around her waist to steady her as they both stood together. He felt the soft press of her breasts. He felt her hand wrap around his neck as she pulled him down. He went because he could not refuse her.

An embrace, body to body for comfort. And yet he felt so much more. Every part of him bristled with a wariness that only made his perception of her all the more intense. He felt her breath catch when he pressed his lips to her hair. And he felt the grip of her fingers as she pressed her body intimately close.

He pulled her higher on his body, his groin thickening as she rolled over him. His thoughts narrowed down to her hair, her grip, her breath. She unbalanced him with urgency, and he stumbled slightly beneath her weight. He spun them around, pressing her against the wall while shutting the door with a quick flick of his wrist.

The door banged into place, and he flinched. He tried to pull away, but she would have none of it. Her body was shuddering against his. Reaction? Need? He had no idea. He knew he was vulnerable with his back to the room. She could be hurt, and he could not allow that.

So, he set her apart from him. And while he searched every shadow, he knew that he was undone. No soldier allowed himself to be distracted as he had. No warrior protecting anyone put his back to the room while taking his fill of a woman, no matter how tempting. It had only been a hug for comfort. She'd been attacked. Every man, woman, and child would need to be held after a thing like that.

She touched his back with a tentative stroke.

"Lucas? What are you looking for?"

Threats. Attackers.

"Nothing," he rasped. There was no one there. Then he glanced at the door and remembered how it had slammed shut. "We made noise," he said.

He felt her look at the door. He didn't know how he felt it. She had only her hand on his back, but he knew when she looked and realized what they'd just done.

"Oh God," Diana whispered. "What is happening to me?"

It was the aftermath of battle. He'd seen countless men indulge in every aspect of the body as a way of suppressing what had happened, what might happen tomorrow, and what couldn't be accepted by any rational, moral person. He would not read anything more into it than that. So rather than think of Diana and all his confusingly aroused thoughts of her, he focused on his immediate task. Had anyone heard him slam Diana's door, and did it matter?

"It's quiet," he said. He went to the door and eased it open so he could look through the crack. He scanned the hallway. "No one is there." He listened to the steady snores of her husband. "His lordship rests—" *No, wait.* Oscar wasn't sleeping. His gentle breaths were interrupted by a wet cough followed by a low moan. He turned to Diana. "Is that normal for him?"

He glanced back at her long enough to see her frown and shake her head. That was enough for Lucas. He moved quickly to his lordship's bedroom door and eased it open. The smell hit him first. The man had fouled the bed. But that didn't stop him from checking every shadow before he let Diana into the room.

She brushed quickly past him as she headed to her husband's side. "Oscar?" she said. "Oscar!"

She flipped back the bedcovers and gasped in horror. There was blood in the sheets where he'd fouled the bed. Diana grasped the bed pull and hauled on it hard, even as she was touching her husband's face.

"Oscar! Oscar, wake up!"

But the man's eyes didn't open, even when Lucas lit an oil lamp set by the door. He could see the panic in Diana's eyes as she shook her husband's shoulders. He knew it was too late. Death was upon him. They only waited for the rattle that would signal the end.

"Oscar!"

Footsteps came running up the stairs, and Lucas turned to see who approached. His lordship's valet and the butler, Simpson. He let them hurry inside and watched when they recognized what was happening.

"Quickly!" Diana said. "Fetch the doctor!"

It wouldn't help. Indeed, even as Simpson ran back to do as she asked, he heard the rattle. A gasp and a choke combined. Diana heard it, too, and she grabbed her husband's hand.

"Oscar, breathe! You must breathe!"

Some things couldn't be ordered, and Lucas kept an eye on the shadows and the valet, just in case. But he was also aware of the tension in Diana's body. The horror in her eyes and the way she put a hand to her husband's chest, hand flat, fingers extended.

"Oscar, please. Not like this. Not..." Her voice broke. "Oscar...please breathe."

He did not. And neither, it seemed, did she. Her breath caught and held, and while everyone in the room strained to hear his lordship's inhale, they heard nothing but the pounding of their own hearts. At least that's what Lucas heard until Diana's body forced her to draw breath.

She did with a choking kind of gasp. And then the valet spoke gently into the silence.

"My lady, perhaps you should go into your room. I'll clean up here."

"But I don't understand," she said. "He was fine earlier. He said he felt better. But this..." she gestured to the bed. "This is wrong!"

He concurred with that. He could tell by Diana's reaction that this was not the normal course of her husband's illness. But the valet didn't understand what she was trying to say.

"I'll take care of it, my lady," he said. "You may rely on me."

She shifted such that she was gripping her husband's hand. "I don't understand," she said to his thick knuckles. "He was sitting up. He drank his tea."

A discordant note sounded in Lucas's thoughts, but he couldn't isolate it. For all that he did nothing but stand by the door, his senses were filled with her distress. He couldn't ease her pain. He couldn't even go to her side and hold her. That wasn't his place. The best he could do was stand guard at the door and protect her from harm. But even as he scanned the shadows again, his mind churned over what she had said, sifted through his memories of the evening, and finally— slowly—he remembered something important.

"You said the tea had gone off." He looked at Diana. He could tell she hadn't understood what he said. "His tea. You told Tina to have it thrown out. That you would order more in the morning."

She nodded, though it was clear she didn't comprehend. "Yes. He said it was too sweet. That Mama had probably doctored it with something to help him."

"Your mother?" That didn't make sense.

She straightened up. "She's always talking about special herbs and teas. Thinks the right leaves will cure anything."

Or kill. He looked at the sheets with clearer eyes. This wasn't normal sickness. This was the result of poison.

"Where?" Lucas rasped. "Where is the tea kept?"

"Belowstairs, in the kitchen with all the other tea. Why?"

Lucas didn't wait to answer. He was already rushing down the stairs. He heard her call after him, but he had to get that tea. He wasn't an expert in poisons by any stretch of the imagination, but he knew some basics. Simpson was just coming up, no doubt, after dispatching a footman for the doctor. Lucas dodged him and headed straight for the kitchen, where anyone could have gotten into the tea.

He hauled open the cabinet, but the special tin wasn't there. Likely already thrown out by Mrs. Hopkins. He knew where the garbage was kept, and sure enough, the tin was there at the top of the rubbish. He pulled it up and pried open the lid. There were white crystals like sugar in the tea, and when he sniffed, he smelled nothing beyond the usual scents. But the tea leaves were strong, and many poisons didn't have a scent.

He pulled up a bit of it on his finger and tasted it. Sweet, but not like sugar. There was a metallic tang to it that suggested something more sinister. He set down the tin and watched as the butler came into the room, followed closely by Diana.

"What are you doing?" she asked as her gaze took in what he held.

"Send for the constable," he said. "I think that's filled with arsenic."

CHAPTER THIRTEEN

L UCAS WANTED TO help her. He saw her shock and pain, then watched with admiration as she took control of her home despite the way her voice shook, and her hands trembled. She ordered the cook to provide food and strong tea for the staff just now rousing in the middle of the night, and for the people who would soon arrive. She commanded the poisoned tin to be set back in its customary place for the constable to see and then went to her bedroom to dress for the arrival of the Watch.

He could do no more than order a man to be sure the tin remained in its place without tampering by anyone, and he sent another to rouse Elliott and his wife. Though Diana would likely object, they would provide support for her where he could not. Then he climbed the stairs and stood guard outside her bedroom door while he stewed over what to do.

He was a soldier, not a constable or barrister. He knew Geoffrey was the murderer. Indeed, now he understood why the man had left so easily earlier. He'd practically crowed victory when he'd heard that Oscar was upstairs drinking tea. He'd known his father would soon be dead from poison, and most would assume that Oscar'd finally succumbed to his illness.

After identifying the enemy, a soldier's job was to eliminate the problem with lethal precision. Indeed, the urge to find Geoffrey and slit the bastard's throat was burning in his gut. Unfortunately, that wasn't possible because he wasn't in the middle of a war. This was London, on a night already filled with violence. He doubted Diana could handle another incident without breaking, and his job, first and foremost, was to protect her. He couldn't do that if he was off killing Geoffrey while she faced the constable and Oscar's other children alone.

So, he remained outside her door while frustration coiled in his gut. Fortunately, the Watch arrived with speed and the constable soon after. They met him down in the front parlor. Diana led the way with Lucas a half step behind, ready to spring into action, though there was no immediate danger anywhere.

The constable was a dour man with a square jaw. Simpson led him upstairs to view the body—only partially cleaned. With the help of the doctor who arrived soon after, the man agreed with the determination of poison and also helped identify the additive in his lordship's tea as arsenic. All good, but then the night took on an appalling twist.

"So you were at a party when his lordship was poisoned?" the constable asked as they returned to the parlor. "And who gave his lordship his tea? It was your mother, wasn't it? At your direction?"

Diana answered with the poise expected of a lady. She remained calm and, though her hands tightened to white where she gripped them in her lap, she did not react to the man's increasingly hostile tone.

That was left to Lucas as his temper finally broke. "Those are some very specific questions, sir. Where did you get this information?"

"I'll ask the questions, boy. If you interrupt me again, I'll have you removed and whipped."

No one had called him boy even when he was a lad, but he'd long since learned not to respond to a jibe with unthinking anger. "I am a member of her ladyship's household, and you have no authority to have me removed from the room much less whipped. Now I ask again, how do you know to ask such questions?"

"It's a logical question, boy. Who gave the poison—"

"No, the logical question is who put the poison in the tea, and I can tell you that. It was Mr. Geoffrey Hough, who is anxious to inherit before his time."

The man's eyes narrowed as he lifted his chin, triumph in his gaze. "As it happens, this isn't the first time I've been asked to investigate her ladyship. Earlier this evening, Mr. Hough told me of his concern for his father. Said that he thought her ladyship might do something dire to his father. Likely poison, he said, as she is the one who controls his food, all the way down to the tea he drinks each night."

Diana gasped. "And why would I kill my husband?"

"Mayhap, you got tired of caring for him. That's why you went to the party, is it not? To escape endless days and nights in the sickroom? Seems to me a pretty young girl like you would find it hard to care for a sick old man."

"Seems to me that the murderer spoke with you to throw suspicion elsewhere," Lucas returned.

"And who are you to question my investigation, boy? You're pretty hot to defend the lady. Mayhap you were the one who got her the poison, eh? Are you her lover?"

"Don't be insulting," Diana snapped, her tone as imperious as a queen.

Unfortunately, the constable was a man who enjoyed his authority over his purpose. He liked intimidating people, and if he could hand a story of a murderous wife and her lover to the papers, then that would only increase his power. He wouldn't be surprised if Geoffrey had already offered the man a generous gift for his help. The truth wouldn't matter. Attention, advancement, or money were his only motivators, and likely Geoffrey had sewn those up.

Which meant Diana's only hope of not being caught up in a nightmare was to show the constable that she had powerful friends on her side. And pursuing Geoffrey's version of the story would damage the constable.

There was no choice now. Elliott wasn't here, and Lucas would not subject Diana to one more minute of this obnoxious man while undefended. So Lucas took a breath and said the one thing that he'd been denying for years.

"Careful, constable. I am Captain Lucas Crosse, Lord Chellam, and the son of the Earl of Wolvesmead. Lady Dunnamore's brother, you know him as Lord Byrn, asked that I position myself here because of Mr. Hough's threats to her person. He's most anxious to get his inheritance, and obviously, he's finally managed to do it."

It was a significant moment for Lucas. He'd resisted telling his identity to everyone, including his family. That he had to reveal himself now, to this toad, made his throat tighten with disgust. And if there was any reward for what he'd just done, it was the way Diana turned to him, her mouth parted in shock, and her eyes wide with sympathy. She knew what revealing himself this way had cost him. But she was the only one who seemed to understand.

Diana's servants seemed to nod as if they had expected something like that. His men already knew. And the constable—the very person he'd meant to impress—seemed completely unaffected.

"All the more reason to suspect you are her lover and a partner in her crimes."

Geoffrey must have offered the man a great deal of money. With a grimace of disgust, Lucas looked at Simpson. "I believe it's time to summon her ladyship's solicitor." The butler nodded and turned to speak with a footman while Lucas turned to Diana. "Perhaps you should go upstairs and rest. At least until Elliott arrives. He should be here soon."

Diana arched a brow at him. And though her blue eyes were filled with pain, she shook her head. "I will remain here and face my accuser, even in the guise of a constable more interested in courting favor than in finding the truth."

It was well said, but it had little positive effect. The constable sputtered with outrage, and he was then cemented in his opposition. Lucas had to stop himself from punching the man. He couldn't even step in front of Diana to block her from his attacks. She wouldn't tolerate the insult to her authority, and it would do no good in any event. So he stood by her side and counted the seconds until help could arrive.

It came in the form of Elliott and his wife. Amber went straight to Diana, taking her hands and soothing her as only women can. Elliott checked that his sister was safe, then turned to him. Lucas responded without even needing the question.

"Someone placed arsenic in his lordship's special tea."

"Geoffrey, obviously," Elliott said. "But how?"

"If you can keep Diana safe, I will investigate," Lucas said. "Someone will tell the truth, and then the whole thing will unravel."

Elliott nodded, his expression troubled. "So, the man takes one last go at Diana in Vauxhall, then poisons his father's tea before making a big show of leaving."

Ignoring the constable's attempts to insert himself into the conversation, Lucas turned to Simpson, who was listening with a deep frown on his face. "Who could have done it?"

The butler shook his head. "Anyone, my lord. The tea wasn't kept under lock and key. We all knew it was for Lord Dunnamore."

Diana spoke up. "I drank the tea with him. Sometimes." Then her eyes widened. "But it didn't agree with my stomach—"

"And so you stopped," Lucas finished for her.

Diana pressed a hand to her mouth in shock. "You think Geoffrey has been poisoning the tea all along?"

Elliott took her hand. "We will likely never know. But it is assured that he has been pushed into drastic action now. We must make sure you are safe."

Lucas concurred. "The solicitor is on his way. Get the will read immediately. He's less dangerous to her after he inherits. And it will give us time to investigate."

"She'll stay with Amber and me," Elliott said firmly.

His wife concurred. "Come along. I'll help you gather your things."

Everyone seemed to be in agreement. Everyone, that is, except Diana. Looking at her, he saw determination coupled with an angry kind of resignation, but he couldn't fathom why.

"Diana?"

She looked at him with a frustrated expression, and this time, he couldn't stop himself from going to her side. He touched her shoulder and studied her face when she looked up at him. And then she gripped his fingers as if grounding herself with a touchstone.

"It won't make it better," she whispered.

"Why? Whyever not?"

She blinked away her tears. "Do you really think Oscar was that much of an idiot? That he didn't see the way of things with Geoffrey? At least financially? From the moment Oscar became ill, I began to manage the household affairs. And then the full estate. The more unmanageable Geoffrey became, the more Oscar turned affairs over to me."

Elliott nodded. "Then he had more sense than I thought."

She shot her brother a frustrated look. Obviously, he didn't understand what she was saying. But Lucas did, and he was terrified of the implications.

"You took control of the money," Lucas said, verifying the details as he said them aloud. "You took control of Geoffrey's allowance, which is why he is in such bad straights now."

"Yes," she whispered.

"And you convinced Oscar to change his will such that Geoffrey wouldn't beggar the estate as well."

She nodded. "Geoffrey wouldn't manage the land well. Likely not at all."

"But you would," he said.

She nodded. "He left it to me rather than destroy his tenants' lives with a bad heir."

The constable chose that moment to speak. He pinned her with a hard look. "So, you have the true motive to murder your husband, not Mr. Hough."

Lucas couldn't believe the man's idiocy. "What motive? She already had control of the money. She had no need to kill anyone."

Meanwhile, Elliott was still thinking of the terms of the will. "Isn't the estate entailed? Doesn't Geoffrey get it anyway?"

She shook her head. "Just the castle and the near lands. And the title, of course. But nothing able to sustain itself. And certainly not to fund his lifestyle."

"Did he know?" Elliott asked. "Did Geoffrey know that the will had been rewritten?"

Dianna nodded. "Oscar told him a few weeks ago."

Right before Geoffrey's nastiness had increased. Which was when Elliott had brought Lucas into the household to protect her. It all made sense now. But it was still left to him to voice the biggest problem.

"And if you were to die?" Lucas asked, voice deadly low. "If the men at Vauxhall had succeeded in killing you?"

She touched her throat, as she no doubt remembered every detail of the attack.

"Diana!" Elliott demanded, his voice tight with urgency. "Answer him. If you die—"

"Then it all goes to Geoffrey," she said. "It wasn't meant to stay with me anyway. I was to manage the properties until I married or died, and then it returned to the regular line of succession." She looked to the ceiling. "It was to give Geoffrey more time to mend his ways."

"Or find a way to kill both you and his father," Lucas said.

No one said anything to that, which is just as well because it was clear to Lucas that his job of protecting her had just gotten that much harder. Geoffrey had already killed his own father. Nothing would stop him from killing Diana and getting his hands on that money.

CHAPTER FOURTEEN

WHAT TO DO?

Diana stood in the middle of her bedroom, completely frozen with indecision. Her family wanted her to leave for the safety of Elliott's home. The constable wanted her questioned for murder. And she wanted to hide away from it all, in a place where no one spoke to her of anything beyond what sweet to offer at dinner. How could anyone kill their own father? How had she become so important that her life was threatened? She couldn't comprehend it.

In less than twelve hours, she'd been attacked, held by Lucas, and her husband had been murdered. The doctor, the constable, and now the undertaker were here. She'd managed to write notes to Oscar's children. They would likely arrive soon, and the idea of facing Geoffrey made her sick with dread.

But as much as Diana wanted to run, she knew she couldn't. As the eldest daughter of an earl, every aspect of her life had been proscribed by duty to family, duty to her husband's title, and duty to future generations. It was why she married and how she convinced her husband to turn over the estate management to her. Geoffrey certainly wasn't going to be an appropriate steward. Which meant she couldn't run away on the very day her husband perished.

How would she manage? Her knees could barely support her, and her hands trembled when she did the smallest task.

"Shall I tell the modiste you need more dresses in black, my lady?"

Diana turned to her maid with a confused frown. When had she walked into the room? "What?"

"You have only the one," she returned kindly as she gestured to the gown Diana already wore. "You'll be needing more."

Of course, she would. "Oh, yes. Thank you, Tina."

"And shall I pack you a bag? So that you can stay with your brother?"

Yes! The word echoed in her head, but she couldn't voice it aloud. That wasn't where her duty lay. But rather than say the word, she mutely shook her head.

"No one would think less of you—" Tina began.

"I would," she said tartly. "I would think less of me." Oscar deserved as much from his wife. He'd been murdered, likely by his own son. She would stand by his side in his death as she had throughout their twelve years of marriage. It was what a proper woman did.

Tina took the rebuke well, dipping into a curtsey, and Diana saw respect in the woman's eyes. Diana would do her duty even if it meant Geoffrey had an easy target here. He'd managed to get poison into her home. Should she start questioning everything she ate now? Did she worry that every cup of tea now held a lethal dose of arsenic? What about the eggs she ate for breakfast? The bread that came with every meal? How did she cope with a life where everything was suspect?

The thought had her dropping into the chair between the fire and the window. She barely noticed when her maid left. She just sat and remembered the many hours she'd spent here as the days of her life slipped by. She'd often wondered if her life would ever change. Well, it had, and now she wished it would stop.

She heard footsteps as someone entered the room. She knew who it was even as he shut the door and came to kneel down before her. She didn't open her eyes. If she did, her vision would be filled with him, the man she had been holding while her husband lay dying. The man—if truth be told—she still wanted to touch. But more than that, she wanted to be in his arms while he held the rest of the world at bay.

"I will go away if you want me to," Lucas said, his words like the first step into a warm bath. She felt surrounded by his voice.

"Stay. Please," she said. She wanted to sit here while he spoke to her in that way. It didn't matter what he said, only that he used that special timbre of voice.

"The constable is interviewing everyone. He still tries to implicate you, but the staff is adamant in their love for you. They do not believe you could possibly hurt his lordship."

"I wouldn't. I never—"

"I know." His fingers slid up her forearms to stroke the back of her arms just past the elbow. It was a strange place to be touched, and yet she felt it as deeply as any other caress in her life. "I've been speaking with everyone as well. I think I know who did it."

Her head shot up as she looked into his eyes. "Who?"

"You have a footman named Donald Fisher?"

She nodded. "Yes." Then she grimaced. "He gambles foolishly. I warned him that he would lose his position and worse if he continued to play. I've seen other men destroyed by it." Men like Geoffrey.

"I don't think he listened. In fact, I think he gambled against Geoffrey and lost."

"Oh." Such a foolish boy. "Where is he?"

"I have sent one of my best men to look."

She shook her head. "You must find him. He could tell the constable who is behind this. He could testify—"

"Yes. But I won't leave you alone, Diana. Until this is done, I will not leave your side unless I am sure of your safety."

She bit her lip. "You think Geoffrey will try again."

His expression was grim. "I am certain of it." He took a deep breath, then eased a little closer to her.

"You must find Fisher." She tried for a smile and failed.

He nodded, but it did not soften his expression. If anything, his jaw became more pronounced as he held back whatever he wanted to say.

"I am too tired to play games, Lucas. What is it that you want to tell me?"

He nodded once, and she read it as a gesture of respect. And that was rare indeed. "I believe Geoffrey killed his father. I believe he will stop at nothing to kill you."

She blanched. It never got easier to contemplate. "So you've said."

"I can end this for you, quickly and quietly. You need never fear him again."

The relief she felt at just his words made her lightheaded. She'd wished for it all to end for months now. Years even. Ever since it became clear that Geoffrey was not the man his father wanted him to be.

"How?" she whispered. "How could that be possible?"

He waited a moment until she looked directly at him. And then he spoke in very soft tones. "I will kill him, Diana."

She didn't think she'd heard him correctly, but the seriousness with which he looked at her froze the breath in her lungs. "You cannot mean to…" She couldn't even say the word.

"I am a soldier. I have killed many men—"

"In a war! This is—"

"And even then, I fought for less than I do now. Diana, we cannot keep you under guard forever. Eventually, someone will make a mistake, and he will strike."

She shook her head, the idea too much for her to absorb. "I will not have you murder for me."

He took her hand, covering it where it trembled against her knee. "It will be for me then. My choice. Because you will never be safe until—"

"No!" She jerked her hand away. And as she shrunk back into her chair, she pressed them to her temples. The world had gone insane.

"Diana—"

"Stop!" she said as she dropped her hands and glared at him. "Why would you suggest such a thing?"

He didn't answer. Probably because he already had. She was in danger, and he was her protector.

"Why are you doing this, Lucas? I cannot possibly mean this much to you."

He frowned as he looked at her. "I would do anything for you."

"That's ridiculous! We have barely spoken in twelve years! Before a few weeks ago, we have known nothing of each other."

"That's not true," he said. "I wanted to marry you."

"We were children."

He blew out a breath, and his tone took on harder notes. "I was old enough to go to war. You were old enough to marry. Even then, we both knew what we wanted."

She shook her head. She thought of the silly child she had been then. She had believed in magical possibilities. She'd actually thought the boy of her dreams could find a way to save her from an evil marriage. It hadn't happened. And even more, she'd discovered her husband wasn't bad. That it was possible for two strangers of disparate ages to find common ground.

"I'm nothing like the girl I was then. And you are nothing like that boy." She touched his face. "You're a man who understands the consequences of his actions and that nothing is as easy as it seems. And so, I ask you again, why do you profess such..." Her voice trailed away. Neither of them had spoken of "love" since the night before her marriage. She wasn't even sure she believed in it anymore. And yet he seemed to have no problem at all.

"Love, Diana. That is what I profess for you. Pure and simple love."

She shook her head, rejecting the notion. "You cannot mean that. We don't even know each other!"

"But we do. I do. And I have thought of you every day since your wedding. Your image pulled courage from me when I was afraid. I recalled your laughter during battles and your smile in the endless times between. My fever dreams were of you. My waking dreams, as well. They were all of you."

"They were *dreams*. And they are much too insubstantial to let them dictate your actions."

"No," he said. "No!" He gripped her hands and pulled them to his mouth. "Diana, dreams are the only things that should dictate our actions. And for the dream of your safety, I will end this problem for you."

End her problem? "That's a clever way of speaking of murder. You could be hanged!"

"Have more faith in me than that. With the places he frequents, a knife in the gut—"

"Stop!" She pushed him away as she jumped to her feet. "Just stop!" She paced to her bed and back. Not once but three times, and with every step, she grew more agitated. He was speaking nonsense, and yet the seductive power of it was clear. It was the height of romantic fantasy. He was her knight in shining armor, sweeping away her troubles with a flash of his bright sword. "You cannot rescue me, Lucas. Not that way." Then she slowed, her steps faltering as her mind finally began to work logically. She looked at him. He had risen to his feet as well, and so now she had to tilt her head. His hard jaw seemed cut from stone as he looked down at her. He might as well be a Grecian statue of a warrior in his prime.

"Diana—"

"Why did you ask me?"

He blinked. "What?"

She swallowed. "A knife in the dark." She shuddered. "You hardly needed my permission for that. Why did you come here and ask me such a thing?" It didn't escape her that this was the exact place where he'd been holding her a few hours before. Here where she had broken down into emotion and need as she sought comfort in his arms. "You could have done it and told me after. Or not at all."

"Is that what you want? The deed done, and you none the wiser?"

"No!" She was emphatic on that point. "Absolutely not!" If such a thing were to be done in her name, then by God, she would know it and not shirk from the fact.

"That is why," he said. Then his shoulder lifted in a small shrug. "I did not know what you would want, and I feared…"

His voice trailed off, and she nearly stumbled as she tried to follow his thoughts. "The hangman's noose?" she asked. "Perhaps missing the mark and getting a knife set in your ribs instead?" The very words tasted hideous in her mouth.

He raised his hands in a helpless gesture. "I feared losing your regard. You are a proper lady, Diana, and I mean that with all reverence. I would not have you despise me for this act."

"Only for the offering of it?"

He flinched at that, and she regretted her words. She didn't hate him for the offer. Merely that it seemed so very appealing to her when she should despise it from the very core of her being.

Lucas took a step forward, coming close enough to touch her but not actually reaching her. "I wanted you to know all your options. You have been making your way on your own for so long, Diana. I knew you would want control of the next steps." Then he lifted his chin. "I can lift the burden from you if you want. I would shoulder this for you if I could."

"It is my responsibility! My duty and my—"

"Promise to a husband you didn't want, to his family who despises you, to generations that may not be. Damn it, Diana, when will you choose for you? What do *you* want?"

She stared at him, fury building up inside her. Anger, hatred, and all those black emotions that she so carefully locked away. They burst from her in a scream that tore through her throat. It was loud and raw and didn't make a dent in the emotions tearing through her. Without even planning it, she started raining blows down on him. It was how he made her question things she believed were absolute. And how he made her feel everything. Pain, fear, desire—all of these emotions had been locked away for so long. Why did he insist on making her feel?

He took her blows without flinching. He let her beat at him again and again until he was cradling her in his arms as she sobbed against his chest. She gasped and cried and wanted to rip out her own heart for the display, but she could not stop.

"Shh," he said. "It's all right. It will be all right."

Nothing would be all right ever again. "I hate you," she rasped, though she didn't mean it.

"You have that right. I should have married you twelve years ago and damn the consequences."

She snorted. "Starving would have been better for us? Neither of us had any way to survive."

"Maybe. Who is to tell?"

She said nothing. He held her with his lips pressed to her forehead. And he whispered such things as only lovers would say. That he would take care of every detail. That it would be just as she wanted when nothing was at all what she wanted.

"Do you know why I hate you?" she asked when he finally ran out of nonsense to say.

"Why?"

"Because you make me feel, Lucas. You always have. And it has been so long since anything has touched my heart."

He took those words from her. And in the end, he pressed his lips to her temple.

"I understand that very, very well."

CHAPTER FIFTEEN

D IANA DIDN'T SAY any more. She simply allowed the feelings to wash through her as he held her. Safety and gratitude welled up, but also a dark, blind fury at everyone and everything. She didn't want to feel that. It ate at her insides and choked off her breath. She focused instead on the feel of a man's arms around her body. There was strength in him, enough to carry her for a time, and she couldn't ever remember feeling that since her father had lifted her up while she still wore leading strings.

A knock sounded at her bedroom door, and she silently cursed Simpson as he spoke through the heavy wood. "Your mother has arrived, my lady."

"My mother?" she mouthed as she looked at Lucas. "Did you send for her?"

He shook his head as he released her. Then he stepped toward the door and raised a brow in question. Did he open the door? She nodded. Might as well. All the staff likely knew she'd been behind closed doors with Lucas.

With a nod, Lucas opened the door and stood to the side. Simpson looked every hour of his fifty-seven years, but he still bowed to her with the elegance of a man half his age. "The dowager countess says she has come at your hour of need to provide comfort."

If his words were sarcastic, she didn't hear it. But in her mind, she heard every self-serving, dramatic word her mother must have uttered. And with those images came a rage that climbed up her throat and began to choke her. The nerve of that woman coming to comfort her when it was her fault that Diana was in this situation in the first place. Lucas blamed himself for being unable to rescue her from her marriage. Diana blamed her mother for foisting it on her in the first place. And at this moment when the floodgates to her emotions stood wide open, Diana would eviscerate her mother for daring to show her face—

"Tell the countess that the lady is indisposed," Lucas said. "She will see no one."

"It won't work," Diana rasped. "She'll rush upstairs—"

"No, she won't," Lucas said firmly. "If I have to stand in the door and carry her downstairs, she will not pass. Not if you don't want her."

"I don't," Diana said as she tried to swallow down a black hatred toward the woman who had sacrificed her to an old man. But with every gasp, she remembered how she'd felt on her wedding night when his arthritic hands had touched her. How alone she'd felt in a house where even the servants despised her. And how her mother had visited her every day to "comfort her" when in truth, she had wanted to make sure Diana didn't cause a scene in her new life. *A scene!* As if the mistress of the house couldn't do whatever she damned well pleased in her own home!

"Perhaps," Simpson said, "she can be called upon to act as hostess to Lady Beddoe."

Diana reeled, and Lucas grabbed her elbow before she fell. "Penelope is here?" she asked. Oscar's daughter was a shrew if ever there was one.

"Not as yet, but—"

"Soon." Diana looked at the clock. It wasn't even nine in the morning, and she was overrun. She put her hands to her face. "They'll come up here. They'll—"

"No," Lucas said firmly. "Simpson, inform the countess that her daughter needs her to keep everyone away. She is understandably upset and not ready to see anyone yet."

"Of course—"

"They won't listen," Diana said. Her mother certainly never bowed to any butler.

"They will because the constable is still here. He'll want to interview them, I'm sure."

Diana's head snapped up. Of course. He was here investigating Oscar's murder. Good God, why couldn't she think?

Lucas gently guided her to sit in her chair. Back to her seat between fire and window. "Let your mother handle things for now. It's the least she can do, and she's well up to the task."

True. "I'm not putting my faith in my mother," she snarled.

"Then put your faith in me," he said as he dropped down to face her eye to eye. "Let me have the command of your staff, and I shall see—"

She laughed, though the sound came out hard. "They already listen to you."

"No. They are your people and will always care for you."

She wasn't sure she believed it. She had spent too much time demanding respect for her to believe it was there even when she faltered. But Lucas clearly believed it. And when she looked to Simpson, he gave her a firm nod.

"You are the head of this household, my lady. There is no other."

Except for the one who had poisoned her husband. Except when Penelope reminisced about the times Simpson had indulged her as a child, and he caved to her every whim. Except for—

"Have faith in them, Diana."

She looked into Lucas's eyes, and the words came out—not exactly easy, but she voiced them, nonetheless. "I will leave it your hands," she said. She looked down at her fingers. "For now. Until I can catch my breath."

Lucas nodded, then turned to Simpson. "You understand what's to be done? For the first time in her life, the countess is to protect her daughter. She is to see that no one disturbs her ladyship." Then Lucas straightened. "I will be down in a moment to lend my hand."

"Of course, my lord."

Diana's head snapped up, and she saw Lucas jerk in reaction as well. Everyone in this household called him Mr. Lucifer. But he had revealed himself, and Simpson had been in the room. So, of course, the staff now knew his true identity.

"There's no need to call me by anything new—" Lucas began, but Diana interrupted him.

"The news is out. You are Lord Chellam, and it is foolishness to try and hide that."

Lucas exhaled. "I'm not trying to hide it. At least not anymore. I didn't want my sins to land now, as well."

She didn't speak. She didn't need to. They both knew that there was no avoiding any of what was to come. And suddenly, after that flash flood of anger, now she just felt tired. Not just weary in body, but exhausted from emotions. From relaxing her guard for one night, only to have her entire life destroyed around her. It crippled her.

"Enough," Lucas said sharply. "Simpson, I'll be downstairs in a moment. My lady, I insist that you rest." And so saying, he scooped her up off her chair.

She gasped in surprise but did not object. Now of all times, it felt too wonderful to settle into a man's strong arms as he took care of her. She was not proud of this weakness. She needed to be strong. But for this moment, she allowed herself to rest in his arms.

"It will be done, my lord," Simpson said as he bowed himself out of the room. Diana clearly heard him shut the door before his footsteps thunked down the hallway.

Meanwhile, Lucas was settling her gently on her bed. She didn't choose her next action. Like so much of the last twenty-four hours, her body acted without consulting her mind. As he set her on the pillow, she wrapped her arms around his neck. She had no thought as to why she did it, except that she didn't want to lose this moment. When he made to withdraw, she pulled him tighter.

"I can't, Diana," he said. "I want to. God, how I want to, but this is not the time. You'll hate me afterward."

"Never," she whispered. Even when he had failed to save her from her wedding, she had never hated him.

He dropped his forehead to hers. "How quickly you forget. You said you hated me not ten minutes ago."

"I lied."

"I know." He gently untangled her hands from his neck and drew back. "When this is over," he said. "When you are safe, then we shall talk again. I have more to offer you now. Even without any money from the title or your estates, I could support us. Not like this, of course. Not with servants tripping over themselves to serve you. But I could keep you well, my lady. And we might be happy."

What a pretty picture he painted. Her settled comfortably in a bed while he slew all her dragons. Right then, she wanted it as she wanted her next breath, though she knew the need wouldn't last.

He nodded as if he expected as much, though she saw a flash of something in his eyes. Disappointment? Whatever it was, he quickly hid it.

"We don't have to speak of this now," he said. Then he straightened up. "I'll send your maid—"

"No," she said softly. "If you will not remain, I will rest alone."

He nodded. "Simpson and I will guard the stairs, and your windows are locked. Not a soul will disturb your rest, my lady." Then he touched her face. A soft caress down her cheek until his thumb rolled across her lips.

She felt the tingle of his touch and a desperate yearning inside for more. For him. For everything he offered her.

She held her breath again, relishing the sensations even as she kept all her thoughts inside her. This was not the time for her to speak. She was much too likely to say something rash. Then he straightened off her bed, bowed to her as the courtliest knight of old, and left her alone in a suddenly cold room.

CHAPTER SIXTEEN

W HEN HE'D BEEN a soldier, everything he did had a purpose. The cleanliness of his body and uniform kept him from disease. Marching kept him fit, developed unity, and had a tradition as old as England. Even sleep allowed him to trust the men who proved over and over again that they had his back just as he had theirs. And his rank instantly gave him a measure of authority that allowed him to serve England and the men who trusted him.

The minute he came home, all that had been lost. He was back to a life of aimlessness that only stabilized when he found his work at the Lyon's Den. There he guarded good people against unruly gamblers, and his company became the veterans who worked under him to watch the doors and the women who eked out a living under that roof. That was the real reason he hadn't gone home to his parents. They weren't his family anymore, and he refused to go back to the empty life of privilege.

So it was with some bitterness that he headed downstairs to where Simpson bowed to him and called him "my lord." He was about to navigate through people who would assume he was another frivolous gentleman filling his time with stupid amusements and none of the serious work of a man: protecting the vulnerable from other people's sins. It was fortunate that the first person he encountered after Simpson was the one woman with whom he'd wanted frank conversation for twelve years.

Diana's mother stood at the base of the stairs with an imperious air.

"I will see my daughter now!"

"You will do no such thing," Lucas snapped, his voice as hard as if he disciplined the rawest recruit.

"How dare you—"

"Are you aware that the constable suspects you of murdering Lord Dunnamore?" He didn't wait for her to process the words but kept dropping facts like sharp rocks tossed at a rat. "He has little evidence beyond your presence here last night. But you were alone with him and had ample time to poison him."

"What the devil are you talking about?"

"Arsenic in his tea, my lady. The very same tea you ordered for his lordship, and the very same tea that killed him."

Her eyes widened in horror as she looked at Simpson. "Arsenic?" she gasped. "But why?"

He didn't leave Simpson time to answer. "Because, my lady, you sacrificed your daughter to your fears, forcing her to marry Lord Dunnamore because he promised to help manage your finances."

"You...you have no right," she cried.

"Over the years, you've seen to your great embarrassment how badly your daughter is treated by her stepchildren and indeed, by yourself, who preens about town with no thought as to the woman who paid for your fripperies with her freedom." He gestured with a disdainful flick of his wrist at her very fashionable gown.

"That's not true."

"It's not true that you regret it? Well, you should have, my lady. Because the very daughter you claim to be here to support has been miserable for twelve years thanks to your cowardice." He lifted his chin. "A mother should protect her daughter."

The woman shook her head. "She has a husband, status, and mon-ey—"

"The constable thinks that perhaps you regretted your actions and, in a misguided attempt to save your daughter from her fate, poisoned his lordship's tea with arsenic."

"I did no such thing!" she cried.

"Of course not," he agreed. "Because you do not have a caring bone in your body for your daughter. You'd never think to help her unless it benefited you somehow."

"I was here last night to help her. Do you think I enjoyed sitting with a dying old man all evening while she went to a masquerade?"

He looked at her, his lips curled in disgust. "And yet you married her to him when she was but a child."

That shut her up, and well it should. He could tell from her expression that she knew what she'd done. And perhaps she had regretted actions taken in fear after just being widowed. Even so, he couldn't forgive her.

"If you wish to avoid the hangman's noose, then you will do exactly as I say."

"The noose!" She was all but choking on her shock.

"Yes," he said as he leaned down to tower over her. "The constable is in the housekeeper's office conducting interviews. You will go there now and tell him the truth—every single bit of it. How you sacrificed Diana to your fears. How you know that she has been treated to insults and abuse from Oscar's children. And that you did nothing, absolutely nothing to help her."

She opened her mouth to argue, but no words came out. Not a single one, but the glitter of tears shone in her eyes. And into that taut moment, Simpson gestured with a slow movement of his wrist.

"This way, my lady," he intoned.

She started to move. And in that place of vulnerability, he poked her one last time.

"How did you know?" he asked her.

"What?"

"How did you know to come here now?" She had been here last night after Diana's attack but had gone home before his lordship expired. Elliott knew of the situation here, but he would not have told his mother. Not without Diana's agreement. "Was it because you knew about the poison? Perhaps put it in the teapot yourself?"

"No!" she cried.

"Then, how?"

She swallowed. She clearly didn't want to say, but he kept his expression implacable. And when she still didn't speak, he arched a brow.

Finally, she huffed out an answer. "Tina sent a message last night that his lordship had passed. She didn't say how."

"Diana's maid? She sent a message? You pay her to spy on your daughter for you." He shouldn't be surprised. Of course the woman snooped. That's what women of the *ton* did because gossip was the life bread of their set. Still, it repulsed him to think that she would—

"Of course I did!" she snapped. "I watch her because I knew. I knew about Geoffrey. I knew that Oscar was too ill to protect her." She dashed away tears. "But what could I do? She was already married."

Lucas felt his gut tighten. "You know you did wrong."

"Yes, damn you, yes!" She looked away. "It was one mistake. One horrible mistake and—"

"And Diana was one to pay for it."

"Yes." The one word sounded miserable and carried with it a load of guilt.

And suddenly, Lucas felt ashamed. He had thought forcing the woman to admit what she'd done would ease some of his fury. Because of her, he and Diana had been robbed of a normal courtship. Instead, he just felt empty.

What good was it to force a mother to admit she'd betrayed her daughter? Perhaps he should have a séance and force Oscar's ghost to

122

admit that he lusted after a child. That he'd used the situation to get what he wanted. Did he also look to Diana's father, then, for failing to provide adequate income for his family after his death?

All of these people were at fault, and the burden of payment had come to Diana. And if he were truly to point fingers, he needed to confess his own guilt. Twelve years ago, she would have run away with him. He had managed to get the three thousand pounds he needed so they could escape together. He could have found a way to survive for the rest of their lives. They would not have lived in the same way, not with servants and fine food, but Diana wouldn't now be in mortal danger from her stepson.

How useless it was to blame. He saw that so clearly now. He took a breath, reoriented his thoughts, and gestured the countess belowstairs. "Tell the constable everything. Don't try to hide from it."

"He'll think I did it to save Diana."

"He might," Lucas admitted. "He might also see how Geoffrey was the one who frightened everyone and that he is the only one cold-blooded enough to do the deed."

The countess was no fool. She heard his words and straightened, knowing now what she had to do. Without lying about anything, she would likely point the stupid officer toward the true villain. With a crisp nod, she headed down the stairs just as the knocker sounded.

Lucas knew who it was. The only other people who would sound the knocker at this early hour were Oscar's children.

He moved to the door, feeling undecided on how he would handle seeing the adult daughter who had tortured Diana. He was still humbled by his revelation with the countess. How could he stand in judgment of Penelope, who had likely been victimized by her family as well?

He pulled open the door and did his best to understand her sour expression and angry demeanor. She'd just lost her father, after all. But within a minute of opening the door, he banished any thought of sympathy. This woman deserved no compassion at all.

CHAPTER SEVENTEEN

"W HO ARE YOU? Where's Simpson?"

Lady Beddoe's expression was as tight as her hair, which pulled her face up until she looked perpetually startled. And that looked very odd given her sour frown.

Lucas performed a modest bow as he opened the door and stepped back to allow Oscar's only daughter and her husband to enter. Lord Beddoe, however, remained outside, his gaze on Geoffrey, who was just now sauntering up the street.

When he looked back, he shook his head. "This is bad business. Bad business indeed." His words didn't appear to be for anyone but himself. He handed his hat to Lucas—who hadn't offered to take it— and then headed straight for the parlor and then the sideboard to pour himself a drink.

Meanwhile, Lady Beddoe stood at the base of the stairs. "I suppose Papa's upstairs, then. I suppose I'll have to see him."

Lucas set the hat on the entry table, then stepped to watch Penelope's expression closely. "Your father is upstairs, but he hasn't been cleaned up yet. The results of poison can be messy."

Her gaze cut hard to him. "Yes, Geoffrey told us that shrew poisoned our father." Then she sniffed delicately. "I'll wait until things have been properly prepared before I see him."

"And how did Geoffrey know that?" Lucas asked. "The constable is still completing interviews."

"As if that matters," she said as she headed for the parlor. Her black skirts made her look like a burned-out tree. "I hope she hangs for it."

"I assure you, it matters a great deal. How did your brother know Lord Dunnamore was poisoned?"

She turned to stare at him with a huff. "He pays a footman to tell him things. Do you think we would allow a murderess to run wild in our father's home without some form of watch?"

"And do you know this footman's name?" He would bet anything it was Fisher.

"I don't concern myself with my brother's spies. Only the information he gives." She looked around the parlor. "Where is Diana? With the constable, I suppose?"

Lucas didn't answer. The knocker had sounded again—Geoffrey, no doubt—and since Simpson was still belowstairs, Lucas took a perverse pleasure in forcing the man to cool his heels on the stoop. Meanwhile, Lord Beddoe turned from the sideboard and, after taking a full measure of claret, spoke to Lucas.

"How was it done? Was it truly poisoned tea?" He shuddered as he spoke and quickly took another gulp of his drink.

Lucas studied the man, trying to gauge possible guilt. If he had to guess, he'd say that the husband knew nothing about the business beforehand and was horrified by the idea of death. Indeed, he could speculate that Lady Beddoe was of a similar mindset. Anything that brought knowledge of death was turned upon with the viciousness of a mad dog.

The knocker sounded again with the force of a battering ram. Apparently, Geoffrey wasn't happy with being left outside. Lady Beddoe frowned at him.

"Aren't you going to answer that?"

"I'm not the butler," he answered smoothly. Let the bastard wait until Simpson came back.

Lady Beddoe pinched her lips tight. She looked him up and down, taking in the dark clothes of his Lord Lucifer attire. He'd discarded the mask and cape, of course, but she could see the excellent fabric he'd been forced to wear. That betrayed him more than anything else. He was not a servant, and she was just now realizing that.

"You're her lover then," she said. "Did you know? Did you help?"

"Penelope, must you?" her husband huffed.

"I am brutally honest. I'll remind you that it's a virtue," she snapped at her husband. He responded by pouring himself more claret. Meanwhile, she turned back to Lucas. "Well? Did you?"

Obviously, she used her so-called virtue to badger people into her way of thinking. It was a crude tactic and one that proved she had no subtlety in her. But just to be sure, he leveled her with a hard stare.

"No. If you must know, Geoffrey was the poisoner, as I think you already know."

Lord Beddoe set down his glass with an audible click. "The devil you say!" Then he turned his stricken eyes to his wife. "Penelope?"

The woman gaped at Lucas, her eyes wide with shock as the color drained from her face. She didn't speak but just gaped at him. It was a true reaction and one that told him she had not played a part in the deed. Then her skin flushed hot, and she lifted her chin until her head was tipped halfway back.

"You, sirrah, are offensive."

Her husband, however, would have none of it. He shied back a step, horror in his expression. "Penelope! The truth, now!"

She turned angry eyes on her husband. "I know nothing of the sort!"

"But you suspected," Lucas said, disgust in his tone. "You both know your brother's character. It is your sin that you would rather believe the worst of the woman who cared night and day for your father than turn your rancor on your brother."

"Don't be ridiculous!"

126

"I should call you out!"

Clearly, neither husband nor wife would tolerate his disgust, and they turned on him in unison. They cried insult and any number of other things. He ignored them, his attention shifting to the door as Simpson finally arrived and pulled it open.

Mr. Geoffrey Hough stood there, an angry sneer on his face. "You are not long in this position, Simpson," he said. "I do hope you have saved something for your old age."

Simpson said nothing. Indeed, he didn't even react as he performed the duties of a butler with a flat, almost bored expression. And here Lucas saw the true face of a murderer. Geoffrey wasn't cold-blooded or even very smart. There was no cleverness to be seen in his calculation, only the angry demeanor of a petulant child. And the more that Simpson ignored him, the more furious Geoffrey became.

And what was even more interesting was that Lord and Lady Beddoe saw it, too. Lord Beddoe swallowed the last of his claret with an audible gulp. His wife dipped her head and looked away. There was a new slump to her shoulders, and for the first time, she looked like she truly grieved. Had she loved Geoffrey? Most likely. Spoiled children came from too much doting.

Geoffrey sensed the mood of the house, and his gaze zeroed in on his sister. "Pen, dear, what have you said?"

"Nothing," she answered, though she did not meet his eyes. Then she squared her shoulders. "We cannot see Father yet. The body has not been prepared."

"And his lady wife?" Geoffrey said with a sneer. "Has she been taken by the authorities yet?"

The pair looked at Lucas. He took a moment to draw out his pronouncement, relishing his words. "No one suspects her."

Geoffrey's eyes widened, and he looked to his sister, the one he'd already prepared to push Diana as the perpetrator. But before he could say anything, Penelope finally got her nerve. She faced her brother and said in a low tone that everyone could hear.

"Did you do it?"

Her brother strode forward, his legs covering the ground with shocking speed. Penelope squeaked in alarm as she leapt backward from him. Clearly, she was used to her brother's temper. Fortunately, Lucas had been prepared. While Penelope cringed against her husband, Lucas stepped directly into Geoffrey's path.

"There will be no more violence done in this household," he said.

Well, maybe just a little more. He saw Geoffrey's punch coming. The man was not a skilled fighter, and Lucas had ample time to avoid the blow. But Geoffrey did not have the capacity to hit very hard, and Lucas needed witnesses to say the blackguard had attacked first.

He let the blighter hit his jaw hard enough to bruise but not break anything. Penelope screamed, and her husband gasped in shock, while Lucas grabbed Geoffrey's arm. And when Geoffrey kicked out as every inexperienced fighter did, Lucas tipped him over such that his face landed hard on the rug. Then he held onto the man's wrists and waited for Geoffrey to exhaust himself from squirming and cursing.

He heard the knocker sound and guessed it was the solicitor. He didn't bother to take his attention off of Geoffrey. He leaned down and spoke hard into the man's ear.

"You're beaten," he said softly. "Run to the colonies if you want to avoid hanging. I won't allow you to live any closer."

The man reacted with more curses and threats. Lucas didn't bother listening. He heard much more inventive ones at the Lyon's Den. And the more insanely violent Geoffrey looked, the easier it would be to prove his crime in court. What he didn't expect was the high-pitched scream that cut through the room. It wasn't Diana, but it was startling, and his head jerked up as he scanned the room.

And then a cold sweat broke out on his brow. Of all the ways for this to happen, he had not wanted it while brawling on the parlor floor. And yet, he would not let Geoffrey up. Not until the man calmed down. So he stayed where he was, waiting for a pause in the man's continuing diatribe so he could speak into the silence. It took another minute. Geoffrey, apparently, knew a lot of ways to insult his parentage. And then—as Geoffrey drew breath—Lucas finally spoke.

"Hello, Mother, Father. I had not expected you to find me so quickly."

That should have been dramatic. His mother was the one who had screamed. She was now leaning heavily on his father, who frowned down at his son.

"What are you doing?" his father demanded. "That is not appropriate behavior. Release him this instant."

Such was the power of his childhood that he felt the impulse to obey. He didn't. He wasn't a boy anymore. "I'm afraid I can't," he said. "Not until he calms down enough to not kill his sister." He glanced at Lady Beddoe to make sure that she remembered her brother had been coming for her. Apparently, she did because she shrank even further behind her husband.

"Don't be ridiculous," his father continued. "No one is going to kill anyone."

And wasn't that the sin of the civilized elite? They just didn't believe what they didn't want to know.

"On the contrary," came Diana's voice from the stairs. "I'm afraid there has already been one murder in this house, and your son is acting most appropriately."

Lucas grimaced. "You were supposed to be resting," he said.

"And miss all the punching and screaming?" She walked the rest of the way down the stairs. She appeared composed as she moved, though he saw the dark smudges beneath her eyes. "Simpson, where is the constable?" she asked with weary patience. "I would think the screaming would have drawn him out."

"It did, my lady," said the man as he stepped out of the shadows. "But his lordship had things well in hand."

"And do you?" she asked dryly. "Do you have enough information yet?"

He looked like he wanted to argue, though about what Lucas had no idea. But after taking a thorough inspection of Geoffrey on the ground, he grabbed his hat from the side table. "I believe I do for the moment. There's a footman who needs talking to. And I may need to ask a few questions of the family in a day or so. After things have been laid to rest, so to speak. If that's acceptable to you, my lady?"

Lucas could feel Geoffrey grind his teeth in fury, but there was no dignity in spouting insults from his place on the floor. He kept his peace as Diana graciously saw the constable out. Then she turned to the parlor. "Oscar's body has been prepared." Her voice trembled a bit as she spoke, but there was no wavering in her stance. "Penelope, you may see him as you wish. Geoffrey—"

"I have no need to see the old bastard, may he rot—"

Lucas raised Geoffrey's arms enough that the man's words were choked off.

"Very well," continued Diana. "The family solicitor is due very soon. I shall await him in the library. You all know the terms of the will. He was most clear." She looked down at Geoffrey. "If you think he changed his mind about your inheritance, you gave him no reason to."

Geoffrey was purple with rage. Every time Lucas eased off his arms, the man started cursing loudly. Meanwhile, Diana shook her head.

"You cannot see the solicitor in this frame of mind. Leave, Geoffrey, until you are more rational."

Lucas didn't wait for the man to respond. Instead, he shifted his weight and quickly hauled him to his feet. Simpson had already pulled the door open and stepped neatly aside as Lucas shoved the idiot outside. Simpson slammed the door shut before Geoffrey had time to turn around.

Done. At least for that moment.

Lucas turned back. He saw first that Penelope and her husband were being escorted up the stairs, presumably to view the body. Diana stood to the side with her back straight, and her chin lifted as they passed by her without even looking her way. Which left the last two—his parents—with their backs pressed against the far wall and their lips curled in distaste. He didn't even want to acknowledge their presence, but his father left him little choice. The moment Penelope and her husband disappeared from sight, his father spoke.

"How could you involve yourself in something so sordid?"

Childhood habits reared as he felt his lip curl in an identical expression of disdain. After learning that he was alive, all they could do was criticize him? Or scream? Fortunately, Diana interrupted him before he gave voice to any cruel response.

"Your son saved my life last night. I am most grateful to him."

"But why is he here at all?" his mother gasped. "We declared him dead."

"How did you find out I was here?" he asked.

"We didn't," his mother said. "We heard from others that you left some masquerade with *her*." She clearly included Diana in every sordid thing she could conceive.

"And we came to find out the truth," his father continued. "Only to see you brawling on the floor like a common guttersnipe."

Diana blew out a breath. "He was saving my life," she said dryly. "And I find your reaction to your son's continued existence extremely odd."

"Odd?" his mother sniffed. "You can say such a thing after what we just witnessed?"

"You didn't witness anything," Lucas said, suddenly weary of the whole affair. "You're just angry that I have the audacity to be alive." He straightened to his full height and brushed back his hair with his damaged hand. Now she could see his scarred face clearly. "It's me, alive and not as well as you no doubt want."

"Stop it, Lucas," chided Diana. "That isn't kind of you. They've had a shock."

They've had a shock? Diana's husband had just died, and the murderer had come to gloat. But none of that reflected on her face as she gestured to the parlor.

"Come in, everyone. Let's sit down to a cup of..." She winced, no doubt remembering that her husband had been poisoned with tea. "To some refreshments. Then we can sort things through."

"No, Diana," he began. "On today of all days, you need not..." His voice trailed away at her fixed stare.

"You saved my life, Lucas. I'll not abandon you now."

"You don't need to stand by my side. I'm in no danger from them." That was true. No physical danger, at least. But inside, he felt a war going on between what he feared and what was real. He'd been avoiding this moment for years, and he barely understood why. Until he looked at his parents' hard expressions and knew that, even though he was a man, there was still a child inside him. One who had been hurt over and over by them.

As if she understood his tangled emotions, Diana answered him with a calm air he appreciated. "Even so, I will not leave you." Then she called for refreshments.

CHAPTER EIGHTEEN

HONESTY WAS SUCH a horrible thing; it was no wonder everyone avoided it. Such was Diana's thought as she hosted the most bizarre tea ever at barely ten o'clock in the morning.

Lucas's parents were polite as they sat down to food that no one wanted. Still, they directed her to milk and no sugar as if it were of international importance. Lucas had nothing to drink, of course. His body was so rigid, she suspected he was trying to turn his cells to stone. And then all four of them suffered through the most banal small talk. They were sorry for her loss and embarrassed to intrude, the weather was appropriately dismal, and what a delightful tea blend.

Normally, Diana would have allowed the polite farce to go on without interruption. It was not her place to intervene in their family affairs. But Lucas sat like a man waiting for his execution. His expression was tight, and she could feel tension vibrating in him. His hands were clenched on his thighs, there was no sign that he breathed at all, and his gaze remained as sharp as a stiletto on the empty space between his parents' heads.

"You might as well ask your questions," she finally said. "I doubt you will get another chance."

The earl's gaze snapped to hers. "Why?" he asked, his voice a hard knock of sound.

He meant why they wouldn't get another chance to talk to their son, and in answer, she simply looked to Lucas's rigid posture. Did the man know nothing of his son? It was only out of deference to her that he was sitting here at all. She knew that if he had his choice, he would be anywhere but with them. The earl must have understood at least some of what she was thinking, so he voiced that same question again in an equally hard tone.

"Why?" This time the word encompassed so much more. Why had he played dead? Why hadn't he told them he was alive? Why had he acted as he did? And that was her question as well.

In answer, Lucas looked to his mother. He didn't say a word, just stared hard at her until she clenched her jaw so tight that the muscles trembled along her neck. When her words came, they were like shards of broken glass spit out at Lucas.

"How could you do this to your brother?"

"I didn't. You did."

"What?" his father asked, obviously confused.

"I didn't die," Lucas explained. "I know it would be more convenient if I had, but I'm afraid I couldn't manage that. I leave it to you now to decide if I am truly to live. Nathan loves the land and its heritage more than I ever will. Perhaps you should leave me dead."

"But you aren't dead," his father said. "You're here, you breathe. I don't care what you've done. You have a duty."

And wasn't that a cold thing for a father to say to his son? That he had a duty to live?

"Actually, I don't," Lucas answered. "Not when there is a spare to take my place."

The countess pursed her lips. "Too many people saw you last night. It's on everyone's lips this morning."

"I spoke to no one, confirmed nothing."

"Actually," Diana interrupted. "You did admit it to the constable." For her sake. As a way to defend her from the man's accusations.

Lucas shrugged. "The man can be bribed. Obviously."

That much was true since Geoffrey had likely already done it.

"Nathan won't do it," his mother said with a sour twist to her lips. "He will not deny you."

His father nodded agreement. "He won't, and neither will I. You are my son. How could you think we would lie about your existence?"

Because his mother wanted to, that much was clear. His mother had given all her love to his brother and was now shattered inside at the thought that Nathan would not inherit the title. It made no sense, and yet, the reality of it was clear as day on her face.

"It's settled," the earl said as he pushed to his feet. "We will go now to the solicitor and inform him of the happy news." For a man reporting "happy news," he certainly sounded matter-of-fact about it. If anything, his expression was one of firm dedication to appropriate behavior, as there was not a hint of a smile on his face.

"You go ahead," Lucas said as he, too, rose. "I am sure you know what's to be done far more than I."

"That's the reason you must be there," his father said. "So you can learn—"

"I can't." His gaze cut to Diana's. "I have duties here."

"What duties?" his father snapped. "You're my heir, and you're obliged to me."

"Actually, Father," Lucas said in equally clipped tones, "right now, you come in a distant third." As if to prove the point, one of his men came into the room. He was dressed as one of her footmen, but he was clearly a soldier reporting to his commanding officer as he waited, hat in hand, for a moment to speak. Lucas turned immediately to Diana and gave her a quick nod. "If you'll excuse me a moment," he said.

"Of course."

All three watched as he crossed the room to confer with his man. They spoke in low tones that Diana could not hear, but his mother's remarks were loud enough.

"Did you see that?" she remarked to the earl. "He doesn't even look at me. Such abominable manners. And did you see his hand? It's like a crow's foot."

Her husband didn't respond; neither did Diana, which apparently was normal for the countess. She just kept speaking as if everyone was fascinated by her observations.

"He needs to cut his hair in a more fashionable style. One that hides that scar along his face. A little paste would cover it up as well, but the haircut is vital." She lifted her chin. "We shall tell everyone that we have known from the beginning but that we remained quiet out of respect for his delicate health."

Diana meant to be quiet, but a snort of laughter burst out. And at the countess's outraged expression, she quickly apologized. "I do beg your pardon, but surely you see that no one will believe a word of that." She gestured back to where Lucas stood strong and tall. His muscular figure was on display. Indeed, Diana had just been admiring it.

"Of course, they will," the lady responded. "With that scar on his face and whatever has happened to his hand." She shuddered. "It's repulsive."

Diana's humor faded. "It's what happens to men during a war. He was at Waterloo, you know. That's where he was wounded. I haven't learned much more except that he's a formidable fighter." That much she had seen when she was attacked.

"We were told he'd died," the earl said, awe in his tone as he stared at this son.

"I wore mourning for months," the countess added.

Diana had no response to that, so it was fortunate that Lucas dismissed his man and strode forward to speak to her. "I need to go. Do not leave the house. I have a man watching Geoffrey and several here inside the house. If you—"

"I can't go anywhere. I'll need to receive visitors all afternoon. There are many who will want to pay their respects."

Lucas nodded as if he expected that. "I don't expect this to work. The news is unreliable at best, but I need to check it out nonetheless." He looked back as another one of his men stepped into the room. "This is Caleb Matthews. I trust him. You'll be safe, provided you keep him with you whenever you're outside of your bedroom."

She looked back to see Mr. Matthews square off as if saluting her. And she didn't miss the sheen of pride that came over him when Lucas said he trusted him. It was a sharp contrast to Lucas's parents' attitude. In that soldier turned footman, she saw true feelings for Lucas. He loved him in the purest, brotherhood sense of the word, and from what she could tell, Lucas returned the emotion in full measure.

Meanwhile, his mother was just now gaining her feet. "Whatever this business is," she said with disdainful tones, "pray it ends quickly. We must reintroduce you to society."

Lucas turned to his mother, his expression grim. "Shall we open a ball together, Mama? Perhaps I shall lead you out for a quadrille." He extended his maimed hand to her as if inviting her to dance. He wasn't wearing his customary glove, and so the scarred, crab-like digits hovered in the air between them while she visibly recoiled. He waited a moment, then a second, before pulling on his glove with sharp movements. "Perhaps we should wait a bit until you are more in command of your emotions."

Diana winced. In that one exchange, she saw years of damage inflicted from mother to son, back to mother in an endless cycle of anger. And standing off to the side was Lucas's father, who watched with an air of helpless despair. If she had to guess, she would say that he had not caused the problems between the two, but he certainly hadn't helped. It all lay before her like a tapestry of pain, and she found herself grabbing Lucas's deformed hand in her own. He had the glove half on by then, and she tugged it back off with a firm jerk of her wrist such that she held his bare hand.

It is the first time that she had touched his scarred flesh, and he seemed to freeze at the contact. She gentled her touch, doing her best to caress his scars, even as she tightened his fingers over his.

"You have not rested in two days," she said to him. "Surely you can trust someone else—"

"I cannot. If there's a chance to prove Geoffrey's villainy in court, I will find it." He left the rest unspoken, but it was there in his eyes. If he couldn't find a way to end Geoffrey's threat legally, he would do it by any other means available to him. He would see her safe, even if she didn't like how he chose to do it.

"I trust you," she said, and she watched her words settle into him. His shoulders eased down for the first time since she'd come down the stairs. She even noted some softness in him, if only around the very edge of his mouth.

"See that you listen then. Let Caleb protect you." His gaze cut to the footman.

"I will."

Which is when he slowly drew her hand up to his mouth. He kissed it with a courtly elegance befitting a future earl. But he was nothing like a dandy gentleman. He had harsh edges and a family that hated him so much that he'd played dead for years rather than reveal himself to them. He dressed more like an impoverished soldier than as a gentleman, and when he moved, it was with the sharp purpose of a soldier.

He couldn't have been more attractive to her if he were a royal prince. And as he pressed a kiss to her palm, she saw in his eyes something she'd never seen before—herself as reflected in a worthy man's eyes. He seemed to worship her, while her mind was caught up in how amazing he was. He disregarded everything, including his own parents and title, in order to save her from Geoffrey. Just as he'd tried twelve years ago to give up everything in order to save her from her marriage.

He was an extraordinary man, and for whatever reason, he felt she was worth saving. For twelve years, she'd fought for respect from her servants, her husband, and her stepchildren. Odd how something she'd sought all her life was now gifted to her from a man who was much more powerful than her. Lucas could easily dismiss her as he pursued his own life. And yet, he gazed at her as if she were everything to him.

The walls around her heart crumpled. In that moment, her heart gave in, gave up, and gave herself over to him. She loved him.

She loved him.

Then he left.

Just as he'd done so long ago. She knew he'd come back. If it were at all possible, she believed he'd return to her. Because that's what great men did when protecting the women they valued above all else. And that knowledge was enough to keep her strong throughout the hellish hours that followed.

Hours that turned into days. And days to a very long week.

Damnation! Where was he?

CHAPTER NINETEEN

Ireland, Two Weeks Later

I RISH MUD SMELLED ten times worse than London's mud. Such was Lucas's thought as the wet from the ground seeped into his clothes. He heard the distant bark of a dog and smelled the pungent scent of sheep that could only be found in the country, and he cursed the weeks he'd spent skulking about in Irish mud, English mud, and London muck.

A week in Ireland! Two weeks since he'd last seen Diana. And now he reeked of Irish mud while he wondered if he'd made a very bad choice somewhere along the way.

He'd thought he was being clever. He decided to hide away from Diana, disappear on the search for Fisher, the missing footman. In truth, he had other men on that task while he skulked about waiting for Geoffrey to attack Diana. He'd guessed—obviously incorrectly— that Geoffrey would be more likely to make his move when Lucas was in the wind.

Except there had been no attempts on Diana's life that he could see. None in England as she greeted mourners for several days in their London home. Nothing on the trip to Ireland where the now-deceased Oscar had his titular estate in all its crumbling ruin. And none yesterday after the service and burial in the family tomb. He'd remained nearby, failing completely to hide from the locals given that he wasn't Irish, didn't speak with an Irish accent, and had no reason to be loitering about. Fortunately, English coin spent very well in famine-ravaged Ireland, and he'd managed to remain relatively undetected, he hoped. Or maybe not, given that Geoffrey certainly hadn't shown his hand. Lucas was a soldier, not a spy, and he feared that he was ill-equipped to discover Geoffrey's plans.

With the funeral over, the Beddoes left, and good riddance to the shrew and her husband. Geoffrey never arrived, clearly uninterested in giving any respect to his father or viewing the ramshackle disaster that was his castle inheritance. So now all who remained were Diana and a small staff, all staying at the dower cottage that was not part of Geoffrey's inheritance. It was a comfortable property, easily able to hold Diana, her maid, and the two bodyguards he'd sent along with her—Caleb and Egeus. Everyone had retired now, except Diana, who leaned out her window as she turned her face to the moon.

Lord, she was beautiful. A true English goddess with her flaxen hair, blue eyes, and sweet, bow-shaped lips. At least that's what he'd say if he were writing poetry about her. In truth, as beautiful as she was, his mind lingered on other aspects. He'd heard from a tenant this morning how his lordship had saved everyone from famine by forgiving rents and even paying for hard cheeses for every tenant. He'd bet anything that Diana had done that, not Oscar.

He also thought about how she'd kept her head in Vauxhall. Certainly, she'd become terrified afterward, but during the attack, she'd been an asset, and that was rare indeed among women of her set. But what his thoughts returned to over and over was the moment when she had touched his scarred hand. He'd shown it to his mother, knowing the woman would recoil in horror, but Diana had taken his fingers in hers and held on. Her touch had been light. He couldn't remember the last time anyone had touched his deformity.

The memory still rocked him to his very foundations.

That's what he dwelled on as she gazed up at the moon—the caress of her hand and the aching desire for her to do that again. He wanted her to touch him everywhere. It wasn't what he said, though. Instead, he hissed at her and gestured her back.

"Diana! Get back from the window!"

Anyone with good aim and a passable weapon could have ended her. And even the worst marksman got lucky every now and then. What were his men thinking, allowing her to lean out an open window?

And right there was the measure of how weary he was. He forgot that she didn't know he was there. For him—she'd consumed his waking thoughts and inhabited his dreams every second of the two weeks they'd been apart. For her—she thought he'd disappeared with no word. So it was no surprise when she looked down and saw him that she gasped in surprise. Far from pulling back from the window, she leaned over and peered into the darkness.

"Lucas?" she asked.

Damnation, he was an idiot. But there was no help for it now. With a muttered curse, he slipped around to the back door and made his way inside. He identified himself to Caleb in the kitchen, then used the water there to quickly wash himself. "She was leaning out the window," he said before he ducked his head straight into the bucket.

Caleb sighed as he handed over a towel. "I told her not to."

As if that made the least bit of difference, and so his glare said. But he didn't stop to debate the issue, especially as Diana came rushing downstairs.

"Lucas? Lucas! Where have you been?"

"Hush," he said as he pulled her back up the stairs. She wore a dressing-gown of light blue, a dull sight compared to her eyes. And her hair was falling down her back in a disorderly braid. She should not be seen in such immodest attire, but he was too busy drinking in the sight of her worried expression to comment. She had been afraid for him. Enough that she was now growing angry the more she reassured herself that he was safe.

"You look exhausted. Are you all right?"

"I'm fine. Upstairs. You need to stay away from the windows."

"Where have you been?"

"Right beside you from the beginning—"

"What?"

"I never went anywhere." He shrugged. "I was trying to draw Geoffrey out."

"He hasn't been around. Didn't even come to the funeral."

"I know."

"You've been here?"

"Within a hundred feet of you always."

"The whole time?" Outrage was creeping into her tone. "I've been worried sick!"

"You're a terrible actor, Diana. I couldn't let you know."

"I am no such thing! No one knows what I'm thinking. No one!"

"No one saw your wan face? Or that you jumped at every knock on the door? No one knew that you rub your arm when you are thinking of the attack at Vauxhall or that your hands shake when you serve tea now?"

She flushed as they made it into her bedroom. "How do you know that?"

Because he'd watched her constantly. He knew the tempo of her breath when she slept because he'd spent the night beneath her open window. And what he hadn't seen, his men had reported to him.

"I'm sorry," he said. "I needed Geoffrey to think you were abandoned." He studied her face, praying she understood.

She smiled at him, though the expression still held some irritation. "I never thought you abandoned me on purpose."

That was something, he supposed. He ought to go back out on patrol, but now that he was finally talking to her, he needed to know how she was really doing. Especially now that he saw telltale redness in her eyes.

"Why were you crying?" He shut her bedroom door quietly, then turned to study her.

"What? Oh." She pressed her hands to her face. "No reason, really."

He arched his brows, challenging her with his expression.

She shrugged. "I was thinking about melancholy things. And worrying about you."

He gave her a weak smile. "I am safe. What melancholy things?"

Her gaze grew abstract as she wandered about the room. It was large for an Irish cottage but small for what she was used to, and he wondered if she felt cramped. She didn't look uncomfortable as she dropped down onto the edge of the bed and looked at her hands. "Oscar and I had a normal marriage," she said. "Despite the way we began, we learned to rub along well enough."

He winced. He did not like thinking of her in a marriage with anyone other than him, normal or not. And he absolutely did not need to hear the details. But she appeared to need to talk, and so he would stand and listen, no matter what it cost him.

"You miss him," he said when she fell silent. "You were married for twelve years. That is only natural."

"He fell ill nearly three years ago. And though he would get better for a time, he never fully regained his strength." She took a breath and exhaled. "Do you know, I have not been touched in three years? His skin became so sensitive, you see. At times he could not tolerate even the slightest brush of the sheets."

He shuddered. That sounded horrendous.

She looked at him, her eyes bright in the moonlight. "I have only kissed two men in my life. Him and you." Her smile took on a mischievous bent. "I am a wealthy widow now. I begin to wonder what that means for me."

He jolted, very shocked. He knew what becoming a widow meant for many young women. Free of the restrictions placed on them by their husbands, they indulged many immodest appetites. Indeed, he'd seen several such women at the gaming hell where he'd been working. The women's side of the building catered to all kinds of sins. The idea of Diana—this goddess—descending to debauchery left him physically ill.

He took a hasty step forward. "You cannot know what you are saying."

She cocked her head to the side. "Why can't I? Men indulge themselves from the moment they hit adolescence until the day they become too infirm. Why do you think a woman has no appetite?"

Women did have appetites. He knew that very well. He just had not thought that she... That Diana would... He swallowed and looked away. "You're a proper lady," he finally said.

"I have been," she admitted. "But I find time and experience have changed me. Maybe I don't need to be so very proper anymore." She stood up until she came close enough to touch him. She didn't, and he didn't reach for her. But his skin prickled at her nearness, and his breath heated as his heart sped up. "I am a woman finally free," she said softly. "My elderly husband is gone after being ill for years. Why shouldn't I experience a man's touch if I want to? Someone I choose."

He wanted to do it. He wanted to take her in all the ways a man fantasizes. But in his mind, she was a lady and a goddess, as holy for him as the Madonna. To possess her now as a matter of appetite felt profane. And yet she stood before him in a dressing gown light enough for him to see the outline of her nipples, tight and perfect. Lust surged through him, lifting his cock to attention.

But he did not move. He couldn't. It wasn't right. She was a new widow, and he was supposed to be protecting her, not seducing her, and...and...what kind of man took advantage in a situation like this?

She waited a moment. A very long moment, then she sighed and wandered away. This time she went to the window, which still stood open to let in the evening breeze.

"Keep back—" he rasped.

"I know." She stayed far enough away from the window that she would be difficult to see from outside. But he saw every part of her outlined by the moonlight. Her sweet curves, her full hips, and the way her hair tumbled into the fabric of her gown to create a kind of veil. It made him hungry to slowly reveal that which was already filling his thoughts.

"I have spent so much time thinking about our kiss," she said. Her gaze settled on the distant moon. "We were teenagers, and every time you looked at me, I thought I would burn up. When we kissed, I felt like I'd become the sun." She abruptly spun back to him. "For twelve years, I have been a good wife to Oscar. I never strayed and always acted for his best interest and that of his family. And yet on the night he died, I was in your arms. How could I do that? I think back to that moment and wonder what madness possessed me."

"Diana." He did not need a replaying of what they'd done. He'd already relived it a thousand times. He'd held her. That was all. But in his fantasies, they'd done so much more.

Her gaze cut straight to his. "You were the perfect gentleman, but I wanted…" She shook her head. "Such things that I wanted from you."

He had been far from a gentleman in his thoughts. "You'd been attacked. It's natural to want to feel alive again."

She seemed to consider that. "Maybe. You do not understand the loneliness of my life. Years at the bedside of a dying husband with no companion except servants or the occasional hateful visits of his children. My family would try to visit, but I often put them off. I fought hard for respect because that was all I could hope for. Until you walked in."

"I am here to protect you," he said because that was the only honorable thing he could confess.

"And what of the tenderness I see in your eyes when you look at me? What of the need that burns there when you reach for me? Am I not allowed those things?"

"Of course, you are," he said. "In time." When the danger was past. When he could approach her with the reverence she deserved instead of the pounding lust that beat in him now.

She looked at him, her expression slowly shifting to disappointment. And how that cut at him. He couldn't fail her again.

"Do you know what I did today?" she asked.

"After Lord and Lady Beddoe left?"

"Yes."

"You spent the day inside resting."

"Resting?" she scoffed. "You think I went to my bed and slept in pristine beauty? Am I a hothouse flower to you?"

He blinked. "You were inside. You were safe—"

"I was with the estate steward. We have been corresponding for years now, but there is so much more to be done face to face. Improvements to the tenant farms. A school for the children. Sheep and pigs and crops. That is what we discussed."

"You and Nathan would get along famously."

Her lips quirked. "Yes, I should very much like to talk with him."

He nodded. He could arrange it once they were back in England.

"I spent my day as a man does, seeing to the needs of my tenants." She looked to the ceiling. "Why shouldn't I spend my evenings as a man does as well? Enjoying whatever pleasures are at hand."

"Enough," His voice became harsh as he took control of the situation. She'd had her say. Now it was his turn to bring her back to sanity. "You are speaking out of grief and guilt."

"Am I?" she challenged.

"Of course, you are. It has been two weeks since your husband passed. You just buried him."

"It has been years, Lucas. Oscar took to his bed *years ago.*" Her voice throbbed with those words. "We knew he was dying. And though there were good days, he was never a husband to me after that. More like a fond uncle. And now, finally, I am free."

"You want everything. Every experience, every indulgence, things you have been denied up until now."

"Yes!"

He arched a brow. "Have a care, Diana. Not every experience is pleasurable. And too much—"

"Do not lecture me. I am done with being told what I can and cannot do."

He didn't intend to lecture her. But he certainly wasn't going to stand around and allow her to be self-destructive. "Do you know what you want to do first?" And with whom? That was the main question, but he didn't voice it.

Her chin lifted. "You know I do." And when he didn't respond, she rolled her eyes. "I told you I was thinking of you."

He took a breath, his mind running quickly through the risks and dangers. He had seen no danger, heard no hint of betrayal, nothing untoward. He or his men checked her food, watched her drink, and stood guard. She was as safe as it was possible to be. And she would be that much safer if he were in the room, though every man was vulnerable when absorbed in a beautiful woman.

Then he looked at Diana. He saw the need in her for an experience—any experience—that was for her and her alone. Her pleasure, her entertainment, her delight.

He took a breath. Was he really going to do this? Apparently so, because he spoke softly after making sure her door was locked.

"Have you ever experienced a woman's quickening?"

She frowned and shook her head. "I'm not sure what that is."

"You would know."

Her brows lifted in interest.

"Do you trust your maid and cook? They will tell no one?" He knew his own men wouldn't dare breathe a word.

She nodded. "They will keep my secrets."

He licked his lips, his heart thundering. "Even so, you must try to be silent."

"I understand." And when he still didn't move, she huffed out a breath. "Do you intend to talk about it all night long? Or shall we—"

She spoke no more because he was already kissing her.

CHAPTER TWENTY

DIANA LOVED HIS kisses. She loved the way he looked at her—all brooding intensity—but when she finally broke his reserve enough to let the passion free? Well, then every caress, every taste, every second, was filled with his hunger for her. *Her!* She fought daily for every scrap of respect from her world. His complete adoration was intoxicating. She didn't have to gauge her words with him. She didn't have to moderate her emotions or calculate her actions. She simply felt and responded without consequence, and in that freedom, she found her own bliss.

It started with a kiss. Quick and sure, he caught her body and her mouth in the exact same instant. She tensed in surprise, but that didn't last long. As he thrust into her mouth, she arched into his arms. Then he explored her lips, her tongue, and her teeth with the thoroughness of a man intent on leaving no part of her untouched.

She allowed it. She gloried in it. And then she grew bold enough to touch him back. She gripped his back muscles that bulged with strength and stroked her fingers across the curve of his bottom. She had no fear of hurting him no matter how wild her passions. More, she trusted him to keep her safe within the confines of his shelter.

His clothes frustrated her, so she pushed at them, worming her hands between buttons and beneath fabric. He let her strip away his shirt, but he demanded more as he pushed her dressing gown off her shoulders, then gripped the bottom of her nightrail. He drew it off her in a single sweeping movement. She emerged from the volume of fabric with a gasp, then shook her hair away from her face. It was already wild, and she pulled out the tie so that not even her braid would restrain her.

He helped her, running his hands through her hair to loosen the plait. His gaze was rapt, and she smiled as she watched him. No one had ever looked at her as he did. No one thought even her wild curls worthy of anything more than a passing glance.

And while he stroked his hands through her hair, she let her fingers explore his broad shoulders and chest. She saw scars there. A small c-shaped cut near his collarbone, another jagged rip below his right nipple. The more she looked, the more she saw other signs of damage. And she touched every one, including the most obvious one along his face near his ear.

"So many hurts," she whispered.

He turned his head enough to press a kiss into her palm. "I was hurt badly at Waterloo. Most of these are from there."

His words didn't come close to describing the damage suggested by every single mark on his body. She'd known about his hand, of course, and the scar on his face. But all of this? There was no part of his body untouched. "I can't believe you survived all this."

"Cuts heal," he said as he lifted her face until they locked gazes. "I don't even notice the scars anymore."

She grabbed his maimed hand and pulled it to her mouth. "I see only you," she said and pressed her lips into his palm. "And every part of you is glorious."

She meant it, but he didn't seem to hear it. Instead, he trailed his mouth along the curve of her neck. He nipped at her shoulders as he stroked his free hand down her back. She arched, letting him support her as she stretched herself along his body.

"It's the fever that saved me," he said.

She was so absorbed in how easily he held her that she didn't at first hear his words. And when she did, they didn't make sense. "That cannot be," she said as he gently set her down on the bed. He came with her because she would not release him. And as he pressed his forearm into the mattress beside her head, she took his mouth, tasting him as he had her.

He let her, he opened for her, but only for a little bit. All too soon, he broke from her hold to look at her as he stroked her face, her hair, and even the curve of her ear.

"I had fever dreams of you just like this. So beautiful in my arms. Your hair spread out around you." His gaze followed the curls that he coiled around his fingers. "I dreamed about your face and about your body." He smiled. "Such things we did in France."

She stroked across his jaw. "I am no imaginary woman," she said. And to prove it, she pulled him down for another kiss. She tempted him as much as she knew how. She thrust into his mouth, she dug her fingers into his shoulders, and she did all the things she'd never dared before. She took what she wanted and demanded his response.

He was more than up to the challenge. While she possessed his mouth, his hands began to stroke her breasts. He began gently, but as she reacted, pushing herself against him, he grew bolder. He kneaded her flesh and pinched her nipples. And when their mouths separated to breathe, he moved lower on her body until he could take her nipple into his mouth. Soon sensation overwhelmed her, and she moaned with need.

He took his time while she writhed. He was stronger, heavier, and very sure of himself as he played with her breasts. And it was playing for him, she abruptly realized, because when he lifted up to look at her, his face was pulled into a wolfish grin. He loved it when she had so little control of her body.

She wanted to say something. She wanted to ask, "What happens now?" Because already, this was so much more than anything she had ever experienced. But she had no breath, and she doubted he would answer anyway. Instead, he reached above her head and grabbed a pillow. When she frowned at him, he gently pressed it into her hand.

"Use this when it becomes too much."

"What?" she asked, but he didn't answer. Instead, he moved down her body, pressing kisses onto the underside of her breast, her belly, and then to the junction between thigh and hip. She felt his hands stroke down her sides to cup her bottom. And then he slid lower— down the backs of her thighs—until he gripped just above the backs of her knees.

His mouth was already at an intimate place, and she was more than willing to accept his cock. Indeed, she wanted to feel the fullness of him stretch her. There would be such strength in his thrust.

He pulled her legs wide, but it wasn't his cock that found her entrance. It was his mouth and tongue. This was no blunt object ramming into her, but a dance that probed into her, stroked her, then teased and sucked while he shredded her composure. Never had she felt such things. Never had she realized how electric her body could feel. How sensations could pile one on top of the other while her belly coiled and her breath caught.

She tightened her knees as she tried to draw back. He shifted his grip on her legs until he pushed her knees wider. And while she lay fully exposed, he feasted on her everywhere. No part of her was left untouched, no place forgotten.

Then he found a place that shot lightning through her body. Over and over, he kissed her, his tongue doing things she couldn't even process. She was all feeling then, all gasping need.

Then he pulled back. He stopped everything while she still writhed, waiting for something. He grabbed the pillow, still clutched in her hand. He pressed it gently toward her face.

"Scream, beautiful Diana. Scream loud."

She wasn't going to scream. She was a lady who never raised her voice.

He must have understood her thoughts. Likely read the expression on her face. But instead of being insulted, he looked smug.

"You will," he said. And then he gently urged her to put her face into the pillow.

She didn't. She wouldn't. But just then, his thumb thrust upward across that spot. It was a sharp feeling at a place that had begun to cool down, and his movement startled a soft cry from her.

"You will," he repeated, and then he knelt down again. He put his mouth between her thighs. He thrust fingers into her, in and out of her slick center. She arched into the feel. It wasn't what she wanted, but it was delightful enough that she stopped trying to anticipate. No need to do more than feel, to learn, and to…to…

Oh, yes.

His mouth on that spot again. His fingers deep inside her. *And all was, yes, yes! Please!* She whimpered. She gasped. And yes, she even put the pillow over her face because of the sounds she was making.

Then he stroked her in earnest. He pushed, sucked, and whatever else he did took her over. The coil inside her tightened unbearably. Harder. Then it burst.

Ecstasy.

Did she scream? She didn't know. So consumed was she in the waves of pleasure—joy bursting in waves that crashed through her.

She was amazed.

CHAPTER TWENTY-ONE

S HE WAS STILL floating as he gathered her up. She helped him a little, but truthfully, she felt too boneless to do more than lie there in languid delight as he held her. Plus, it was fun to feel his strength as he effortlessly maneuvered her beneath the covers.

And when she was finally settled, she frowned at the pillow he casually tossed aside. "I think I screamed."

"Yes."

Such smugness in the one word. She didn't mind. He deserved all the credit for that, and she was very grateful.

She raised her hand and caressed his jaw. She realized that she was tracing the line of his scar. How close had he come to dying? How many times? Whatever had caused this could have killed him. A few inches difference, and he would be dead. But that was nothing to the fever. She knew infection often killed more after the battle than during it. And yet he had survived it all.

"You astound me," she whispered.

He ducked his head, and it startled her enough to laugh. Was this the man who had just grinned at her with smug satisfaction? Now he was embarrassed? To cover, he pressed his lips to her hand while his hair fell to hide his expression.

"It was my pleasure," he said gruffly.

"I'm fairly certain it was mine," she said. Then she gently extricated her hand such that she could turn his face to hers. "Was that a quickening?"

"Yes."

"I like it."

Now that cocky grin returned. "I like being your first."

He was her first kiss, her first quickening, and her first and only love. But she wasn't ready to tell him that. Not yet. Not before she understood what that meant for her life. Would she take him as a lover? Would she wed him? He was an incredible gift as he settled beside her on the bed. He sat with his back to the headboard as she adjusted to lay in his arms. Would he still do that with her after they took vows? Or would he disappear in search of new ladies to entertain?

Questions ate into her bliss despite everything she did to shove them away. For once, she did not want to strategize for her survival. She wanted to stay in this happy place.

"Kiss me," she said.

He did. He kissed her with the intense passion that she relished because it spoke of his need for her. But then he ended it, pulling away while hunger still burned in his eyes.

"Lucas?"

"I will not do more, Diana. Please do not tempt me."

"But—"

"No. You have had your first quickening. Is that not enough for you?"

Of course it was enough for her. She had been surviving for so long on so little that tonight's experience felt like enough happiness to fill an entire life. But she wasn't thinking about herself. She knew that men needed their release.

"I don't understand you, Lucas. Why won't you take what I freely offer?"

"Because it's too soon."

She lifted her head, the joy in her body fading as she faced yet another man who tried to tell her what was best for her. "You think you know better than I?" she asked, her voice silky-smooth.

He arched a brow, clearly hearing the warning in her tone. "Diana—"

"Why do you think you can tell me how to behave? Have I not proven I can survive? That I can stand when everyone else wants me to crawl?"

"Diana!" he said, his voice exasperated. "You have done that and more. Of course."

"Then—"

"I have my own honor," he said, his voice rough. "War stripped everything from me. My title was not proof against the resentment of my own men. My skills were not enough to stop artillery. My body was not strong enough to keep fighting when my men still needed me. And I could not stop my parents from declaring me dead and being grateful for the loss."

She blew out a breath. "That's not true." At least it wasn't for his father. His mother clearly had a favorite child, and it wasn't Lucas.

He brushed her words away. "When I lay shivering with fever, not knowing if I lived or died, one question kept plaguing me."

She held her tongue, waiting for whatever he was struggling to express. And while she waited, she settled differently on the bed such that she was still touching him, but she could now see his face clearly.

"I kept thinking, why am I still alive? Why haven't the bullets, the fever, or even the enemy put paid to my existence? Why did I still breathe when all I wanted was to finally rest."

She bit her lip. "What's the answer?"

He shrugged. "I don't know. That's the answer, Diana. I don't know why I still breathe, but as long as I do, I cannot put faith in anything I once believed. Not my country, my title, my body, or even my own will. I couldn't even force myself to live or die. That was in God's hands."

She stroked her hand across his clenched hand. How had he gone from what they'd just done to this angry place where he banged his fist down on his thigh?

"You are a man of extraordinary willpower. I doubt you would have survived otherwise."

He shook his head. "It's not my willpower that is strong, Diana. It's the knowledge that I will choose honorably where I have choice."

"Of course," she said as she sat up and faced him, but even as she spoke, he shook his head.

"It's not 'of course.' A man has two choices when he is stripped down to nothing. He can indulge in every whim to satisfy the moment, or he can decide to give meaning to his actions."

"And that's honor?"

"It is for me. Did you ever wonder how I ended up as a guard in a gaming hell?"

"You know I do." She leaned forward. "You don't usually answer my questions." She was grateful that he wanted to talk now.

He shrugged. "Sometimes it's hard to explain. I went into the Lyon's Den because it was warm, and I was cold. Normally I wouldn't have been allowed in." He smiled. "Their clientele dresses much better than I do, but the doorman, Nick, was inside trying to subdue a violent drunk. As I watched, he got punched hard enough that he lost his front teeth. For the rest of his life, Nick had to chew on the side of his mouth rather than eat like a normal man, all because a drunkard cared more about what he wanted than what his actions meant for everyone else." He shook his head. "I saw it happen and grew so angry that I stepped in, got the idiot in a headlock, and marched him out the door. I was offered a job five minutes after that."

A beautiful story, but she didn't understand how it related to everything else. "And that's honorable. Because you helped a doorman?"

"Because I see how actions affect everyone else. I think ahead, and I choose a path that causes the least suffering."

She touched his face. "Or perhaps the most joy?"

He shook his head. "Joy is fleeting. Suffering lasts a great deal longer. Do you still feel your quickening?"

Her cheeks flushed in memory. "Not that exactly, but I am happy to be here with you."

He nodded. "And I with you. But if I were to take my pleasure with you now, that would give me great joy—"

She grinned. "Then—"

"But the future would hold suffering. You might regret your choice in the morning. And if there was a babe, how would you explain that? I don't want to father a bastard."

She shook her head. "Babes can be prevented in other ways." She'd learned that at the beginning of her marriage when she hadn't wanted a child. "And even if I regret my actions, I would never blame you."

He sighed as he lifted her hand to his lips. "Don't you see? I want my choices to have meaning. If I were to lay with you now, it wouldn't have meaning. Just lust."

It would have meant something to her. To make love with someone by her choice would have been a momentous thing for her. But once again, someone else forced his choices upon her, and she resented it.

"I chose you tonight," she said, and though she tried to hide her anger from him, he likely heard it anyway. "I may not do it again."

"To give in to my lust now would betray my own honor. I will not risk our future on the needs of the moment."

"Even if they are my needs?" she challenged. Then she held up her hand to stop him from talking. "I have spent my life measuring my life by other people's demands. Tonight, I choose for myself and no one else." He didn't respond, but then again, he didn't need to. Making love was a choice made by two people, not just herself alone. She blew out a sigh. "I will not damn you for making another choice."

His expression softened. "You act as if my heart isn't pounding for you. It would be so easy for me to fall."

Her eyes widened. "You're not acting as if that's true." Was it a crime for her to wonder at her own attractiveness? She was a matron now and not as dewy fresh as the eighteen-year-old debutantes. "As Lord Chellam, you will have your choice in brides this Season."

He wrapped her hand in his good one, then slowly drew it down his body. He pressed it to the hot bulge beneath his falls, and she heard his hiss as her hand began to shape the length and breadth of his cock.

"I want you," he whispered. "I have wanted you since the day we first met."

She took her time feeling him. The heat was intense but more interesting was the way his head dropped back, and his breath stuttered as she played. Even through the protection of his clothing, she found where he was sensitive. She learned a little about how he liked to be touched.

"Would you like it?" she asked. "If I did to you what you did to me?"

His eyes widened. "How do you know of such things?"

She arched a brow at him. "I was married for twelve years."

"But you..." He swallowed. "Diana, I do not want to risk our future. I do not want to go too quickly—" His words were strangled off as she unbuttoned his clothing.

"My choice," she said. Then she bent her head to him.

This was an intimacy she knew, but the differences were clear. His musk was intriguing, the shape and power of what she kissed obvious, but what startled her was the joy it gave her to pleasure him. She listened to his sounds, felt the shudder that went through him when she engulfed him and knew the exact moment when he surrendered to what she made him feel. He released a low groan that rolled through his body into hers, and his hips began to pump in earnest. She grew wet as he lost himself in her. And she found her own delight when his fingers cupped her breast and pinched her nipple.

Heat coiled through her. Hunger made her ache. And when he

pulled her off him and caught his release in a handkerchief, she found herself watching him with hunger. His chest heaved, and his hands shook.

He wrapped his hand around her head and pulled her close for a kiss. And while she wrapped her arms around his shoulders, she felt his hand slip between her thighs. Still wet. Still sensitive. He worked her with his fingers, while she gasped into his kiss.

Quickening. Again!

Heat. Bliss.

Him.

Afterward, when she lay there panting, he pressed his lips to her neck. He nipped her there in lazy tastes as he brought his mouth to her ear.

"I cannot wait to make you my wife," he said.

Her breath caught. "Wife?" she whispered.

He pulled back, his gaze luminous. "Of course."

Not.

No.

Never.

She knew this is what he wanted, but the reality of it hit her broadside. Not his desires, but hers. She never wanted to be a wife again.

"Diana?"

CHAPTER TWENTY-TWO

LUCAS WAS NOT a man given to doubts. Though he often wondered about his worth in God's eyes, he did not question his worth from the world's perspective. Especially since his family now knew he was alive. He was Lord Chellam again and would one day become the Earl of Wolvesmead. The idea that the lady of his choice would not agree to marry him never entered his thoughts. And even if it had, the lady he wanted was right now in his arms. She had begged him to make love to her. And he had brought her to fullness twice this night.

And yet, he could see by her expression that she would refuse him.

"Lucas," she said. She licked her lips, and her gaze darted away from him. She meant to roll out of his arms, but he held her tight. "Lucas, I am just now widowed."

"And we will wait for an appropriate amount of time. But this I swear to you—"

"I will not be forced into marriage again, no matter what you swear!"

He swallowed his temper. "You just this night said you chose me."

She sighed. "Do not be dense. I meant for this night. For this pleasure."

"And you assumed that I would pleasure you without thought to our wedding?"

"Yes!"

"No."

Her head dropped back, and she looked at the ceiling. "There is not a man among the peerage who does not look for a wealthy widow to bed with no thought of marriage."

He snorted. "There is one. Me."

"Just my luck."

He didn't respond to her dry tone. It hurt to hear it. He had no wish to continue the conversation. He released her and reset his attire. He threw his handkerchief in the bucket and would see that it was disposed of in a private way. Meanwhile, she drew the covers up until he could see no more than her face and the wild crown of her hair. Beautiful, but defensive.

"Be reasonable, Lucas. I have not had a great deal of time to think of my future."

"That's a lie," he accused. "You do nothing but think of the future." He was standing beside her bed and now dropped his hands on his hips. "Is it the money? I have savings, and my title carries funds as well. I do not know the particulars, but I can keep you in good style."

She sat up, obviously offended. "I have my own savings," she snapped. "But if you want to think of estates, then recall that the people here are under my care until I wed. Upon that day, everything here returns to Geoffrey's exploitation." She shook her head. "Ireland has suffered greatly. I will not leave them to his mercy."

He had forgotten that detail in the heat of the moment. Damn it. She always had a reason to deny him. "And if the problem of Geoffrey could be resolved? Would you marry me then?"

The way her gaze slid away was answer enough, but she made it worse by trying to explain. "I have just now gained my freedom."

"Marriage to me is not prison."

"Marriage to any man is." She turned to face him. "Surely, you see that."

He did. It made no difference to him. "How lonely have you been these last twelve years? Was there companionship between you and a man double your age?"

She grimaced. "We found ways to get along."

"And was that enough for you?" He leaned forward, dropping his fists on the mattress beside her. "You have been terribly lonely. You said so yourself!"

"Yes."

"So why would you want to remain alone? Why sentence yourself to more years in isolation—"

"Isolation?" she mocked. "A wealthy widow chooses who she spends her time and her money on." She straightened up onto her knees. "A married woman goes as her husband wills."

He shook his head. "I would not restrict you."

"You have been restricting me from the first moment you came into my house! You have been locking my doors, following me everywhere, keeping me within sight—"

"For your own safety!"

"And when will you cease worrying about that?"

"After Geoffrey is dealt with."

"Then I shall be free to go where I will, do as I want? If I chose to shop in Cheapside or come back here?"

"Why would you want to do either of those things?"

"What if I want to take a ship to India or the colonies?"

"You've never wanted to do any of that!"

"That's not true! I've never had permission before."

He blew out a breath. "All of these things can be done with proper precautions. Except for Cheapside. There is nothing there for you."

She shook her head. "Can you not see it? I don't want to bargain with anyone for my choices."

"And you would toss me aside so you can visit Cheapside?"

She swallowed. "That would be your choice. There are ways to prevent pregnancy. Ways to have pleasure without a wedding ring."

He knew that. Hell, he had spent the last years in a gaming hell that had upstairs rooms for all manner of entertainment. But he could not think of her like that. Not Diana, the woman who had reigned as an angel in his thoughts. He couldn't imagine her as yet another merry widow in search of entertainment. He wouldn't.

"I need to take another circle of the property."

She blew out a breath. "Geoffrey is not here."

"You don't know that. You have no idea what a man will do get what he wants."

She could not miss his dark tone, but did he truly intend the double meaning? Geoffrey would go to any end to get hold of more money. Would Lucas do the same to possess her?

Maybe. He wanted her that much, but he had to be smart about it. He had to let her choose him. She would not be forced, that much was obvious. And so he would leave her side now and think about it. He would plan his campaign as carefully as he would a war. And in the end, she would see that she wanted him so much that she would give him everything, including her hand in marriage.

"Lucas," she said as she let the covers slip. Her breasts were stunningly beautiful in the shimmering light of the moon. "Leave the protection to your men. Stay the night here with me."

He wanted to, but that was not going to happen. "I trust your safety to no one but myself and God."

She sighed. Then he pressed his point harder.

"I want you by my side for life. And I will not grace your bed until you can give me that promise."

CHAPTER TWENTY-THREE

LUCAS HAD A long night of patrol to think about his decision. He relieved every moment of their time together. Not just this night, but every shared look, every word, every touch since they'd first met twelve years ago. And after all that, his decision remained the same.

She was the woman he wanted for his wife. She was smart, resilient, and she fought hard for what she wanted in life. He just hadn't expected that what she wanted would be so different than what he did. She seemed consumed by her desire for independence. As a man who had spent the last twelve years learning he had to rely on others, he knew exactly how lonely it was to go it alone.

He finished his circuit and decided to go to the kitchen for a moment. He slipped inside the dark to see the bright tip of a cheroot burning. He didn't have to say a word before his friend was speaking.

"All quiet, sir. Not even a wolf is howling tonight."

Lucas smiled. "Do I hear a little boredom in your voice, Caleb? Don't like Ireland?"

"I was born here, sir. I left for a reason."

Lucas shook off the wet before turning toward the fire. "I thought you left because your girl married someone else."

Caleb grunted his agreement. "Ireland's got plenty of pretty girls. I left because I wanted more than the moors." He shrugged. "There's lots more of everything in London."

"Can't argue that."

Caleb tossed him an apple, which he caught. He was halfway through it before Caleb spoke again.

"Sir, if I could ask…?"

"Yes?"

"What's to happen now that you're back in the world?"

"I never left the world, Caleb." It was the truth, but it also wasn't what the man meant, and they both knew it.

"You're Lord Chellam again, sir. That type can't man the door at a gaming hell, no matter what his hand looks like."

He thought about walking away from the whole conversation. He'd had enough thinking about his future while he wandered the grounds. But Caleb deserved better than that, so he finished his apple and turned back to his right-hand man.

"I haven't come to any decision. I didn't mean to reveal myself. It just happened, and now I'm caught without a good plan."

"Women have a way of making things just happen, don't they?"

"Ain't that the truth—"

"But you can't blame this one on her, sir."

His brow lifted in challenge, but he didn't say anything. His look was dark enough to warn Caleb to be quiet. It didn't work, because the man kept speaking.

"You never shirked once from the hard work, sir. Not once in battle, not once before or after. You were in the mud and the fire right with us every minute."

Good that they noticed that. And good that he'd done it because there had been plenty of times he'd wanted to run as far away as he could get. "You're my brothers. Why would I leave you?"

"Nathan's your brother, too, and you let him think you were dead. I know you had your reasons, but it still didn't sit right."

Lucas winced. Caleb wasn't one to reprimand anyone, least of all his commanding officer. But this cut pretty close to censure, and damn it, Lucas knew he deserved it. He looked down at his clawed hand and was acutely aware of the scar that cut down the side of his face. It was a silly thing to worry about. He knew that looks meant nothing about the true value of a man. And yet, he recoiled at the idea of appearing in society with his injuries.

"My mother doesn't like damaged things," he said. "She'd throw out anything with the slightest flaw." He paused as he remembered all the food she'd refused because of blemishes, the vase she destroyed when she found a mistake in the painting of it, and the times she's sent him away because his hair wasn't brushed or he sported dirt on his shoes. But a man didn't use others as an excuse for failing in his responsibilities. "I should have told them."

Caleb shrugged. "You were too sick at first. And then busy finding us."

But that didn't explain the last year, and they both knew it. "I just wanted to be me for a bit, doing what I do best." Leading men not into battle but into protecting something of value. And though gaming hells were everywhere, he'd come to respect the people in the Lyon's Den, most especially Mrs. Dove-Lyon, who was doing her small part to help the people in her employ advance to bigger and better lives.

"And now that you're back in society?" Caleb prompted. "What are your plans?"

The conversation had just come full circle, and he still had no real answer. "Your jobs at the Lyon's Den are safe if you still want them. I'll see to that." Then he pulled out a chair at the central table, sitting down as he looked at the one man who'd been at his side all his adult life. "You can be the new Titan at the Lyon's Den if you like." Being the man in charge of all the security at the den had been Lucas's job, but Caleb was more than capable.

"I'd like that, except it seems to me you have something else in mind."

Lucas shrugged. "I might." He looked up at his friend. "Don't know if it'll make money yet, but I'd be happy to talk over some thoughts with you. If you felt like talking while we're watching the house."

Caleb looked about the kitchen. "I'm sick of sitting indoors. Let's go walk the perimeter again."

"I was just out there for an hour."

"Two weeks as a peer, and you're already complaining about a little walk."

It was several miles of walking that he'd already done twice tonight while he was thinking about Diana. But he wasn't going to let anyone suggest he'd gone soft, even in jest, so he pushed to his feet. "You wake Egeus and tell him we're walking. He's got watch of the house."

Caleb nodded. "Yes, sir!"

"I'll just be a moment," he said, purposely hiding where he was going. It didn't work. Caleb knew him too well.

"She's sleeping, and about time. I've never seen a society woman work as hard as her. She's doing a man's job here. Ireland could use more like her."

"She's good at it."

"Yes, sir, she is. Better than anyone else for generations, according to the people here."

He nodded, waiting for the rest. With Caleb, there was always a little more. "What are you getting at?"

"That I can't really blame her for wanting to keep hold of doing what she's good at. I hear she'll lose it if she marries. That true?"

Lucas blew out a breath. "Yes." Then he looked straight back at his friend. "But do you think she'll trade working like this for being a mother? She's not one to have bastards, and she can't keep this if she wants to have children of her own."

Caleb acknowledged that with a grunt. "Seems to me a smart man would find a way that she can have both."

"Seems to me," Lucas countered, "that I've got plenty to think about what with managing jobs for my men, protecting the lady from her murderous stepson, and finding my way back into being Lord Chellam."

"That does sound like a lot. Well, mayhap you can find someone who'd be willing to help you out with some of those tasks."

"And maybe that someone ought to go wake Egeus so we can talk about it."

"Yes, sir!" he said, saluting with a quick flick of his wrist.

Lucas watched him go, his thoughts turning toward the future with renewed hope. He might not have his lady love yet, but he had his comrades in arms, and for the moment, that would be enough. Or so he thought until he slipped quietly into Diana's room to see that all was safe there. She was asleep, her breath steady as she lay curled on her side. He looked at her face, saw her body outlined by the moonlight, and wanted desperately to climb in beside her.

He didn't, though he did touch her cheek. What would he give up to be with her? Everything. But would she do the same?

He didn't think so, and that saddened him enough that he left her side to talk about his future with someone else.

CHAPTER TWENTY-FOUR

London, three weeks later...

THEY STAYED TWO more weeks in Ireland. Long enough for him to see ever more clearly how good Diana was at management and how desperately her tenants needed her expert guidance. It was disheartening because he knew how much they would suffer under Geoffrey's negligent care.

He never graced her bed, though she caught him looking at her often enough. She made it very clear that she would welcome his advances, but he had sworn not to dally with her, and so he kept away. But that didn't stop him from becoming obsessed with her safety. There were no attacks, nothing untoward, and even the travel back to England was completely uneventful. Was that because he did everything he could think of to foil an attack? He had them travel under different names and pretend her maid and cook were her sisters. All three returning from a holiday in Ireland. Perhaps he was overre-acting, but he counted the uneventful travel worth all his hard work.

And then the day they arrived back in London, he learned how useful his planning had been. An hour later, Lord Beddoe sent a request to see him. Not Diana, but Mr. Lucifer, along with the hope of discretion.

He agreed, of course, and met the man in the downstairs office that had once been Diana's but was now his. It suited his work with the staff to be down here, and she had acceded to the wisdom of keeping her work abovestairs. Lord Beddoe, however, curled his lip as he sat in the tiny chair, but he was too agitated to refuse.

"We were attacked," said the older man.

Lucas's brows shot up, and he leaned over to shut the door. It wouldn't give them total privacy, but it would help. "Where and when?"

"On the ride back to London. Coarse men. Terrified us all." Beddoe lifted his chin. "Shot and killed my coachman, and for that, I will never forgive Geoffrey."

"Geoffrey?" Lucas's mind had gone there immediately, but he was surprised to see Beddoe so ready to accuse his brother-in-law. Up until now, Lucas had thought the man inclined to be tolerant of Geoffrey's tendencies. Now he spoke as if he wanted the man strung up. "Why do you think it was him?"

"I didn't. Not at first. These things happen, though never before to me."

"Tell me what happened exactly."

"I heard shots. Woke me out of a sound sleep, I tell you." He spoke brusquely, but his hands were trembling enough that Lucas didn't bother offering him tea. He poured a strong measure of brandy for the man who drank it down with unseemly haste. "The horses pulled to a stop, and the carriage door opened. Penelope screamed, of course, and a gun was forced in our faces, and the man asked for her." He looked up at Lucas. "He asked for *her*."

"Your wife?"

"No. He asked if she was Lady Dunnamore."

"I told him who we were and that I'd see him hang, the bastard." He paused a moment to finish off his brandy.

"And then?" Lucas prompted when he didn't start speaking again.

"Then he searched everyone and asked again, where is she?"

"She being Diana?"

"Yes. I told him, still in Ireland. I didn't tell him in a friendly way, you understand. So he hit me." He rubbed his chin. Lucas didn't see a bruise there, but it had been over two weeks. Any mark could have healed by now.

"Did he hurt your wife? Your servants?"

"Other than killing my coachman? No. Took the jewelry and my coins. Fortunately, Penelope wasn't traveling with anything of much value. She didn't trust the Irish not to steal it," he said, and it was clear that he recognized the irony of fearing the Irish when they were robbed on an English highway.

"And then what happened?"

"Happened? Nothing. They took our valuables and left with my coachman lying in a ditch." He shuddered. "I had to tell his wife."

"I'm sorry." He would not wish that task on anyone.

Beddoe nodded, but his gaze was far away. "I didn't want to believe it. Not of my wife's brother, but they were looking for Diana. They thought Penelope was her at first and were about to drag her away to do God knows what." He shook his head. "They must have known that we meant to take Diana home with us. Penelope offered it to her, you see. Said she should visit with us for a bit. To show that there are no hard feelings between them."

But there were hard feelings, and Diana had wanted to stay and take care of matters in Ireland.

"I went over this with Penelope, just to be sure. There's no mistake. She told Geoffrey her plans. Told him that she would insist that Diana join us because it was proper. A woman can't stay alone in Ireland. That just invites gossip."

"But Diana refused her."

"Surprised us both, I can tell you, but thank Heaven she did. Because what those men might have done to her, I don't know."

"They would have killed her. Possibly after doing worse." He needed Beddoe to understand Geoffrey's depravity. Fortunately, the man looked like he already knew.

"They asked for Diana. Asked after her again and again. They weren't there for us. The robbery was an afterthought. We were an afterthought!" There was true outrage in that last part, but to his credit, Beddoe was focused on the real issue. "No one has reason to target Diana except Geoffrey. Penelope didn't want to think it either, but we've been over it many times. There's no one else who hates her. No one."

Lucas let the words hang there. He believed everything, but even so, he needed more details, more ways to trace the attack back to Geoffrey in a way that would hold up before a magistrate. And though his blood burned with the need to kill the man, he had promised Diana that he would try to find another way.

So, he kept Beddoe with him for another two hours. They went through more brandy—enough to keep the man steady—and in the end, Lucas had all the details Beddoe could remember.

"Penelope's terrified. Cries in her sleep and hates it when I leave the house."

"Does she think the highwaymen will come back?"

Beddoe nodded. "She thinks Geoffrey knows that she's turned against him. He's a monster, and she's afraid of her own brother. I keep telling her it's Diana who needs protection—and she agrees—but she's frightened, and I can't say as I blame her."

"Any attack is terrifying. She will calm down in time."

"I hope so, but I wondered…" Beddoe toyed with his empty brandy glass. "You've got men here protecting Diana, and I approve. But do you have a few more? Some who might stand guard over us?"

Lucas's brows rose up in surprise. "You have servants, yes? Large footmen—"

"But they're not military men like you. Like the footmen you've added here. Do you know of a few more who would like to earn money? Just until this business with Geoffrey is settled once and for all."

"I do. But this business may take a while. And good men don't come cheap."

Beddoe nodded. "I'm well-heeled enough to afford it. And it would give me an extra measure of rest. Penelope's increasing, you see. It's not good for the baby for her to be anxious like this. We want to go back to my estate in Staffordshire, but I won't risk another ride. Not without extra men who know what they're about."

"I know just the men you want," he said. "He's been with me through the war, and there's not a steadier hand in all of England."

"But will he be loyal? Will he protect Penelope, even if Geoffrey promises him more than I can pay?"

And right there was the problem for Beddoe. Any man he might hire would be vulnerable to bribery from another source. Lucas smiled. "Caleb will not betray you. I'd stake my life on it."

"Then, we'll leave for Staffordshire as soon as it can be arranged."

"I'll get Caleb started on the details. Don't worry. You and Lady Beddoe will be safe."

Beddoe stood, then abruptly held out his hand to shake. "I didn't trust you at first. Who goes by the name Mr. Lucifer? But now that I know you're Chellam, I've got better respect for you. Elliott swears you're the best, and you've done well by Diana. If you do well by Penelope and me, then I know a few others who might need a steady hand with a gun now and again."

Lucas shook Beddoe's hand with a firm grip. "You'll be safe with us," he said firmly. "Lucifer's men won't betray you." And just like that, he and Caleb had a new business venture.

CHAPTER TWENTY-FIVE

E XHAUSTION DOGGED DIANA even as she sat in the upstairs parlor and drank tea. She never understood how sitting in a carriage for hours could be so tiring, but it was. Or maybe it was her thoughts that had worn her down. She could not stop thinking about her argument with Lucas. It had happened three weeks ago back when they were still in Ireland, and still, she wondered if she'd erred.

It wasn't wrong for her to want to be independent. There were sound financial reasons for her to stay free of a man's control. For her entire life, others had the final say over her decisions, but no longer. And yet, independence came with loneliness.

Since the night Lucas had touched her so intimately, he had kept himself scrupulously apart from her. They spoke as needed, but he remained well out of arm's reach no matter how she tried to entice him. She hadn't been blatant, but they'd had several very frustrating conversations in her bedroom. She'd worn her thinnest dressing gown and even once had appeared to him only in her nightrail.

Nothing.

Certainly, his eyes had raked her from top to bottom. His gaze had narrowed, and she thought he would break when her hair tumbled down out of her pins. He didn't. He watched her intently throughout the day, his expression dark and hungry. But he never acted on it, and she was not brazen enough to demand he touch her. She doubted it would work anyway. The man was as immovable as a mountain when he wanted to be.

They stayed apart while she questioned her decision to remain a wealthy widow. And now, after weeks of frustration, she was ready to do something brazen, but it couldn't be tonight. This evening she was fully dressed, and she'd called Lucas to her parlor for an entirely different reason.

She had just poured herself another cup of tea when he knocked on the door. She motioned him inside and then failed to hide her grimace when he kept himself on the opposite side of the room from her.

"Oh, leave off," she snapped. "Just sit down, take some tea, and answer my question. Please."

His eyes widened in surprise, but he was gentlemanly enough to sketch a bow to her before taking the chair opposite her. "Are you feeling well?" he asked as he scanned her face.

"Tired and restless, which is an annoying contradiction."

"I understand the feeling, well."

She looked at him, seeing that exhaustion hung on him, too. Whereas she had spent today's travel dozing in a carriage, he had ridden ahead and was likely sore from top to bottom. "I'm sorry, Lucas. I have only a single question, and then you may seek your bed."

He nodded and didn't respond, which she took to mean that he would head for rest when he deemed it safe. Damn him for being the one man in her household she couldn't order to bed for his own good.

"Fine. Keep your own counsel. I just want to know..." She looked up at him, needing to judge his reaction. "Did Geoffrey attack Penelope and Walter? Are they all right?"

He nodded, his expression grave. "Lord and Lady Beddoe were attacked on their way back from Ireland. The thieves killed their coachman and robbed them. But Diana, they were expressly looking for you."

She swallowed. "For me." It wasn't a question. She had heard as much from her maid, who had learned it from the cook, who had been listening at the door when Walter was belowstairs speaking with Lucas. And yet it was still a blow to hear it confirmed. "Was it Geoffrey?"

"I believe so," Lucas said. "He's not one to commit crimes himself. He hires someone else to do it for him."

"Which is why it was done badly, I suppose. If he'd thought for two seconds, he would have known I will never travel with Penelope."

"Really? Why not?"

"The motion of the carriage bothers her, and she complains constantly. Besides, you already know there was too much work in Ireland for me to leave."

"Geoffrey is not one to understand work."

No, he wasn't. "What am I to do?" she whispered. "I cannot live my life in a cage for fear he hires assassins. And where is he finding the money for these highwaymen? Isn't he in debt all over London?"

Lucas shrugged. "Desperate men find each other." He took a breath. "Do you regret the restrictions you have placed upon me?"

She met his eyes. "I still do not want you to kill him," she said firmly. "Not for him, but for you. I would not add that burden to your soul."

His expression softened. "My soul can bear it."

"Even so. We are a civilized society. He should be tried and sentenced, as is lawful."

He was silent a moment. "You know that if I must, I will—"

She held up her hand. "I know you will do what is required," she said, struggling with her own thoughts. "But this is a not battlefield, and we are in England, which is a country of laws." She could see from his expression that he agreed in principle but that he would act as a soldier if he had no choice.

She should not be comforted by that. She was a woman who stood by her convictions. And yet, she remained desperately grateful that, thanks to Lucas, she would not die for her principles. She blew out a breath. "I am a hypocrite. I don't want you to kill him, and yet..." She lifted her gaze to the ceiling. "He set highwaymen on Penelope. Did you know she is pregnant? Who would hire thieves to rob his own sister?"

He was silent as she dashed away tears.

"This is ridiculous," she said. "Geoffrey was a sweet boy once. By all accounts, his mother loved him. Oscar certainly did. He had good nannies and all the benefits of wealth. Why has he turned so wrong?"

Lucas touched her hand, where she fidgeted with her teacup. His fingers were thick with calluses and yet brushed so lightly across her own. "I don't have any answers, Diana. I cannot take the time to wonder how he became who he is. I can only end this as quickly as I know how."

Her gaze went to his. "And how will you do that?"

"I have a man in my employ with connections throughout London." He squeezed her hand. "He has found Mr. Fisher for me."

Her head snapped up. "My footman? The one who poisoned Oscar's tea?"

"Yes. I am heading now to speak with him. He must testify that Geoffrey paid him to kill your husband."

"Then Geoffrey can be arrested and punished lawfully for his crimes."

"With luck, this will soon be over."

She had the strongest urge to kiss him. She did, in fact, grip his shoulder, stilling him for a moment as he started to get up so that they were nearly nose to nose. She searched his face as he gazed at her, his eyes turning dark and intense.

She wanted so very much to kiss him. Not just because he made her heart beat fast and her legs go liquid with desire, but because he made her feel safe. No one would harm her while he was here, least of all him. Not with casual neglect nor overwhelming authority. He simply remained beside her, caring for her as she accomplished her tasks. It was a heady experience having a man be a help rather than a hindrance. And she wanted him beside her always, but most especially now when she felt so vulnerable.

His hand came up to cup her face. She watched the movement of his lips as he whispered her name. "Diana." There was longing in her name, and she echoed it a thousand times.

"Lucas—"

But then he shut it all down. "I must go." He pulled away from her. "Ruben has already called for the constable. If I am to have a chance at speaking with Fisher first, then I must make haste."

"Ruben?"

"My associate. The one who found Mr. Fisher."

She nodded, then made a quick decision. "I will go with you," she said as she pushed to her feet.

"What? No. You're safe here. Well protected—"

"I need to see it for myself, Lucas. Mr. Fisher was a part of my home for three years. I need to know why he would do such a thing." It was the truth, but it was also a lie. She certainly wanted to speak with her footman, but mostly she wanted to stay with Lucas. It was only with Lucas that she allowed herself to feel, and she was reluctant to give that up even to the point of inventing excuses so she could remain at his side.

"Diana, this is not a place a gently reared woman should go."

"I am never safer than I am beside you." Then she resorted to doing something she swore only weak women did. She softened her expression and used every feminine wile she had. "Please," she begged. "I swear I won't interfere and..." She blinked tearful eyes at him. "I want to be with you."

He exhaled in a kind of growl. "I am a weak man around you."

She brightened, seeing that she'd won. "Really? I've found you incredibly, almost frustratingly strong."

He shot her a heavy look. "Flattery is a cheap trick."

She laughed. "It is the simple truth," she said. "I shall be but a moment."

"Bring a cloak," he said. "One that covers your face."

Five minutes later, they were in a hackney that smelled of boiled onions. Not a pleasant odor, but she overcame it by pressing close to Lucas's side and turning her nose toward him. He had bathed recently, so he smelled clean, though she could still detect his own personal scent. It never failed to capture her attention, and she smiled as she inhaled deeply.

He set her firmly away from him.

"Lucas?"

"This is beneath you, Diana."

She jolted, her tone stiff. "What are you talking about?"

"You cannot toy with me like this. I would swive you right now, right here if I could."

A shiver swept down her spine as she was unexpectedly titillated by the thought. "I—"

"But you know my conditions."

She blew out a breath. "It is too soon for me to give up my freedom again. Surely you understand that."

"Of course, I understand it. But I want a wife, not a passing fancy."

How like a man to be so black and white. "It is too soon for me—"

"All I ask for is a promise that you will be mine. We won't have the banns read right away. We can wait for that, but I have been too long in limbo as I wait for my life to begin." He shrugged. "I see that now, thanks to you. But I'm ready now to be the man I was meant to be."

She smiled. "That's wonderful, Lucas, but I hardly think I had anything to do with it."

He pressed his lips to her forehead. "Every day I watch you stand your ground, fight for what you believe in, and hold firm, despite being a woman. It shames me that I have done so little since—"

"Returning from war? Healing from near mortal wounds? You have men who still follow you long after the war is done. Believe me, I know how hard it is to get anyone to follow, and you do it effortlessly."

He was silent as his cheek rubbed across the top of her head. She felt every catch of his evening beard and relished his closeness. Nothing could ever hurt her while he held her so close.

"I want a wife and a family, Diana. It will not be easy for me to be an earl with all the pomp and circumstance that it entails. But I could do it with you." He pulled her fingers to his lips. "Swear you'll be mine eventually, Diana. I know you will keep your promise."

She would, which is why she couldn't say yes. Not yet. Not when she had yet to take a walk outside as a free, independent woman. When she hadn't gone shopping without wondering if Oscar would scold her for her purchase. She hadn't even danced once at a party without worrying over who cared for Oscar in her absence.

"Not yet," she whispered. "I can't."

He accepted that with a grim nod. Then before she could say more, the carriage came to a halt. He pulled the hood of her cloak down over her face, then said in a harsh whisper. "Stay right behind me. And don't say a word until I tell you it's safe."

He waited for her nod and then stepped out of the carriage into an area of London so rank that she was grateful for the darkness. It hid whatever foul thing was festering nearby. It also gave her a moment's terror. Just where were they going?

CHAPTER TWENTY-SIX

S HE WAS DRIVING him mad with wanting. Even as he led her into the dark rooms beneath the Lyon's Den, her scent teased his nostrils, her breath whispered across his thoughts, and heat burned on his skin whenever she was near. It was distracting as hell, and damn if he didn't ache to give her everything she wanted in every way possible.

Instead, he focused on the miserable man tied loosely in a chair. On the opposite side of the room, Reuben Bates lounged with a cocky expression on his perpetually happy face. Lucas had met the man in the army, and they'd become fast friends. But it was only in London that Reuben's real skills had come to the fore. He had a huge family and connections throughout the upper and lower society. If ever there was an unacknowledged king in London, it was Reuben. So it was no surprise that he had been the one to find the missing footman, Donald Fisher.

Reuben acknowledged Lucas with a jaunty whistle and a cock of his head toward a side door. The constable would be waiting there, listening to every word spoken. The official would step out when it was time, but for right now, Lucas needed to see the idiot footman face to face and ask a few very important questions.

That is, after Diana stepped around him and gasped at what she saw. "What have you done?"

Lucas couldn't tell who she was speaking to. Did she ask the footman about his crimes? Or did she ask Lucas why the man had a dark bruise on his cheek or why he was bound at the wrists and ankles?

Whatever the truth, the footman seemed to believe it was directed at him because the man started protesting his innocence in the most hateful voice.

"I've done nothing but visit me mum, you filthy witch!" he spat. "A cow like you, you've always had it in for me. Wanted to have me, you did, and when I said no, you set your dogs to grab me out of my mother's arms—"

Lucas punched him straight in the face. He held back another blow. He didn't want to kill the man, but it was enough to snap the bastard's head back and cut off his words. Beside him, Diana blew out a breath and spoke with admiration in her tone.

"You cannot know how often I have wished I could do the same."

He glanced at her in surprise. "It's less effective than you might think but enormously satisfying."

And as he guessed might happen, the man quickly recovered his breath and started spewing insults that were so commonplace as to be boring. He had heard it all—in multiple languages—during his time in the Lyon's Den. Except, obviously, the words were new to Diana.

"Do you know what he is saying?" she asked.

"Nothing worth repeating. Or hearing."

"But I've never heard some of those things. What do they mean? Beyond the obvious, of course."

Lucas shook his head. He should have known she wouldn't be thrown by a man's curses beyond a little curiosity. Meanwhile, Reuben grew tired of the noise, so he quickly looped a rope around the man's neck. He didn't tighten it, but just the drop of the thick cord on Fisher's chest was enough to set the footman to screaming the same insults in a louder voice.

Lucas blew out a breath as he caught Reuben's eyes. "You've made it worse."

"Not if I tighten it." To prove his point, he began pulling the rope high enough that it just touched the man's throat.

The scream was ear-splittingly high, and it went on a very long time. Fortunately, he didn't have endless lung capacity, and when he paused to draw breath, Lucas spoke.

"Scream again, and I'll have him kill you now. You're giving me a headache."

Mr. Fisher choked off his next screech only to sit there and glare resentfully at the entire room.

"Why did you poison Lord Dunnamore's tea?" Lucas asked.

"I never did! I liked the old bastard!" He would have gone on, but Reuben picked up the edge of the rope again. He didn't pull it, but Fisher took the hint and cut off with a squeak.

"Several people saw you put something in his tea tin. They saw you and will testify to it." It was a lie. They didn't have a witness. In fact, the only proof they had was that Fisher disappeared the day Lord Dunnamore died.

"They lie! I didn't!" He spat at Diana. "She poisoned him. I gave him medicine. I kept him alive for weeks while she tried to kill him!"

Now there was something interesting, but he didn't have the chance to pursue it as Diana took a step forward. She even squatted down so she could look at him eye to eye. "Mr. Fisher," she began, then she moderated her stern tone. "Donald. I gave you money when your mother was ill. A great deal of it. I forgave it when you came in late to work with bloodshot eyes and shaking hands. I could have sacked you any number of times, but you pleaded with me that you were the only support of your ailing mother and pregnant sister."

Reuben spoke up from behind Fisher. "He's got no sister. His mum isn't actually his mum, but she gives him a bed every now and again. That's where we found him. Drunk as a sot in her back parlor." He looked up at Lucas. "She's the one who contacted me. Said she'd be glad to be rid of him."

Diana sighed. "Lies, then. I thought as much, but Oscar liked him." She straightened up. "They played cards together, and he told Oscar jokes." She shrugged. "Jokes Oscar wouldn't repeat to me, but some days it was the only thing that kept his mind off the pain."

"Cards, you say?" Lucas asked, and at Diana's nod, he knew exactly what had happened. Reuben, too, by the expression on his face. But mindful of the constable, he had to walk everyone straight to the truth.

"I bet you're pretty good at cards, then," Lucas said in a casual way. "To play with the likes of Lord Dunnamore. He was pretty good, and if you held your own with him, then you're a right dab hand."

Fisher straightened up at that, and his sullen expression softened.

"You probably win most of the time, too," Lucas continued. "If the game's played straight, that is. But I bet you didn't win with Geoffrey, did you? He's a good cheat. Doesn't even have to play with a bad deck. He starts early, you see, with your cards. And as he plays, he starts to mark them. You don't even notice because you're winning. But as the night goes on, he can see what you got 'cause he's marked them. And pretty soon, you're in too deep. You owe him."

Phillip's eyes widened, and the confirmation was on his face. The more Lucas talked, the more his lip quivered as he realized he'd been duped.

"What did he want you to do?"

"Nothing," he said, the word thick with hatred. "Said he knew she was poisoning his father. Just wanted me to put medicine in the old man's tea. I'd be doing his lordship a favor, he said. Saving him from his wife's poison."

Diana sighed. "I wasn't poisoning him."

"Says you!"

"Who gave you this medicine?" Lucas asked.

"I picked it up from the potion place in Cheapside. Straight from the doctor there."

Reuben shook his head. "He's not a real doctor. What did you tell him?"

"To give me Mr. Geoffrey Hough's medicine." He glared at Diana. "I put a couple spoonfuls in the tin once a week. It was to keep him alive."

"It was to poison him with arsenic, and he made you the perfect gull. Why'd you put in more the night he died?" Lucas asked.

Fisher was sweating now, and he shook his head as he spoke. "Mr. Geoffrey found me and gave me a pouch of medicine. Said the mistress were getting desperate, and I needed to put it all in or his lordship would surely die by morning." He looked back at Lucas. "It must not have worked! She must have given him too much poison, 'cause he died!"

Diana sighed. "You don't really believe that."

"You witch! You killed your own husband, and he never did nothing against you!"

"You know that's not true," Diana shot back. "You know I'd never—"

Lucas stopped her by touching her shoulder. She cut off her words, tears in her eyes as she turned to him. He spoke to her in a gentle tone. "He does believe it because he can't think otherwise." He looked to Reuben, who gave him a nod.

"I already talked to the doctor. He told the constable a week ago that he gave rat poison to this idiot."

"It's not true." Fisher's eyes were wide with panic. "You forced him. You forced him to lie. You're going to make it looked like I killed him. I didn't! It was her! I swear it, it was her!"

Diana pressed a hand to her mouth. Lucas could tell that she was shaking, and he pressed a gentle hand to her back.

"We can prove all of this," he said to Fisher. "The doctor has already given his statement. You've just confessed to putting the poison in the tea tin."

"It were *medicine!*"

"Do you think Geoffrey will admit he played cards with you? A servant? Never. He's going to say he had nothing to do with it. That you did it all yourself just to ingratiate yourself with him. That in your deluded mind, you thought you were doing him a favor."

"It's not true!" the man kept screaming. "You're lying!" His voice was hoarse by the time he stopped screaming enough to hear Lucas's next words.

"It's what he'll say. Unless you tell your side first. Every word. Every honest and true word."

"I will! I will tell the constable. It was Mr. Geoffrey's medicine for his father. Against her poisoning. It weren't me! It were her or Mr. Geoffrey. Not me!"

No one responded because, at that moment, the constable pushed through the side door. He was followed by two of his men, and all three had grim, disgusted expressions. Fisher saw them immediately and turned his pleading eyes on the constable.

"They tied me up. Hit me. It wasn't right what they did. You can't believe a word they say!"

"I don't," the constable responded in gruff tones. "I believe what you said. How you put a powder in his lordship's tea."

"Medicine!"

"So you say. But if it were medicine, why didn't you stick around and tell us instead of making us search all of Cheapside for you?"

"I was afraid. She killed her husband. What was she going to do to me?"

"Or maybe you were afraid Geoffrey would find you and kill you to keep quiet for what you did for him."

Fisher blanched and looked down. His shoulders were hunched as he shook his head. "No, no. I was afraid of her."

"Do you know where Geoffrey is now?" Lucas asked. "Might go a long way to helping your case if you tell us where he is."

Fisher shook his head. "He said it were medicine. That's what he said."

Meanwhile, Reuben smiled. "Don't worry. I know all the steep gambling that goes on in London. He'll show up at one of them eventually."

Diana spoke up. "But he doesn't have any money. Everyone knows that now."

Reuben chuckled. "Gambling's like a poison in his blood. He can't stop doing it. And once he shows, I'll have him."

Assuming Geoffrey didn't get some sense and bolt for the colonies. But with Fisher handed over to the constable and Reuben on the watch, there was nothing left to do but take Diana home. They had to wait for Geoffrey to make his move. Whatever he did would bring him out of the dark, and they'd get him. He was sure of it.

"Thanks, Reuben," he said as he took Diana's arm.

"Just pay my bill, and we'll be square."

Lucas chuckled. Reuben's bill would be a long night of drink and chess. He had so few worthy opponents that he would go to a great deal of effort just to have a good evening's entertainment. And though Lucas lost more than he won against Reuben, he was one of the very few who could win occasionally, and that made his company valuable.

"I'll be waiting for your missive," Lucas said. Then he escorted Diana up the stairs and out into the fetid night air. She went easily enough, but once outside, she stumbled. Or not quite a stumble as a retch. She lurched to the side and cast up her accounts into the street sewage.

He held her, of course. He held her while her body shook, and her belly heaved. And when she was done, he realized she was a great deal weaker than he thought. Her knees kept buckling, and she would have been on the ground if he didn't hold her up.

"Diana?"

"I just need—" She heaved again. "I can't—" Nothing was coming up, but her body kept rejecting the very air she breathed. "Lucas—"

she gasped again. It was a plea for help.

Only one thing to do, one place to take her. "This way," he said. And when she couldn't walk, he swept her up into his arms. A few moments later, they were both inside the Lyon's Den.

CHAPTER TWENTY-SEVEN

T HERE WAS NOTHING more wonderful than being carried in a strong man's arms. And nothing more embarrassing than to be weaker than a kitten in front of the man you most wanted to impress with your strength. But try as she might, Diana's body was not under her control. So when Lucas swept her up in his arms, she buried her face in his neck.

She had ceased casting up her accounts, thank God, but her body still twisted and churned. So she set her head into the space between his shoulder and neck and immersed herself in his scent. She allowed her body to absorb his power and listened with rapt attention to the steady beat of his heart as he carried her someplace unknown.

She could have made a guess. He went inside a building that had a guard. Someone called him Titan and opened the doors for him. She heard an orchestra and the sound of men's laughter, then she smelled cigar smoke. He carried her down a set of stairs and then another before he maneuvered her through a small door.

She spent the whole time curled against him, relishing every second, even as embarrassment dampened the pleasure. And then the door shut behind him, and all was quiet.

"Feeling better?" he asked as he gently set her down on a bed.

She didn't want to let go, but she couldn't hang on to him forever, much as she might want to. She let her arms relax, though she trailed her fingers reluctantly down his arms.

Thankfully, he didn't go far, and she was able to still touch his forearms as he knelt down before her. They were eye to eye as he studied her face.

"Do you want wine? Water? Tea? What would settle you more?"

Him. Just him beside her.

"Anything," she said—anything to clean the taste of bile from her mouth.

He pulled a flask from the drawer of a nearby desk, removed the stopper, then set it in her hand. Brandy, she realized, as he helped guide it to her mouth. She drank lightly, afraid that her stomach would reject it. She focused on the burn of fire down her throat and the steady support of his hands on her. Between the two, her stomach settled.

"I am so sorry," she said. "I promised I would not interfere."

He smiled. "You didn't interfere. We were done."

"I cannot understand what overcame me. I have never been so missish in my life."

His fingers trailed over her arm in a soothing caress. "What you saw was disturbing. What you learned would bother anyone."

She shook her head. "I didn't learn anything new. Geoffrey duped an idiot footman. And Mr. Fisher did not confess to anything. He claimed over and over that I poisoned Oscar." She grimaced at the futility of it all. "He will confuse the issue in a court of law. It is not proof." Then she shrugged. "Either way, it is no cause for me to fall apart."

He smiled. "Murder so close and personal is not something to be absorbed in one go. The mind rebels and rejects, taking it in as it can."

Her eyes widened as she nodded. "It seems to come in waves. I think I understand things, and then it hits me anew. Geoffrey killed his father. And he wants me d—" Her voice caught, but she forced the word out. "Dead." Her stepson wanted her dead.

"I will keep you safe. No one will hurt you."

"I know," she said. And she did. She felt safe in a way that she never had with anyone. Not even the boy he'd been twelve years ago. Back then, she had been the one to think matters through. Now she had no thoughts at all except that she must put everything in his hands, and he would do whatever was necessary. "I trust you."

His expression softened into a look of joy. A quiet, beautiful happiness that she saw in his eyes and pulled into her body. It eased the terror inside her and settled her as nothing else could.

"Do you need more brandy?" he asked.

She looked down at the flask and passed it back to him. "No. I'm much better now. Thank you." The words did not convey the depth of her gratitude.

He nodded and took the flask to his mouth, draining it with a few quick swallows. How handsome a man's neck could be, she thought with a curious kind of surprise. His rugged skin and the steady bob of his Adam's apple. She admired the cut of his jaw and the broadness of his shoulders. And she flushed again in embarrassment as he caught her looking.

To cover, she glanced around the room. It was a small place filled with the pallet on which she sat, a desk to the side, and a washing table. There were papers stacked neatly everywhere, on the desk, beside the bed, and three small piles by the door. Then she saw the clothing—specifically *his* clothing—folded neatly on top of a trunk next to the bed.

"This is your room at the Lyon's Den," she finally deduced.

"Yes."

"There is nothing personal here. Nothing at all. If I didn't recognize the clothes, I wouldn't see anything of you." She looked at him. "How long have you lived here?"

"Two years."

Two years and this was all he had. "Oscar collected books on birds. He recorded birdsong as musical notes in pages and pages of his journals. It was his passion. My brother, Elliott, remembers the smallest facts about everyone he meets. It allows him to find the perfect people for whatever work he sets his mind to. I hum music to myself whenever I can. When Oscar was better, we would go to musical evenings. It didn't matter who played or sang. I could sit and listen to it all." She looked about the room. "What is it that delights you? Is it truly all those papers? Is that the work you did here?"

He looked about his room, his gaze picking out the piles of papers. He pointed to one stack. "That is the details of the people here that I supervise. Each man and his history, schedules, and the like, plus payment records. The next pile is your men and your home. It is also everything on the desk there. The last pile holds my thoughts on the Beddoes and the plans I have for a business to protect people who need guarding."

Her eyes widened. "You plan a business venture for that?"

He grinned. "I do, and Lord Beddoe has already recommended me to a few more customers, should it work out."

"But that is excellent! You will do a wonderful job, I'm sure."

He nodded as if he knew it was true, but then his gaze softened. "But if you look for my own pleasure..." He adjusted so he could reach beneath the bed and then brought out a guitar. It was battered and the strings frayed, but he held it with such care, she knew she looked at a true love of his. Next came a few sheets of music that he dropped beside her. There were smudges and crossed-out passages, but it was obvious that he had labored over each one.

"Did you write these?" she asked, amazed.

"I did. They are silly tunes," he said. "I play because it is good for my hand."

"And because you like it. Because you want to."

He ducked his head as if embarrassed by the idea. "It is nothing like a true composer. I play very simply, and when I like the tune, I write it down to help me remember."

She laughed. "But that is exactly like a true composer." She touched the sheets. "Will you play one for me? Please?"

"Truly, I am not very good. In fact, Ruben has said I am very, very bad."

"I don't care. Please."

He did as she asked, his cheeks ruddy with embarrassment or pleasure. She didn't know which. She watched as he settled himself more comfortably on the bed, cradling the guitar with a gentleness that she adored. He tuned the instrument with care, muttering something about how he would have to buy new strings soon. She resolved that she would buy him enough to last him all year. And then, finally, he began to play.

He was right. The tune he played was simple, but it was so perfectly beautiful that her heart melted. It had a lightness to it, almost whimsical, but beneath it were bass notes that lingered. He thrummed a steady beat of longing. She pressed her hand to her heart as she listened.

It didn't go on long. She knew when he returned to the beginning and played the first strains again as a kind of chorus. And if he missed a note, she didn't notice. He fumbled a bit with his injured hand, but that made it all the more special somehow. And when he was done, she looked at him.

"That was wonderful. What were you thinking about when you wrote it?"

He let his guitar settle into his lap. "You," he finally said. "I have wanted to play that for you since I wrote down the very first note."

She didn't think it was possible for her to love him more. Now she discovered a deeper well of emotion for him. These new feelings weren't based on the safety he provided, but in simple appreciation for how he had expressed himself. Pure emotions set to music, and she wished she could give him something equally beautiful, equally personal. But she had nothing left of herself to give. It was all his already.

"Will you play more for me?" she whispered. "Anything you've written. Everything."

"If you like."

"Please."

So he did. While she lay on the bed beside him, she listened in bliss as his music surrounded her. He played the things he had written, and when he thought she was sleeping, he played more. Random tunes, snatches of melodies, it all came from him, and she drank it in. And when he finally stopped, she stretched where she lay beside him. She put her hand on his arm and pulled him down.

"Please," she whispered when he bent near. "Please let me love you."

His eyes crinkled as he smiled at her, and his hand stroked across her brow as gently as he had stroked his guitar. "I can deny you nothing."

Then he kissed her. She stretched up to him as he pushed down. Their mouths met, their tongues connected, and she played with him as best as she could. She tasted him. And she loved him so much her eyes teared up with wonder.

"Diana?" She saw confusion in his expression and fear. But she touched his cheek.

"You don't understand what it is like," she whispered. "I pushed all my feelings so far down that nothing touched me. But you do. You smile at me, and they come bubbling up. You touch me, and my will disappears. And now I am cracked so open that I feel everything." She shook her head. "That's not right. I feel *you*. And I cry because you are so beautiful."

His mouth opened in surprise. She stroked her fingers across his brow and whispered her words because they were so full of meaning she could not say them with a full voice.

"I love you," she said.

He stilled, his face poised above her. And then a shudder went through his entire body. A tremble that began in his hands until it flowed through both him and her. And when it was done, he was kissing her. His mouth was on her brow, her nose, her mouth, and down her neck. A frantic press of desire everywhere he could reach.

She met him as best she could. She reached for him with equal hunger. And when she could not kiss his skin, she tugged at his clothing, demanding he remove it.

He obliged, stripping out of his waistcoat and shirt with speed. She did the same, yanking at the ties of her dress until she could push it aside. She'd long since discarded her cloak and shoes, but now she wanted nothing between them. He was bare to the waist long before she was. Thankfully, he helped her strip away her corset and lifted off the rest. Her stockings remained, but she would not take the time for those. Not when she could kiss him again. When she could stroke her hand across his chest and feel his breath catch as she caught her nails on his nipple.

He pressed her down to the bed, feasting on her breasts as she pushed her hands into his hair. And while frenzy built in her blood, she tugged at the buttons of his pants.

"All of you, Lucas. Please. I want everything."

In case it wasn't clear enough, she stroked her hands across his cock, outlining it through his clothing. She pressed against the tip and rolled the heel of her hand up and down him. He hissed at what she did, and in the end, he pulled back far enough to do as she bid. He shed his clothing while she waited. And when he stood before her, she grasped his cock where it stretched toward her, thick and proud. She worked it as best she knew how, and then he gripped her hand and firmly peeled it away.

Their gazes met and held. If there was a question in his eyes, she didn't understand it. He simply stood there—a naked man in full arousal. His muscles were taut, his body in its prime, and she felt a surge of lust so strong that it took her breath away. She still had the ability to form words. No breath, but her lips shaped one word.

Please.

He released her hand and abruptly stepped to his desk. With quick movements, he opened a drawer and pulled out a French letter. She watched as he put it on, then returned to her. She straightened, letting her hair fall away from her breasts, as she bared herself to him. She watched as his eyes fixed on her face, then her breasts, then her sex. His nostrils flared, and she slowly spread her knees. The air was thick with the scent of their desire, and she licked her lips, telling him without words that she wanted it as much as he.

Then he abruptly leaned down and grabbed her legs, curling his hands beneath her knees. With a strong tug, he pulled her to the edge of the bed and stepped between her thighs. She wrapped her legs around him as he bent down over her. Then finally, wonderfully, she felt the tip of his cock press to her wet opening.

"Yes," she said as he pushed inside her. A little, the barest of penetration. He was braced on his forearms above her. She had her hands on his shoulders and her body arching toward him, urging him on. But he didn't move, and she whimpered in frustration. "You are the most difficult man ever!"

He grinned and thrust. One push of his hips and he was fully seated. She gasped at the feeling of fullness, of being taken this way by a man she loved. It made her smile as she opened herself to him. It made her arch into him, wanting to take him deeper, fuller, and more wholly inside her body. As deep here as he was in her heart.

And while he worked above her, she watched the muscles of his throat ripple with every contraction. She held his gaze and whispered everything she felt in an unending litany.

"I love you," she said. "I love you. I love you. I love you."

The words were a wonder to her, the feelings wholly new. And with every whisper, his movements became faster, harder, and wilder until he was lost in her body, and she was carried away on his passion.

Climax came with a rush. Pleasure burst through her awareness. He tumbled soon afterward, releasing into her with a triumphant growl.

They clung together, riding the waves, thrilled with every pulse.

And when they tumbled back to earth, he collapsed beside her on the bed. She wove lazy fingers through his hair. And he murmured something incoherent into her shoulder. She didn't know what he said, but she felt his lips press tiny kisses there. And she reveled in the way his arm lay heavy across her belly.

It took a long time before she gathered herself to ask her question. Eventually, she managed it. "Can we stay here tonight?"

He frowned. "Below a gaming hell? Are you mad?"

"Yes, completely mad for you." She turned to face him more squarely. "Just tonight. We'll leave the rest for tomorrow. I am completely safe here."

"Not your reputation. That will be in tatters should anyone talk."

She arched a brow. "They won't. Most don't even know I'm back yet. Besides, I'm a wealthy widow. I can do as I want." She sobered. "Or I can if you want it as well."

He slowly pushed up onto an elbow. She thought he would answer then, but instead, he leaned forward to kiss her. A slow, heady kiss that had her loins stirring again. And when they separated, she smiled coyly at him. "Is that a yes?"

"Yes."

Yes!

CHAPTER TWENTY-EIGHT

M ORNING CAME WITH a stretch of sore muscles and lingering happiness that made Lucas smile.

He didn't fool himself into believing that Diana had agreed to marry him. Last night had been about emotions unfettered from the usual constraints. The morning came with responsibilities and second thoughts.

Still, he couldn't regret a moment of their time together. Not the way she came apart in his arms, not the fevered way she whispered she loved him, nor the sweet way she nuzzled against him in her sleep. He was alive with joy this morning, for all that he had not furthered his goals of getting his ring on her finger. And because he still worried about her reputation, he woke them both early enough to get her home before most of the house realized she'd been gone.

He would protect her honor even if she cared nothing for it. If the situation with Geoffrey ever went to court, she would need every scrap of respectability she could muster.

Mrs. Dove-Lyon loaned him a carriage to get her quietly home. They came in the back and tiptoed upstairs. She was sleepy as he helped her into bed. Her expression was soft, her hair in disarray, and when she looked at him, his heart overflowed with need. He wanted her as his own—forever. But she was not a woman who could be caught in the usual ways. After he kissed her one last time, he whispered the question that had plagued him the night through.

"How can I get you to say yes to me?"

She sighed. "Realize that you don't need me as your wife."

A seemingly profound statement that made no sense to him. "I don't need you to live," he lied. "I want you by my side, honorably. I don't want to sneak in and out of your bed as if we were ashamed."

"I'm not ashamed."

"I am. I will not treat you so shabbily."

She stared at the ceiling. "I do not feel abused! This was my choice." She touched his cheek. "Why can't a woman choose just as a man does? Why can't I have pleasure in my life without giving up everything to a husband?"

He blew out a breath. They were going in circles, and yet he couldn't stop. "I don't want to take anything from you."

"And yet, you would. As my husband, you would take everything, and I would become nothing."

The statement was so absurd as to be laughable. The idea that she would ever be less than the amazing woman he saw before him struck him as ridiculous. And yet she obviously believed it. So he pressed his lips to her forehead and then whispered, "I need to go for a few hours. You are well protected here so long as you don't leave."

She smiled at him. "I know. Thank you."

He swallowed, overcome once again by the faith he saw shining through her eyes. Faith that he would protect her. It was with that thought in mind that he cleaned himself up as best he could and headed for the one place he had avoided since returning from Waterloo.

He headed to his family's London home.

It was not a decent time to visit, being much too early, but that was the point. His father and brother were always early risers, even in London, while his mother often slept well into the afternoon. Knocking now would accomplish what he wanted without the complications of seeing the one woman who never failed to tie him into knots.

The butler answered the door, leaving Lucas cooling his heels on the doorstep for much too long. During the few minutes he stood there, several people passed by and looked at him with curiosity. They were all servants headed out on one errand or another, but as Ruben liked to say, what one servant saw, all of London discussed within the hour. There would be no hiding that he was back from the dead now.

Once inside, he endured the scrutiny of their newest butler. Thanks to his mother's sharp tongue, they never kept servants for long, and so Lucas had the awkward task of explaining himself.

"Lord Chellam, to see my father and brother."

The man stared at him in shock, then nodded, proving that the servants had already been discussing this possibility. "If you would wait a moment here, please."

Lucas considered heading into the breakfast parlor without escort, but he was trying to make nice. So he waited, and in time, the butler returned to escort him. When he crossed into the parlor, his stomach growled at the scent of food. A hearty meal was on the sideboard, and Lucas couldn't stop himself from turning toward it and sniffing appreciatively.

Seated at the table, his brother burst out laughing. "Did you come for a meal, brother? I thought dead mean didn't eat."

"The newly returned to the living do, and it has been..." He shook his head. He couldn't remember the last time he ate a full meal like a civilized man. "A long while," he finally said.

His father was already gesturing to the butler to set another place, and Lucas sank down into the offered chair with gratitude in his heart. Not just for the food, but for the easy way both men accepted his presence. He stayed silent as he was served a large measure of everything, then waited a bit longer to catch his family's attention.

"I'm sorry," he finally blurted. "I should have come here long ago."

His father looked at him for a long moment. His brother, too. But in the end, they both returned to their food as if nothing had been said.

Though, his father did give him a crisp nod before looking back at the morning paper. "Did you see that we're to sign a treaty with the Netherlands against the slave trade?" His father shook his head. "It's all well and good to sign the paper, but if we don't commit money to end the practice, it's no more than hot air and a waste of ink."

Nathan grunted. "Slavery is too big a problem to be handled by one nation. We need everyone else to abhor it, too. Otherwise, the blighters will always find a workaround."

His father grunted. "We must begin at home. Stop slavery here, then we can help others to do the same."

The conversation continued along political lines as the two men discussed the forces that caused one man to declare another as less than human. It was the most erudite conversation Lucas had had in years. No one at the Lyon's Den talked about these things. The clientele discussed cards or how to duck bill collectors. The workers talked of how they would survive through the day. No one thought of the movements of nations except to complain about it.

But his father and brother did, and he realized he would have to as well if he meant to step into the House of Lords one day. That was a sobering thought, but one that sat better on his shoulders than it ever had before. Hadn't he spent years among the common man? The idea that he might find a way to make their lives better through proper government appealed to him. But only in a tomorrow kind of way. Today had enough problems.

Lucas finished his meal and felt well-fed for the first time since heading to war. He was an overstuffed pigeon right now—vulnerable if anyone attacked—but damned if it didn't feel good. He set his fork aside and leaned back with his hands on his belly. His father smiled at him and nodded to the butler. Within moments, the dishes were removed, and the servants were gone from the parlor.

"We're alone now," his father said in a low voice. "Out with it. What do you need?"

Nathan, too, leaned forward, his expression tight. "Have you discovered more about that attack at Vauxhall?"

"Nothing about the attack. As I feared, those thieves are long gone. But I believe we know who is behind everything." He quickly relayed what had happened so far. He kept his voice low to prevent being overheard, and both men listened intently, their expressions reflecting every emotion that could be expected: disgust, horror, and fury.

But his brother added one more emotion. He leaned back with a knowing look on his face. "You look to wed the widow."

Lucas jolted. It was true, but how his brother could know this from his cold recitation of facts was beyond him. His father snorted and gestured at Nathan with a dismissive flick of his hand.

"Don't distract us with the obvious," he said. Then he turned back to Lucas. "What do you need from us to help?"

Lucas stared at his father. Was it obvious to them? Really? Then he reset his thoughts. He needed to focus on the task at hand. "I need a way to bring Geoffrey out into the open. He has gone to ground, and not even my men can find him."

Nathan frowned. "How can we help with that?"

"He's a gambler who cannot stop. Long after it's insane, he still keeps going. His money has been cut off. I won't let him get to Diana, so he has to find funds somewhere. He needs a game, and he cannot go to the usual dens. I have people watching them."

"You need us to stage a game," his father said. "One that would lure him out?"

"Not you." He looked at his brother. "Nathan. I think the idea of taking money from my family would be too tempting for him to resist. If you are wild and angry about losing the title..." He paused long enough to watch his brother's face. Did Nathan resent that loss? He couldn't tell. Nathan nodded as he followed the train of thought, his expression deeply thoughtful.

"I can get drunk and lose money as well as anybody," Nathan muttered. "But how will that bring Geoffrey out?"

"Someone would approach you and invite you to a real man's game."

"A good many criminals, I shouldn't wonder," his father said.

Lucas shook his head. "Most of them know my true parentage by now. They wouldn't want to cross me by duping my brother." He grimaced. "It's not a sure thing by any stretch, and it's dangerous. But there are two things that have been consistent about Geoffrey. He gambles, and he's arrogant. I think he'd believe he could win enough money from you to escape London in style, and he thinks he can do that without me catching him."

His father shook his head. "There are too many risks in this plan. How can you know it will be Geoffrey's man who approaches Nathan?"

"I can't. But as I said, the sane ones won't risk crossing me."

"Leaving Nathan to the insane ones."

"Yes," he said. "But I'll have men watching you. I won't leave you alone."

Nathan smiled. "And better to use me as bait than Diana?"

Lucas winced. "You're my brother. I won't let anything happen to you."

His father snorted. "You can't stop a bullet. You can't—"

"I can," he stressed. "You don't know what I've been doing these last years. I'm good at this. As good as Nathan is at growing things, I am good at protecting those in my care. It's not without risk. In fact, it's damn—"

"I'll do it," Nathan interrupted. "I've been incredibly bored since Vauxhall."

Lucas blew out a breath. "Thank you."

His brother grinned. "It's the least I can do for my future sister-in-law."

Would that were true. "Lady Dunnamore and I are still discussing things. She has by no means accepted my suit. In fact, she has been quite explicit in refusing it."

Nathan waved that away in a gesture nearly identical to his father's. "Besides, there's the other benefit."

Lucas frowned. "What's that?"

"We would have a very public row, wouldn't we? I mean, I'd have to be very angry at you for taking away my title, yes?"

"Yes."

Nathan grinned as he pushed up from the table. "Well then, I shall really enjoy that."

Their father pushed back from the table as well. "Now see here, I'll not have anything untoward in my house."

"Untoward, Father?" Nathan said. "On the contrary, I believe it will be very *toward* Lucas." Then his voice kicked up to a growl loud enough to be heard through the doors to where the servants no doubt listened. "You irresponsible dog! I should kill you where you stand!"

Lucas scrambled out of his chair, making sure to knock it over in the noisiest way possible. "I let you play at being lord for a few years. You should thank me!"

"Thank you!" Nathan bellowed. "Why, you arrogant ass!"

He lunged forward in a way that Lucas could have dodged. He didn't. Instead, he caught his brother by the arms, and they went crashing into the main foyer, wrestling with each other in the way they had as kids. They banged into the wall. They sent a footman scrambling to catch a vase as it teetered above them. The butler squeaked in alarm as Lucas tossed his brother to the side.

Nathan rolled with the throw, coming easily to his feet. There might have been a flash of pure pleasure in his eyes, but it was quickly replaced by what seemed to be deadly intent. "You can't take it from me. I won't let you!"

Lucas arched his brow in the most arrogant expression he could muster. "You can't stop me," he taunted.

He expected his brother's blow. Nathan was powerful, not fast. But damn, he did not expect the raw force behind his brother's massive fist. It threw him back against the wall, while his head exploded in pain. But it didn't knock him out. And while Nathan straightened up to deliver another blow, Lucas launched himself back at his brother, moving with twice the speed. He hit Nathan's face over and over.

Lucas tried to hold back. He didn't want to damage his brother, but they needed this to look real, and Nathan needed real marks on his face. Was that enough?

Lucas slowed his blows, knowing that most of them had landed on Nathan's forearms, not his face. Though, one of Nathan's eyes was already swelling. He'd have one hell of a shiner.

Nathan grabbed hold of Lucas's torso and heaved him across the room like he was tossing a hay bale. Lucas landed in a heap as he gasped for breath. And then another voice cut through the house.

"What is the meaning of this?"

His mother. Her voice boomed through the house, and it brought everyone to a stop. *Oh hell.* He looked at his brother and caught a matching flash of regret. But while Lucas was still rolling to hands and knees, his brother was already standing.

Nathan glared first at her, then their father, and finally at Lucas. "It's not fair!" he finally spit. Then he stormed out of the house.

CHAPTER TWENTY-NINE

L UCAS WATCHED HIS brother rush out of the house, the fury and the pain looking all too real. He knew their fight had been staged, and yet part of him feared that there was true hurt behind the act. After all, he had taken the earldom back from his brother. Any man would be angry at that.

But he had deeper problems now as his mother descended the stairs as regally as a queen. Her eyes were hard, her mouth pinched shut, and she stared at him as she would a rat on her polished floor.

"Lucas," she said, her voice excruciatingly dry. "You've come for a visit."

He glanced at his father, who was hidden half in and half out of the breakfast parlor. The man gave him an apologetic look and backed away. Lucas guessed his father would now disappear through the kitchen to his London club, which left Lucas alone with his mother. Not an experience he relished. But in Ireland, he had seen Diana work with any number of hateful people who despised the mere fact that she was female. The least he could do was try to find common ground with his mother.

"I am here," he said. "And I've come specifically to ask for your help."

She paused on the last step to stare at him, and no wonder. He couldn't remember a time when he'd asked for her help, and her shock echoed his own at the thought.

"If you wanted my help, you shouldn't have come at this hour." She looked out the window at the bright sunshine. "I am never about until after noon."

He acknowledged her statement with a slight bow. "I'd forgotten," he lied.

She arched a brow and took the last step down to the foyer. "Very well," she said with a sigh. "What is it?"

"I find my clothing exceedingly unfashionable. If I am to become an earl one day, I should dress the part, but I have no understanding of what is expected these days. I should like your help ordering clothing, if you would care to lend a hand."

Her scrutiny did not soften as she pounced on one word. "*If* you become an earl?"

He gave her a rueful shrug. "There is still hope that someone will murder me in my bed. And there is always the danger of illness or insanity."

She grimaced. "You think I want you dead?"

"Don't you?" he challenged. He had meant to find common ground with her but found he wanted honesty more. "You want Nathan to inherit."

"I do," she admitted, and he could not restrain his flinch. "He is the better steward. You always dreamed of going far and wide. No nanny could keep you from running, and you even went to war before finishing your schooling." She shook her head. "Your brother likes it at home."

"Which makes him a proper earl?"

"It makes him *at home.*" She held his gaze for a long moment as if her words were self-explanatory. They weren't. Not to him. Did she think a man should linger at home, constantly in his mother's skirts? The idea was ridiculous, and yet, he could see the truth of it in her face. She liked that Nathan preferred the country to the city, that he preferred a quiet life of farming when Lucas had always craved adventure.

"That is…" He almost said "ridiculous" but softened his tone at the last second. "Unreasonable. An earl's political responsibilities require him to be here in the city."

Her eyes sparkled in anger. "It is unreasonable that the first time you are here in years sees a brawl in the hallway. Broken furniture and your brother's disappearance." She pointed to the remains of a table cluttering the hall. At least her vase had been saved.

He bowed his head. "My apologies, Mother. I will remove myself—"

"Stop!" she snapped, her voice both exasperated and angry. "You came here for my help, and you shall have it."

He wasn't sure he wanted it now, but he dipped his chin. "Thank—"

"On one condition." She waited until she had his full attention. "You will eat nuncheon with me."

He blinked, completely confused. One moment she wished him with the devil, and the next, she demanded his attendance at his next meal? "I…If that is what you wish, then, of course, I shall be here for tea."

"Swear it," she ordered. "I know you have never gone back on your word."

That wasn't true. He'd never purposefully failed, but promises in war are often broken. Especially those made to men about to go into battle. "I swear I will be here, provided my other responsibilities do not claim me first." And when she looked at him askance, he huffed out a breath. "Mother, I am in the middle of important matters."

She waved them away. "I should be one of your important matters."

He swallowed away a caustic retort. After all, he had asked for her help. She could have refused him. But that didn't mean he would give her the satisfaction of saying something untrue. He would do his best to attend tea. That was all. In the end, she pursed her lips and nodded.

"Give me a moment to dress, and then I will accompany you to Bond Street."

He smiled and bowed, already itching to be away. He didn't like the idea that his mother would stand with him at a tailor's as if he were a boy still in leading strings. But he had started on this path and would see it through, even if it made him feel like a humiliated child.

It didn't. And what a shock that was!

Several hours later, he was stunned to realize that his mother knew how to shop for a man. She knew how to speak to a tailor with utmost efficiency, explaining things he could only guess at. She picked patterns that gave him freedom of movement and no hint of foppery. And best of all, while he was being measured from top to bottom, she faded away to discuss fabric and buttons, such that she was not even in the same room with him.

It allowed him to breathe and proceed with the task without wanting to hit someone. A miracle, indeed. Still, it was an exhausting morning after a long night. If he hadn't promised to dine with her, he would have made his excuses and sought his bed. But he had promised, and so he nodded wearily when his mother tapped her watch and declared it time to return home. Though, he did offer her an out.

"I woke you early, Mother. Perhaps you would prefer to rest today, and we can dine tomorrow."

The stare she gave him was so cold, she nearly froze his toes. "You promised."

"And I am not going back on that promise. I was simply offering—"

"No. Today."

Very well, then. He bit his lip and resolved to endure more time with his irrational parent. Or maybe not so irrational, because the reason for her demand became clear the moment he stepped into his parents' house.

"Diana?" he gasped. "Whatever are you doing here?"

She looked up from where she was drinking tea in the parlor. She was dressed in mourning, the unrelieved black doing little favor to her already pale complexion, and yet he found her stunningly beautiful. She straightened immediately, her movements graceful even as she stepped out into the hallway to curtsey to his mother.

"Lady Wolvesmead, thank you for the invitation."

"Lady Dunnamore," his mother returned. "I apologize that I was not at my best the last time we met." A vast understatement given that his mother had entered Diana's home screaming upon seeing Lucas alive.

"Totally understandable," Diana returned. Then she looked at Lucas. "You seem surprised. I thought you wanted me here for some reason."

He had wanted her safely away from his poisonous mother, but apparently, something had gone amiss.

"I sent the invitation," his mother stated flatly. Then she pursed her lips. "Prattling about in the doorway is uncivilized. The meal should be served forthwith." She looked at her butler. "Show them into the parlor while I go repair my attire." Then she turned and climbed the stairs without even glancing back at them.

Lucas watched her go, then gave Diana an exasperated look. "It's been a trying morning," he said by way of explanation.

"That sounds interesting. Do give me all the details."

He didn't answer. They were being escorted into the parlor, which was a bare three steps away. They could have walked themselves there, but his mother—and her butlers—were always ones for ceremony. "Where is your guard? He was supposed to watch you."

"He came with me, as well as two others. Last I saw they went belowstairs to oversee the preparation of the meal."

Given that Lord Dunnamore had been poisoned, the precautions were necessary. As was the fact that he now saw his man gesture to him through the window before slipping out of sight. The guard was probably watching the perimeter.

"Why does your mother want me here?"

Lucas shrugged. "I cannot understand the woman."

Diana raised her brows. "Is that a new shirt? And your hair has been cut. Sweet heaven, those are new shoes. Has your mother replaced my disreputable Mr. Lucifer with a respectable Lord Chellam? I am shocked."

He shot her a glare even though he knew she was teasing. More than that, he saw a flash of interest in her eyes. "Do you prefer me this way? Clipped and polished like a dandy?"

She laughed. "You are a far cry from a dandy, but I must admit the new you has appeal. Dark and dangerous certainly has its place, but sometimes a lady wants to sit across from a gentleman."

He studied her a moment, gauging the truth of her statement. In the end, he had to acknowledge her point with a grunt. "If you want a gentleman, then I endeavor to please."

Her expression sobered. "I am pleased whatever you choose to wear."

Then there was no more time for conversation, as his mother stepped into the parlor. "If you would follow me? I believe the food should be acceptable despite the way your men tried to discomfit my cook."

Lucas winced. "A necessary precaution, I assure you."

"No doubt." Her tone indicated the exact opposite.

Would this hell never end? He began to long for an attack just so he could do something that was not spending time with his mother. But at least Diana was here now, and she eased the tension inside him as no one else.

And still the time ground on. They sat and ate. Diana and his mother exchanged pleasantries, and he did his best to join in the small talk. Diana was the bridge for that, of course. His mother would say something that sounded innocuous but still made Lucas bristle. Diana was there to diffuse his anger, softening his mother's words and making him wonder if perhaps he overreacted. His mother certainly did, stiffening at the strangest things, only to have Diana rephrase his words into something more palatable. He had no idea how she did it, only that it worked.

And then finally—blessedly—the meal was done. His mother waved the servants away, but she didn't stand. Instead, she stared hard at Diana, then him. Lucas was so desperate to be done with the whole affair that he considered making his excuses no matter how rude it might appear. But in this, his mother saved him.

"I suppose you wonder why I demanded you both eat with me."

He'd ceased wondering about her reasons when she declared one set of buttons insupportable and another just the thing. But she did have the right of it. There had been nothing so far that warranted his last few hours of misery.

Thankfully, Diana knew how to be more polite than he. "It did cross my mind," she said.

"I wanted to meet the woman my son wishes to marry."

Diana's eyes widened as she glanced at Lucas. He simply shrugged. "They have guessed it."

"Nathan guessed it," his mother said. "And he told me." She looked to Lucas. "Is it true?"

"Yes."

She nodded as if she had expected as much. Then she turned to Diana. "You should refuse him."

It took a moment for her words to penetrate, and when they did, he shot up from his chair. "Mother!" He would have said more, but the furious words choked him in their rush to get out, and in that time, she held up her hand.

"Hear me out," she continued. Then she spoke directly to Diana. "Years ago, his father and I married out of duty. It was what was done, of course, and though neither he nor I wished it, we both complied.

We suffered each other long enough for me to get pregnant, and Lucas was born." She lifted her chin. "I have not allowed him in my bedchamber since."

Again, it took a moment for the words to penetrate his anger, but when they did, he was struck dumb. She'd just admitted that his brother was illegitimate, and his father cuckolded. And still, his mother kept speaking.

"Do not think I was alone in my indiscretions. He has always done as he pleased."

That, at least, was something Lucas already knew. His father had never been flamboyant with his mistresses, but he had certainly frequented women other than his wife.

"I bore Nathan and dared him to say a single word against the boy."

"Father has always raised him as a son," Lucas rasped. And then another thought struck him, one that he couldn't hold in. "Does he know? Does Nathan—"

"I have told your brother everything."

He did not envy Nathan that conversation. Meanwhile, Diana remained more focused while he reeled.

"Why are you telling me this?" she asked.

"Because I *hate* his father." She said the word with venom. "I hate that we wed because our parents wished it. I hate that we are shackled together for life." She took a deep breath. "And I hate that how I felt about his father spilled onto the son." Now she turned to look at Lucas. "I have treated you ill for all your life because I despise your father. That was not your fault, and I am sorry for it." She pursed her lips. "And I cannot seem to change it."

He stared at her, his mouth slack with shock. He could not credit that she'd finally admitted her true feelings toward him. To add, her apology upended his world, but then it was followed by what he had known from the beginning. No matter what she said, her feelings toward him remained hard. She would never love him as she loved his brother.

He gripped the edges of the table rather than stumble. It was too much to absorb in one blow. Meanwhile, she turned to Diana.

"You know something of being forced to wed."

"I do," Diana said, her voice subdued.

"But you are free now. Do not release that freedom under any circumstance. It is not just you who will suffer for it." Her gaze went to Lucas. "Hatred has a way of growing and spilling onto the innocent."

Lucas had no response to that. He was too stunned to form words. And once again, Diana came to his rescue.

"You assume that there is no love between your son and me. There is. Most definitely."

His mother released a short snort of disdain. "It will not be enough."

This time it was Diana who scoffed. "You do not know that, and it does you no credit—"

"The first time he criticizes something you purchased, you will resent him. And when he says you cannot go out to someplace you have deemed important, that resentment will grow. Bit by bit, there will be tiny infringements on your choices, and soon you will hate him." She spoke as if she were saying irrefutable facts like the sun rises in the east and sets in the west.

"That is not true," Lucas said, and he was gratified to hear Diana voice the exact same sentiment. But his mother was undeterred.

"Do you think he will let you pursue your own amusements? What if you wish to go to Ireland, and he deems it too dangerous? What if he does not approve a trip to the theater? He has set three guards upon you. Do you truly think that will ever end? Or that you will not resent him for it?"

"That is for her own protection," he said. "There are dangers—"

"Everywhere," his mother interrupted. "And marrying when one has achieved independence is the biggest danger of all. In the end, it will destroy you both."

"That is not true," he repeated, but he was very aware that Diana had stopped speaking. Instead, she pressed her lips firmly closed as she looked down at the tablecloth.

"Do you think your father is happy?" his mother asked him.

Lucas knew the man was not.

"Enjoy each other if you must. I can see that there is true affection between the two of you. But do not think it will last. And do not think a wealthy widow—a woman finally free—would not come to resent the man who takes it all away."

Lucas didn't respond. He could see the depth of his mother's hatred and the truth that sustained it. She was not free. His father maintained strict controls over her purse and her entertainment. Their income had never been strong enough to support two households such that they could live apart.

Then she delivered her final blow. "Any child born in that anger would be damaged from it. You cannot deny that."

Did he agree? It was true that his mother's hatred had hurt him. Unbearably so at times because he never understood it. And now that he did, the pain of it still cut deep down in a place that would not be soothed.

Then Diana spoke, her voice strong though her face was pale. "Any child of mine would be loved wholly and completely."

"Not when he looks like his father. Not when he so clearly prefers him to you. And not when bitterness carves the wounds deeper."

God, it was true. The impact of that made his hands tremble. The hideous state of his parents' marriage had poisoned any tender feelings inside her. And that had spilled like acid onto him. He had thought himself immune to his mother's gibes, but now he felt how deeply she could still wound him merely by sharing her pain with Diana. By showing the woman he loved that it wasn't enough. Whatever love they shared—whatever love his mother once had for her own son—had been lost beneath an ocean of resentment.

He swallowed, struggling to bring himself to function. But in this, he had forgotten that Diana was made of stronger stuff. Stronger even than his mother's hatred.

"I have never heard anything so sad," Diana said. Her eyes were bright with tears as she spoke. "I grieve for you," she said. "But do not think anyone else is doomed to your fate. I will make my own choices, just as you made yours."

His mother curled her lip. "Love will not be enough," she said. "It does not last. Not when a wife is nothing compared to a man."

Damnation! Now his mother was echoing the very words Diana had said to him. That a woman was nothing compared to a man. "Don't be absurd," he pressed. "She is everything to me."

His mother shook her head, resignation in every movement. "I can see you are resolved."

"I am."

She looked at Diana, who gripped her fingers together. "You have a brain, girl. Think of what you give up. It is a horrid thing that I have done to my own son."

Diana's chin shot up as she met his mother's gaze. "On that, I agree."

"Then, do not repeat my mistake."

CHAPTER THIRTY

"WHAT A WITCH!" Diana huffed out as she let her head drop back onto the squabs of the carriage. Lucas sat across from her, and she saw his head snap up at her words.

"You don't agree with her?" She heard hope and relief in his words.

"That's not the point," she said. "To blame an innocent child for her mistakes is weak, petulant, and irresponsible. I wanted to slap her." She snorted. "I still want to slap her!" Then she looked at him and felt her heart weep for his pain. He was the strongest man she knew, and his shoulders were hunched, and he kept fiddling with his hurt hand. She reached out to him and ended up replacing his hand with hers as she stroked her love into his scarred palm. "I am so sorry, Lucas. I cannot imagine how much you suffered with her as a mother."

He stared at her hand as she worked, and eventually, she felt his fingers relax. "I never understood why she hated me."

"I don't think she hates you exactly. I think she hates her life, and you were just the target. What a horrible way to live. For all of you."

He nodded and seemed to come more fully back to himself. A moment later, he turned his hand such that he held hers. "Was it like that for you, too? You were pushed into marriage just as she was and at a younger age."

How to answer that? "I was very angry for a time, but I had plenty of legitimate targets. I dismissed my awful housekeeper, sacked anyone who sneered at me, and demanded respect from everyone and everything. I even forced Penelope to take her cat back. The damned thing hissed at me."

"Cats don't respect anyone."

"I handed it to a footman and told him to deliver it to her. It was her cat. Why should I shelter it when all it did was claw at my skirts?"

His brows rose. "I shall be very careful about bringing you any pets in the future."

She chuckled. "It was just the one mean cat. I'm actually rather fond of cats, in general. But as I said, it was something to focus all my anger on."

"And how did you change? How did you stop?"

"Feeling angry?" She blew out a breath. "It's exhausting being mad all the time. And Oscar and I became friends. I don't think your parents ever did."

He shook his head. "No, I don't think they did either."

His voice was glum, and she squeezed his fingers. "It's not your fault. The way she treats you was never your fault."

He gave her a half-smile. "I'm grateful you don't agree with her."

She sighed. She already knew this conversation was about to take a bad turn, but she couldn't let him keep denying her choices. "Lucas, she was horrid to you, but what she said wasn't wrong. Forcing children to marry is reprehensible, and it damages the next generation."

His hands tightened around hers. "We're not children."

"No. I am a free widow with wealth enough to live as I choose."

He tugged at her hands just as she tried to slip away from his hold. "You cannot listen to my mother. She is a bitter, old shrew."

Her voice rose to match his. "And she said nothing I have not already said to you. Why would I give up everything now that I finally have it?"

"For me. To be with me." His voice was hard as he answered. It was the first time she'd heard this tone directed at her, and she didn't like it.

"We were together last night and—"

He cut her words off with a quick shake of his head. "Do not make me regret last night," he rasped. "We both wanted it."

"We both enjoyed it."

He agreed with a nod. "But that does not change what I want. You love me, Diana. You said so. Why won't you commit to me?"

It wasn't that simple, and he knew it. She hadn't been blind these last years. She knew that his parents' story wasn't the only hideous marriage. She'd seen couples desperately in love turn against one another within a year. Always, the husband turned to his own amusements, and no one said a word. But the wife was trapped, unable to do anything without her husband's approval.

"I don't want to hate you." And she might if he tried to rein her in.

"I don't want to hate you either," he said. And he might, she realized, if she continued to refuse what he offered.

There was no more to say as the carriage rattled on toward her home. And though they continued to hold hands, there was a coolness between them. She didn't grip him as tight, and there was pain in his eyes when he looked at her. Neither said a word, but with so much already said between them, the silence continued to throb with their disagreement.

Until the carriage stopped. Until he escorted her back to her home, and her bodyguards took up their positions in her house. But he didn't cross the threshold, much to her shock.

"Aren't you coming inside?" she asked.

"I need to arrange things for later. The guards will see no one harms you."

"What things? What arrangement?"

He smiled at her. "My brother." And with that, he bowed deeply and left.

She watched him go, her gaze staying on him as he refused the use of her carriage and instead hailed a hackney. And as he stepped inside the vehicle, she wondered if she already saw the end. After the best night of her life, were they already over? She didn't doubt that he would continue to protect her. Until Geoffrey was handled one way or another, he and his men would remain close. But she didn't want them. She wanted Lucas with her, and that was another thing entirely.

She just wasn't sure she wanted to pay his price.

CHAPTER THIRTY-ONE

L UCAS EXTENDED HIS foot, trying to ease the ache out of his leg. He was sitting half crouched in the shadows of one of the filthiest gaming hells in London. Nathan was at a table toward the center of the room. He drank while grumbling to anyone nearby that his brother had done him wrong. He kept grumbling that he intended to win a fortune ten times what Lucas had stolen from him, see if he didn't.

The good news was that Nathan was a good gambler. He had indeed won in steady increments over three days of determined play. Better yet, his brother was a large man, and though he acted half-drunk, Lucas judged him to be only one-quarter inebriated.

Any minute now, someone would invite Nathan to a high stakes game. Any moment now, Geoffrey would make his move to trap Nathan.

It had to be soon because Lucas was going crazy waiting.

Nothing had changed since the disastrous day with his mother. He had not spoken more to Diana, though he knew through her guards what she did every minute of the day. And he certainly hadn't visited her at night. If he did, he wouldn't be able to keep from touching her. Besides, nighttime was when he watched over his brother, who sat as bait. And of all the people he most wanted to protect, his brother ranked second, right behind Diana. Nathan knew the truth of his illegitimate heritage and still toiled night and day for his family's fortunes and now risked his life for Lucas and Diana.

The truth humbled Lucas. And he swore—as he had every hour of the last three days—that he would somehow make it up to Nathan.

Lucas moved his leg again, trying to ease off the cramp from sitting in the same place for so long. And just as he was focused on his own aches, something happened at the tables. A rat-faced man sidled up to Nathan, bringing an extra drink as he smiled with good cheer and a willing ear. Predictably, Nathan upped his griping while the weaselly man nodded and concurred. It went on for a good twenty minutes before Nathan pushed up from the table, swaying as he found his feet.

This was it. Finally, someone was taking the bait to fleece Nathan. But was Geoffrey behind the invite or someone else?

Lucas leaned forward in the shadows, trying to see the smaller man more closely. Three days before, he'd bet Ruben it would be James Murray, a low life bastard who perpetually caused trouble at whatever pub or gaming hell he managed to ferret his way into. But when Lucas finally got a look at the smaller man, he cursed under his breath. It was Sid Gardner, a seemingly innocuous man, and Ruben's pick as the one to lure Nathan away. Damn it. Now he owed Ruben twenty quid. And more relevant, Sid Gardner was rumored to be deadly with a knife. Lucas knew he kept at least one stiletto hidden on his person.

Too late now. Nathan and Sid were heading for the door. Lucas slipped out of his corner, his back screaming as blood rushed into his lower extremities. With a nod to the owner of the hell, he slipped out the back and heard Nathan's bellowing laugh from the front. His brother was brilliant in the way he kept his voice loud enough for Lucas to follow. Lucas made it to the front just as Nathan stepped into a hackney with Sid. A second after the carriage door closed, a boy leaped upon the back. He flashed Lucas a grin as the hackney moved forward.

The kid was Ruben's second cousin twice removed and was quick as a wink.

On the opposite side of the street, Ruben's own carriage waited for Lucas. Forget flashy vehicles. Ruben's carriage looked like any other hackney except that the horses were fresh and the wheels well oiled. Lucas nodded at the coachman as he jumped up beside the man. It would look unusual for him to be up here, even wrapped in a dark blanket and hunched over, but it was the best way for him to keep an eye on his brother. A moment later, they were moving as they followed the hackney to whatever hole Geoffrey was hiding in. Or so he hoped.

It was a long, anxious ride to their destination. Lucas spent the interminable minutes envisioning his brother getting his throat slit inside the hackney. There was nothing he could do to help if that happened, and he would never forgive himself if it did. He kept his eyes trained on the boy still hanging on the back. He'd react if something was going on inside, but the kid just perched there with admirable balance.

This was madness, he thought. Geoffrey would be ten times an idiot to remain in London. He was probably halfway across the continent by now. Or worse, planning some attack on Diana. Except the blackguard knew that Diana was well protected, and Lucas's men watched every day for poison. It wasn't possible to get at her, so the arrogant man would strike at Lucas through Nathan. That had to be the way. It would get Geoffrey enough money to lay low for months and find a way through Lucas's protection. The problem was that Diana wouldn't last through months of protection. She was already chaffing at the constant supervision. So Lucas had to get Geoffrey now, and he would.

If he had guessed right. If Geoffrey really was that stupidly arrogant. If...if...if...

Finally, the hackney stopped near the docks in front of several squalid buildings, well away from any type of light. The boy jumped off and scrambled to the side to watch where Sid and Nathan would go. Lucas's carriage kept going around the corner. As soon as they were out of sight, he grabbed the bottle he'd left beneath the bench, then jumped off without the vehicle stopping. The carriage would continue around until the coachman found a place to stop and wait.

Meanwhile, Lucas made it to the spot where the boy crouched in the shadows.

"Evening, guv," the boy whispered.

"Evening…Billy?" he whispered back.

"Benny," he said. Then they both fell silent as another hackney pulled up and out came a young man with a scantily clad woman. The boy was wealthy—probably a merchant's son—obviously inebriated enough to risk gambling for higher stakes than he could afford. The woman was just to provide extra enticement as she cooed into his ear about how they'd spend all the money he was about to win.

"Here comes another pair," Benny whispered as he gestured up the street. Two men whistled loudly as they walked, one clearly less drunk than the other. There were other people on the street. Most were working women and their customers, though Lucas had passed several men in a dice game on the way to Benny's hiding spot. It was a busy enough street to take little notice of anyone's coming and going, but quiet enough that the Watch didn't come by too often.

"Have you seen where they're going?" Lucas asked. He'd figured out the building, but not the specific flat.

Benny pointed to the top floor. "I think it's the one with the dim light."

That would be Lucas's guess, too, but it would take following this pair upstairs to be sure. He hoped his brother knew to keep doing his booming laugh. That was as good as a foghorn in a place like this.

Lucas gave the boy a nod, then stepped out onto the walk. He was going to go up right behind the whistling pair, but before he could leave, the boy touched his arm.

"Want me to get the Watch now? Or wait—"

"Now."

"And if you're wrong?"

He shrugged. "Then, I'll pay them for their troubles, but keep them quiet until my signal." He was fast running out of coin thanks to the shopping spree with his mother, but if it came to blows, he wanted the Watch on his side. Not for their help, but because they could testify in court that he'd called them if things went bad.

He waited for the whistling pair to pass, then slipped in behind them as if he belonged. When the sober one looked back at him, he held out his bottle of brandy and put on his oiliest smile. "I'm just 'ere to 'elp."

Thanks to his haircut, cleanly shaven face, and a bit of makeup to cover his scar, Lucas looked better than he had in years. He appeared more like an aristocrat looking for an easy mark rather than the dangerous head of security at the Lyon's Den. And the clearly re-filled brandy helped seal the deal. That helped him appear as someone in on the con.

"Now that's a good friend," the drunk cried as he reached for the bottle.

Lucas held it out of the way. "Have some manners," he chided. "Inside. With a glass."

"Quite right, quite right. Must keep to appearances."

"This is a sophisticated game we're going to," he said with a grin. "That's why we use glasses."

They came to the door, and he let the other whistler get them in. A quick series of knocks and the door opened. Even before he stepped inside, he heard Nathan's booming laugh. That was reassuring. The fact that he'd guessed wrong on which flat they were using was not. They were in the back of the building rather than the front. Well, he'd hope the Watch saw his signal anyway.

He stepped inside and greeted everyone. He saw the six he knew about, plus another lady who smiled warmly as he passed her the brandy. His brother appeared in good spirits as he called for the real card game to begin, and everyone began to gather around the table.

Five players, a female dealer, and an empty sixth place. *Geoffrey?* He could only pray that was true.

He angled for a seat next to his brother and managed it, but then was annoyed to see that Sid took the place on the other side. No way to block a stiletto into Nathan's ribs, but at least he could protect his brother's other side. And then they began to play.

Fortunately, Lucas had brought enough coin to cover the buy-in, and so he gathered his cards and played an indifferent game. He listened to the talk, won as much as he lost, and cursed himself for an idiot. Geoffrey wasn't here.

He was just about to call it quits when the dealer began to struggle. Her words began to slur, and though she had been flirting with everyone at the table, she started to focus on Nathan with singular attention. He returned her teases with a reddening of his ears. Good heavens, his brother was embarrassed as she began to bow deeper toward him, as she showed more and more of her assets. After a few more hands, she waved the hostess over.

"It appears I am tired, gentleman. Do you mind if I allow another dealer to take my place?" She winked at Nathan. "I'll just sit by you in the meantime."

Everyone agreed that they didn't care who dealt and that she should, of course, sit down. And then the trap was sprung. As she sat down between Nathan and Lucas, the door opened, and Geoffrey sauntered in followed by two thick armed brutes who carried their knives openly.

"You've brought another player!" the lady exclaimed as one of the brutes took her place as dealer, the other stood by the door, and Geoffrey headed for the last empty seat.

In the normal course of things, Geoffrey would steadily win all of the marks' money while the others kept anyone from leaving until it was done. Geoffrey would pay his helpers a pre-arranged amount, and everyone would disappear to do it again the next night. In truth, it was all fairly civilized. Or it would have been until Geoffrey recognized Lucas.

"You!" he bellowed, and if a word could carry bitter hatred, that one did.

Lucas smiled, grateful that finally, his plans had come to fruition. At last, he could act.

First, he shoved to his feet while Geoffrey gestured at his brutes. The two menacing men bolted forward, but Lucas was faster. He grabbed his chair and heaved it toward the window. The glass shattered with a loud crack, and someone down in the street cried out in shock as the pieces came tumbling down.

Signal sent. Please, God, let the Watch see it.

The next step was to grab Geoffrey and make sure the man didn't escape in the chaos. Not a problem because the bastard was heading straight for Lucas. Unfortunately, Nathan was in the way, along with Sid, who abruptly had a knife in each hand, and the dealer woman who was grabbing for Nathan's purse.

Chaos erupted. Nathan was quick as he blocked a knife and saved his purse in the same motion. The woman went tumbling back with a curse, while the other two marks looked around with confused expressions. Both were too slow to save their purses. Which is when Geoffrey pulled two flintlock dueling pistols from hiding spots beneath the table.

Lucas kicked the table over, hoping to block any gunplay. But he was too slow to stop Geoffrey from raising his pistols.

Bang! Bang!

The sound was deafening, and Lucas dove to the side. Where was his brother? Where was Geoffrey? Everything was screaming and gun smoke.

CHAPTER THIRTY-TWO

T HE SOUND OF the knocker roused Diana from a fitful rest. Ever since her fight with Lucas three days before, she had tortured herself with questions about her future. Until then, all she'd thought about was her freedom. No more caring for a dying husband, no more coaxing him to give up the reins of control, and—since Lucas entered her life—no more endless nights wishing for a man to touch her the way a husband should.

But now she thought about the cost of her freedom and longed for someone with whom to share her burdens. It was a constant back and forth in her mind, day and night, and she quickly came to hate her own thoughts.

So when the door knocker sounded in the middle of the night, she was out of bed to dress within seconds. By the time her guard scratched at her bedroom door, she was already grabbing her shoes.

"Come in," she called.

He entered, and the look on his face froze her in place. It was dark and hard, but there was a full measure of worry in his eyes.

"Lucas?" she whispered, her heart beating painfully in her throat.

Caleb shook his head. He was newly back from escorting Penelope and Walter out of London, but if the job had given him pleasure, it didn't show. Right now, he looked ragged. "I don't know, my lady. I don't think so, but I cannot tell." His hands twisted together as he spoke. "A man from the Watch is downstairs. With apologies, he asks you to come…um…" His voice faltered.

"Do not hold back," she said sharply. "Tell me it all straight away."

He nodded. "He asks you to come and identify a body."

Her breath caught, and she began to shake. But that did not stop her from pulling on her shoes, though her trembling fingers made it difficult work.

"If it were Lucas," Caleb continued, "I don't think anyone would knock on your door. That would go to his parents."

She looked up, reason finding its way through her panic. "Yes, of course." Then she silently repeated his words to herself. Of course, that made sense. She was not Lucas's wife. "Do you know where Lucas is?"

"No, my lady."

Of course not. Lucas went his own way, always. "But someone has died, and the Watch has come to me."

"Yes, my lady."

She straightened up. "Then, let us not keep them waiting."

"I have already called for the carriage."

"Thank you, Caleb." She looked at the worry on his face. "Would you care to accompany me?"

His expression cleared. "It would be my honor."

She knew he would have come anyway, whether she asked him to or not, but this made things easier on everyone. She went downstairs and met a very uncomfortable man of the Watch. He was young and clearly feeling awkward at having to wake a noblewoman in the middle of the night.

They shared words but no significant information. It was exactly as Caleb said. He asked her to accompany him to identify a body. As soon as her coach was brought around, the watchman joined her sleepy coachman up top to give directions while she and Caleb climbed inside. A moment later, the carriage was moving through the empty London streets while Diana spun through possibilities in her head.

She already guessed who was dead. It had to be Geoffrey. There would be no other reason to wake her. And if that were true, then, of course, she was saddened for his wasted life. Which meant there were things she should be planning. She wasn't exactly sure who inherited the title, what the legal ramifications were. But her mind wouldn't go down those practical lines.

She wanted Lucas. She wanted to know he was alive and well. She wanted him to hold her hand and lend his strength while she sorted through her emotions. She wanted to talk things out with him. He listened so well that even when he didn't have an answer, he helped her think her options through. By the time the carriage stopped, she was a knot of anxiety. She was just reaching for the handle when the door was pulled open, and there stood Lucas, like an answer to her prayers.

Her breath caught, and she launched herself into his arms. He was alive! He was whole! He held her there, awkward as it was with him half in and half out of the carriage, and then while she struggled to catch her breath, he whispered into her ears.

"I'm well. It's over. Everything is fine now."

"It is," she managed to babble. "You are safe." She abruptly pulled back to scan his body. "You are, right? You're—"

"I'm fine. But you're going to have to do a hard thing now. Do you think—"

"Just stay with me. I can do anything if you're with me."

He smiled at her and—just for a moment—traced his thumb down the side of her face. "I've never met a woman more capable than you."

"Only with you," she whispered. No, that wasn't right. Even as she whispered the words, she knew that she was lying. She'd been capable of running a household, managing tenants, and even standing strong against Geoffrey before things became desperate. But she'd done all that inside a hard shell of non-emotion. She hadn't felt much of anything until Lucas came back into her life. And now that he was here, she felt everything that she had denied before and with so much more intensity. Fear became terror. Worry was now crippling anxiety. And happiness had become giddy joy.

Because of that, she needed him by her side to remain strong. Without a numbing emptiness around her, she needed Lucas to ease her burdens, or she'd crumble beneath the strain.

"Stay with me," she begged.

"I'm not going anywhere." He helped her step onto the street.

Beside him stood the constable. She recognized him from the day Oscar had died, and he bowed to her with a gruff kind of grace.

"Sorry to bother you, mum, but I need the name of the man upstairs. I've got my thoughts, but I'd like you to state his name clear for an official record. If you know him, that is."

"I understand." She didn't, but then she'd never focused on the machinery of England's justice system.

"I have to warn you. It's an upsetting sight."

"Can Lord Chellam stay with me?" Her hand remained intertwined with Lucas's, and she did not want to release him.

"So long as he stays quiet."

She nodded, as did he. And so the three of them made their way through a small crowd of onlookers up to the top floor of a building. The air was thick, and there were many smells she wished she could avoid, but she clung tight to Lucas and steeled herself for what was to come.

It didn't work. She wasn't prepared for what she saw. She'd never seen violent death before, and this was horrible. The blood. The broken body.

"That's my stepson, Geoffrey. He is…was…Lord Dunnamore."

Then she turned away. She couldn't look anymore. She focused instead on the smashed table and the scattered cards. There were pockmarks on the wall and someone else she recognized.

"Nathan?" she gasped. "Are you all right?" Lucas's brother was sitting by the broken window, looking tired.

"Most excitement I've had my entire life," he said. Then he mopped his brow. "I don't recommend it."

"No," she murmured. "I can't see how I would enjoy it either."

"Really?" Lucas asked with a grin. "I find myself quite elated." He turned back to her. "You're safe now, Diana. He can't hurt anyone again."

She nodded, tears welling up in her eyes. This isn't how she wanted it to end, but she was so grateful that it was done. Perversely, she felt guilty for the relief that coursed through her body. So many complicated emotions. If Lucas weren't there holding her hand, she feared she'd run screaming into the street just to get away from all the things she was feeling.

Meanwhile, a sweaty young man stepped forward. He had on the clothing of the Watch but the expression of a terrified boy. "I'm right sorry, mum," he said. "So very sorry."

"What?"

"It were me," he blurted. "I came in here first, and he had his guns out. The only one with guns, mum. And he turned to face me."

"Easy, son," the constable said. "You did the right thing."

"He pointed at me, mum. I didn't know he'd spent his shot. I didn't think. I just saw the pistols."

Diana blinked. "You were the one who killed Geoffrey?"

He nodded, his words apparently choked off.

She looked at Lucas. "He was trying to kill you, wasn't he?"

"He was a terrible shot."

That, more than anything else, had her knees going weak. And all the while, the young man stood there sweating as he tried again to apologize.

"I didn't know, mum. I didn't—"

Diana gathered her strength. She could do that because Lucas was alive and well beside her. "Thank you, sir. Thank you for stopping him from hurting anyone else." She gave the boy a quivering smile. "Thank you."

The boy nodded, but he still looked horrified. His gaze kept skittering over to the body and back. Until Lucas touched his shoulder.

"The first is always the hardest, but in this, you did right."

The constable grunted his agreement. "Outside with you, Jeremy. No point in you standing in here."

Diana watched the young man nod and walk stiffly away. Meanwhile, the constable addressed her.

"No need for you to stay either, my lady. We can take care of the rest."

She nodded and was about to leave, but her mind was starting to work again. In a halting kind of fashion. "Constable, did you really need me here? Didn't you know who..." She gestured at Geoffrey's body without actually looking.

"I did, my lady. But for some people, it's good to see it once and for all. To know that it's done now and no questions. I thought you were one of those people."

Yes, she supposed she was. "Thank you," she said. And then she finally, absolutely, and completely exhaled the last of her fear of her stepson. Geoffrey was gone. His threats were over. The terror in which she'd lived was done.

She breathed freely for the first time in twelve years.

"Come with me," Lucas said as he gently guided her out of the flat.

She walked beside him while her head grew steadily clearer. "I thought you'd done it," she said once they were outside.

"Killed Geoffrey?"

"Yes."

"I was prepared to," he said. Then he shrugged. "Turned out, fate had different plans."

Yes, it had. And for that small kindness, she was grateful, though the burden had been shifted to the young watchman. But then her mind turned to other things, as so often happened. Her thoughts left everything else behind as she centered on Lucas.

"What will you do now?" she asked. The question wasn't a simple one. They both knew that his life was in the process of drastic change. He was Lord Chellam again, and she was, finally, absolutely free. No need for his protection now.

He touched her face, that same slow caress of her cheek she adored. "Nothing's changed for me, Diana. I want you as my wife—"

"Yes."

His brows rose. "What?"

Odd how his startled look made her laugh. She hadn't thought happiness had a place here, but she couldn't deny it. Giddiness came on the heels of relief. But under it all was the knowledge of where her thoughts had been taking her for three days now. Maybe even longer. And at his bemused expression, she gathered herself and tried to explain.

"You probably think it's because of this. You think it's the middle of the night, and I was terrified for you." She paused, trying to read his face. He gave nothing away. "But I've done nothing but think these last few days. I think and think about how much I love you."

"I love you, too," he said, but there was confusion in his tone.

"It turns out that I want love more than I want freedom. I don't want to be alone, Lucas. I don't want to be without you. I don't care about the rest. Nothing's right without you."

His gaze blazed in the pre-dawn light. "So you'll marry me? You'll swear yourself to me—"

"If you swear to me."

"Of course."

"Then, of course!"

He grinned. And then they kissed each other. Not a swift mash of teeth and tongues. Not even a refined press of lips. He came to her with a slow caress of acceptance and exploration. But most of all, he came to her with love, and she returned it. That made this moment more than the sensation of their mouths against each other. It was more than the holding of each other's arms. It was a feeling that swelled between them, magnifying with every second they touched. And it kept happening long after their mouths parted.

"There is more that I have to do here," he said. "I need to help the constable see that everything is done properly so that no one can challenge it."

She nodded, though she had no idea what he meant. She trusted him to handle this and so much more. What a relief to trust the man she loved to do things the proper way.

"Come to me as soon as you can," she whispered.

"Nothing could keep me away."

And then they held each other's gaze for a moment longer.

"I love you," he said.

"I love you," she echoed. "And it will be enough," she said firmly. "Loving you will be more than enough for the rest of my life."

EPILOGUE

Seven months later...

T HEIR WEDDING OCCURRED in by special license on the first day of
the new year. Diana didn't care if the whole world knew she was
newly wed, but Lucas was ever careful with her reputation. She was
still in half-mourning, and several people would talk if the speed of
their wedding was known. She didn't care, but he did.

So, they compromised and had a private ceremony at the Adelphi
chapel in the Strand while both their families bore witness. The
announcement of their nuptials would not come until next Season, but
for now, they could live as man and wife in his London home. And
that suited Diana just fine.

The breakfast was lovely. If nothing else, Lucas's mother knew
how to hire an excellent chef. But when Diana smiled at her family—
the new and the old—she realized that her sister Gwen seemed to be
deep in the doldrums.

After the last course was served, Diana could stand it no longer.
With a whispered apology to her new husband, she left her seat to
crouch down beside her normally unflappable sister.

"Have I made a hash of the greenery?" Diana asked by way of
greeting. Her sister was mad for botany and would happily expound
on care of one plant or another. But in this case, Gwen merely blinked
at the collection of pinecones and branches that graced the table.

"How can anyone make a hash of an evergreen?" Gwen asked. "Their branches are so symmetrical, even I could make a decent table arrangement."

"I am relieved that it's not the decorations that have you so glum." She nudged her sister with her shoulder. "So, what is it? Don't you like Lucas?"

"What? Of course, I like him," Gwen said.

"Then what makes you scowl at my wedding?"

"I'm not scowling! I'm happy for you." Gwen grinned at her in such an obviously forced display that Diana burst out laughing. No one, not even her very proper sister, could dampen her mood this morning.

"Out with it," Diana finally commanded. "What are you thinking that has made you unhappy?"

It took a moment for the words to come out. She could tell that Gwen was trying hard to phrase it correctly, but that never worked with her sister. Gwen was a bluestocking through and through, and she simply didn't act or speak like a typical society woman. Diana thought that was a good thing, but even so, she was unprepared for her sister's question.

"Are you getting married so you can have children?"

"What? No!" Though she had to admit, she couldn't wait to have Lucas's babies. What she wouldn't give to be pregnant right now! Or at least very soon.

"Oh. That's good then," Gwen said as her expression turned thoughtful. "I thought you might be."

Which, coming from her sister, meant something else much more astounding. Gwen only asked questions when she was thinking about a thing.

"Do you want children?" Diana asked her sister. Gwen had spent the last twelve seasons avoiding anything having to do with the marriage mart. The idea that she was contemplating children was shocking indeed.

"I don't know about children in general," Gwen finally admitted. "But I'd like to raise a little girl. I would make sure she learned all about science and mathematics and that no one made her dress in scratchy clothes or forced her to listen to idiotic men."

Ah, so there it was. Gwen wanted to raise a girl child to be free as they had never been. Certainly not with their mother teaching them dutiful behavior with every breath. For Diana, that meant marrying a man three times her age. For Gwen, it meant suffering constant criticism for her dress, her thoughts, and how she could not pretend to enjoy conversation with someone less intelligent than herself. Given that Gwen was brilliant, there were precious few men who could interest her for more than thirty seconds.

"Are you considering the marriage mart then?" she asked. She'd always made it clear that she despised the thought of tying herself to a man.

"I am considering a girl child," Gwen answered. "Do you know how I can raise one without the benefit of a husband?"

"I don't," Diana answered. "No unmarried woman of your status could raise a child alone. It just isn't done."

"Exactly," Gwen pronounced as if she were uttering, Doom! Doom! Doom!

Diana giggled. She couldn't help it. "You know," she drawled, "there must be an intelligent man somewhere out there."

"There is," Gwen responded mournfully. "One is our brother. The other is your husband."

"Maybe there are more. Maybe you could find one for yourself next season."

Gwen groaned as if she were facing the most arduous task in the world. And perhaps for her, the societal rounds qualified. "I am dreading it," she intoned.

"I, on the other hand," came a masculine voice from behind them, "am very excited to see who you find." It was Lucas, joining them at the table, and Diana was already standing up just so he could wrap his arm around her. "I might have some suggestions if you like," he said. "I do know some intelligent men."

"No, no," Gwen groused. "I'll do it myself. You two are so besotted with each other, you see brilliance in everyone."

It was true. Ever since she'd declared her love for Lucas, everything and everyone seemed better. The sun shone brighter, the food tasted better, and even the most annoying things—and people—were as nothing to her. Why, just a few moments ago, she'd forgiven their newest maid for saying Diana had the nicest of mothers-in-law.

"Very well," Diana said. "We shall leave you to husband hunt on your own—"

"I'm not hunting for a husband," Gwen interrupted. "I'm looking for an acceptable father for a brilliant daughter."

"Even so," Diana said as she turned to her husband, "try following your heart. I'm sure it will lead you in the right direction." After all, that was the only answer that had worked for her. Her heart had set itself on Lucas and would not let her alone until she said yes.

"Of all the ridiculous, unscientific, silly things to say," Gwen declared. "But that's what comes from falling in love. All reason disappears, and the end result is—"

"Blissful happiness for the rest of our lives?" asked Lucas.

"Joy every morning and delight every night?" added Diana.

"Children!" Gwen huffed. "The only reason I shall marry is so I can have a girl child and raise her in the way she ought to be reared."

If Gwen said anything more, Diana didn't hear it. She was too busy saying, "I love you" to her new husband at the exact same moment he was saying it to her. Then Lucas nuzzled against her ear and whispered something else.

"Did I hear something about you wanting a baby? If so, then perhaps we should begin—"

"Right away," Diana said. "Definitely. Right away."

About the Author

A *USA Today* Bestseller, JADE LEE has been scripting love stories since she first picked up a set of paper dolls. Ball gowns and rakish lords caught her attention early (thank you Georgette Heyer), and her fascination with historical romance began. Author of more than 30 regency romances, Jade has a gift for creating a lively world, witty dialogue, and hot, sexy humor. Jade also writes contemporary and paranormal romance as Kathy Lyons. Together, they've won several industry awards, including the *Prism—Best of the Best, Romantic Times Reviewer's Choice,* and *Fresh Fiction's* Steamiest Read. Even though Kathy (and Jade) have written over 60 romance novels, she's just getting started. Check out her latest news at www.KathyLyons.com, Facebook: JadeLeeAuthor, and Twitter: JadeLeeAuthor. Instagram: KathyLyonsAuthor.

Made in the USA
Monee, IL
23 December 2020